D a s t a r d l y

■ ■ ■

*The story is fiction,
the evil is real.*

A Novel

By Clem C. Pellett

ISBN-10: 1482069245
ISBN-13: 978-1482069242

Library of Congress Control Number: 2013901697

Introduction

The bitter January cold of 1951 enveloped Great Falls, Montana and guaranteed lousy conditions for the poor sap who got roped into baby-sitting the FBI wiretap on some pinko former congressman. The task was too grim for actual agents, so the local Bureau Chief over in Billings farmed out the duty to an assortment of people facing possible conviction, also known as "Confidential Informants." For this job, lucky candidates covered eight-hour shifts around the clock, with each one's dismal duty being to sit alone in a freezing sub-basement and eavesdrop on the compromised phone line of the house next door.

On the midnight shift of the 19th, the undercover operator officially known as FBI Confidential Informant of Known Reliability, Number 3 huddled at his listening post and endured indoor cold so intense that water dripping from leaky pipes had long since frozen. His handlers had explained to him that heat couldn't be used there because it might give away his presence to those on the floor above. The entire operation had been termed "Classified" by J. Edgar himself.

And so Number 3 was stuck in a listening post cold enough to freeze beef until they got something good on former Congressman "Jerry the Red" O'Connell, age forty-two. The main goal, above all others, was that any information gleaned had to have direct value in setting up a blackmail attack potent enough for the Bureau to park the Honorable Congressman's mouth in the closed position and keep it there.

A phone call was in progress. A call was always in progress when O'Connell was at home. Number 3 tried to pay attention to the insipid banter between the former Congressman and his private amusement ride, but boredom gnawed at him. He silently raged at himself for getting stuck with this nasty spy duty, all because of a certain bank embezzlement problem.

Thus a citizen of unproven guilt found himself straining to hear anything Hoover's Bureau could actually use, all so he could get the hell out of there and spend a solid week bundled up next to the fireplace. The sneaky love talk between O'Connell, a married man, and the female on the other end, not his wife, typically tended toward generic nastiness and phrasing from the high school playbook. The pair droned on while she chided him for not seeing her more often and unknowingly inflicted her deepest emotions and her most private thoughts on two men at the same time.

Number 3 could only shake his head. The skirt's tone and vocabulary managed to make her sound like a disappointed child with the I.Q. of a cocktail umbrella. But just as he was about to start tearing at his hair, Number 3's boredom vanished and all sense of despair fell away.

It happened at the instant he realized that O'Connell, unbelievable as it seemed, had abandoned his usual paranoia long enough to get maneuvered into a vulnerable position and give a specific time and place for a meeting with her.

It was a fatal slip that could be exactly what the feds wanted—not done at the hands of trickery by some clever psychological manipulator or by a black widow with a talent for finding men's weak spots. It wasn't even accomplished by the sexual wiles of a clever *femme fatale.* Instead the fool was going to get himself captured red-handed over the whiney owner of two ordinary weekday squeezers.

Number 3 pressed the earphones into his head to capture every trace of sound and listened aghast at O'Connell's carelessness while he made definite date plans with her. The fool was doing this in spite of the fact that he had already mentioned his general suspicion of wiretaps (while Number 3 listened on the very wiretap he feared), but still there he was, talking like nobody was in the henhouse but the chickens. The sensations filling him reminded him of finding serious money in the pocket of an old coat.

The Honorable ex-Congressman planned to meet his honey-pie the next afternoon at her home in Roundup, Montana, a couple of hundred miles away. Number 3 knew of the place—a small town located along the Musselshell River. There was supposed to be great fishing there. It struck him that maybe he ought to visit the place after this, just to celebrate.

This piece of information was a perfect gift for his FBI masters because "Jerry the Red" O'Connell would be easy to track and tail in such a small town. All the Bureau boys had to do was play fol-low-the-moron between Great Falls and Roundup, then hang back long enough to let him get the action going before they came bashing through the door and snapped his picture *en flagrante*, with his hand more or less in the cookie.

Number 3's glee soared while he listened to the former Congress-man confirm that he would indeed be on the next 7:00 a.m. Grey-hound out of Great Falls and arrive at her place by noon. O'Connell bragged that some of his "Party operatives" lived near Roundup and that he could call them and invite himself to dinner. This would justify the trip to his wife—leaving plenty of time in the afternoon for Jerry to play a little backseat bingo with the new doll.

With that, Number 3 got so excited he jumped upright and banged his head on the low ceiling, hitting hard enough to drop him back down to his knees and leave him clutching the floor. He didn't care. He didn't even mind the pain; the throbbing waves only represented freedom because the feds now had a time and a place, and it was Number 3 who picked it up for them. This would truly, as the kids liked to say, razz their berries in assorted flavors.

Of course none of that would ever compensate for the hours bit-ten out of his life in a sub-basement ice pit. But at least with this nasty government obligation fulfilled, Number 3 could step away and let some other sucker play secret agent on the next phase of the case. By this point he'd listened to enough hours of O'Connell's verbal gas that he couldn't help rooting for the feds. If it wasn't for that O'Connell bastard, any other work assigned to Number 3 would have surely been warmer than this.

The way he saw it, somebody needed to pay for all his troubles. Now, finally, somebody would.

Part One

A Dastard Afoot

* Dead Winter, 1951 *

1

Eye Witness

Inside Chester's Barber Shop on Main Street, down near 1st and just up from the railroad tracks, the brand new Hand Held Electric Scalp Vibrator was being used on Sheriff Wade Preston for the first time. Chester the barber was delighted with the result when the curiously soothing little machine lulled the Sheriff to sleep. Chester kept up the treatment while the Sheriff's head gradually tilted forward and his whole face went slack.

Before long, the orbital muscles of the Sheriff's left eye socket lost their grip on his artificial eyeball. The hand-painted glass and ceramic orb dropped out, plopped into his lap, bounced off, hit the floor, and skittered across the room, coming to rest in a little pile of hair sweepings against the back wall. The mélange of black, brown, red, blond, and gray was a fair cross-section of the male population of Roundup.

Preston exhaled with an exasperated sigh and muttered, "Son of a *bitch*, Chester."

"Oo! Sorry, Sheriff," Chester sang out in his practiced voice of permanent good cheer. He carefully set aside the new hand held massager and hustled over to pluck the Sheriff's artifact from the sweepings. He brought it close to his lips and blew it off.

"Soak that in some Barbisol," cautioned the Sheriff. "I don't need a socket full of stubble."

1

"Of course," Chester agreed without a trace of a smirk. "Got a container right here." He picked up the blue liquid soaker, removed a couple of skinny combs and dropped the eye into the solution. But when he turned back to the Sheriff, he saw the driest expression any customer had ever turned on him.

"Can't give you a positive vote on the new machine there," Preston intoned. He avoided looking into the mirror with his good eye.

"No-no," Chester agreed, snatching up his scissors and a fresh comb. "Certainly not the result we're looking for. I'll test it on..."

"Somebody with two good eyes?"

"Now, now—that's not what I was going to say. It's a new device. Only thing to do is try it out."

"Okay. We should move on with the actual haircut," Preston abruptly said while he rubbed his drooping left-side eyelid. "I don't need any of my constituents coming in here right now, get me?"

"Oh! Yes indeed." Chester stepped to the front door, spun the window sign from *Open* to *Closed* and turned the lock. "There," he said with the satisfaction of a man who has just solved a problem. He returned to the Sheriff and made himself busy with the scissors.

You only cut the hair—but you get to know the head, as Chester liked to say. Plenty of embarrassing personal moments passed inside his shop. In the face of a doozy like this eyeball incident, he told himself to drop the topic. But the words "drop the topic" made him need to laugh so hard that he had to fake a sneeze. *Soak your eyeball, trim your nose hair*—all just standard service at Chester's Barber Shop.

Self-control was essential in his line of work. He had managed to preside over a small but steady business by mastering the high-and-tight speed cut and selling it on the cheap while doling out gossip like a bargirl tease. This in a land of frugal working men who didn't much care for the sight of their own hair anywhere above the neck.

However, the customers who frequented Chester's Barber Shop also tended to be those who worked hard and had very little humor in their lives. They loved to laugh at a well-told joke. Laughing customers meant better tips, and Chester knew the eyeball incident had the potential to be money in the bank. After all, Preston was a politician; there would always be people with a grudge to feed.

But he considered it a point of personal honor that he never abused his position, and so he decided the eyeball incident was useless. No, anything he said about *The Tale Of The Hairy Eyeball*, as he already thought of it, would only make Chester look bad for bringing it up.

Of course, if one of the big tippers happened to hear him mutter to himself and as a result started leaning on Chester to fill in the details, well, all right then—who could say?

It was too easy to ridicule Musselshell County's elected Sheriff, and not because of the eyeball but because the whole county knew he had no experience in law enforcement taking his present position. He only got the job because nobody else seemed to want it.

Nevertheless, in a state known for its rugged mountains and windswept high plains, the respect for individualism ran deep. So Chester decided if their old Sheriff had spent the last ten years driving those back country roads with one good eye, then hey, at least somebody was getting it done.

Preston spoke up, "So Chester, you had any run-ins around here lately with a young fellow maybe twenty-one or two, good-looking guy, tough build?"

"Ah, no Sheriff, can't say I have."

"Nothing like that?"

"Not lately. May I ask?"

"Couple of odd reports came in over the last week or so. But with so much itinerant labor around, it's hard to know about one fellow."

"What sort of trouble?"

The Sheriff laughed at that one, hard enough to fail to notice that Chester's scissors took a bite out of the back of his hair when he lurched. "Don't think I can go into detail with a man who gets visited by half the town every week."

"Not that many. By a long shot. Some of the ones with no taste at all have started using those new home cutter kits. You seen those things? Terrible. First time I saw a man who got his hair cut by one of them I like to died, standin' right there."

"We're not even sure there's a problem, or if it's one guy. If he's out there though, I guess he's a cagey one."

"I can tell you in a single instant if your hair is cut with one of those damn kits."

At that moment a young boy appeared at the front door, rattled it against the lock, then began to rapidly knock on the glass. Chester didn't recognize the kid—some punk with a mother who apparently bought one of the new home cutter kits. He couldn't understand why they were even legal.

"Damn it, Chester," Preston sighed.

"Sorry. Sorry. I'll get rid of him," adding under his breath, "Glad to oblige."

He stepped over and opened the door to tell the kid to get lost, but the little shit pushed past him and hustled inside, out of breath. The boy raised his hand in thanks to Chester and immediately turned to Preston. "Sheriff?" the boy began, still breathing hard, "Jeanette over at the Roundup Café sent me to find you quick. I've been looking all around."

"Hello there, Stewie. I've got a pretty full afternoon today. Is this something that can wait?"

"She said tell you that communist guy is at it again. Says can't you get him out of the county?"

"What, old Jerry the Red? Hell he's probably just waiting around for somebody to give him a ride home." Sheriff Preston nevertheless felt a surge of frustration over the idea of Jerry O'Connell harassing innocent diners over at the café again. He sighed, then stood up, yanked off the barber bib, and threw it on the floor. He plunged his hand into the sterilizing liquid to retrieve his eyeball, asking, "Anything else?"

"She said I should remind you the café is the Thornton's family business and the guy is driving customers away."

"She felt the need to say that?"

"I guess."

Preston shook his head, pulled his eyeball out of the Barbi-sol and shook it off while Chester gasped at the sight and bit his tongue. "So he's still there right now?" Preston asked.

"Was when I left. I been gone maybe ten minutes. Went up and down Main Street looking for you. She said if you was in your new radio car she could've reached you herself."

"Oh she actually said that?"

"I couldn't have thought it up."

Sheriff Preston exhaled for a third time while he reached his dry hand into his front pocket and pulled out a fifty-cent piece. He tossed it to young Stewart, who deftly snatched it out of the air and disappeared back through the door on the fly.

Chester felt fine about seeing the kid go. Good riddance to the self-cut crowd. Bastards most likely preferred to pull their own teeth. Set their own bones.

"Here, let me," Chester hurried over and took the eyeball, then carried it to the sink and ran cold water over it. "You don't want to get that solution in your—"

"Damn it, Chester!" Preston shouted, sounding like a man whose adrenalin had just kicked in. "Give me that!" He snatched his eyeball from under the faucet, rubbed it up and down on his shirt a couple of times and then bent slightly forward to slip it in place. He stood back up and blinked hard twice.

"That look right?"

"I'm not sure we rinsed off all the solution," Chester warned. Preston's look made him drop the topic. "The eye looks good. The *haircut* of course is still not finished..."

Preston disappeared through the door without another word. And as quickly as that, it was done. Chester's last cut of the lunch hour rush was over for the day.

The Sheriff's missing chunk of hair would grow right back after a week or two, and he didn't appear to be a guy who spent a lot of time studying himself in the mirror. If he showed up for his usual shave on Saturday morning, Chester would know he got by on that one.

That left him to review *The Tale of the Hairy Eyeball* and consider what an unusual twist it had put on the afternoon. He let out a long exhale and sat with a grunt of relief in the padded barber chair, then leaned over to pick up the bib from the floor. He shook it out and carefully refolded it. However, when he placed the bib on the counter his gaze was caught by the brand-new Hand Held Electric Scalp Vibrator.

The question occurred to him; if that invention could thoroughly unwind a high-strung politician like Wade Preston and do it to the point that he started shedding bits of his anatomy, what would it do for regular people? Hell, Chester thought, it was a good thing the Sheriff didn't also wear a wig, a set of dentures, and maybe a wooden leg. There had to be a limit to the number of body parts that could fall off a person and not get mentioned to his customers later on.

He picked up the device, which he had never taken the opportunity to seriously try, and turned it this way and that, more or less inspecting the thing. Since it was already plugged in, he switched it on, lifted it up, and began to idly run the vibrator across the top of his head.

He started right up there at the crown where the skin always got so tight and sore, then gradually slid the warm, buzzing surface around to the back of his skull, moving down to where his tensions accumulated right there at the back of his neck...

And in that single moment, Chester understood.

The stress-induced knots became butter on a hot griddle. It was a sensation so good it made him feel strangely guilty for enjoying it. He found that the next few minutes were effortlessly lost to stress release so thorough it continued to surprise him with its depth.

The device was a ticket to the door of Nirvana. As a self-employed businessman, Chester could not help but consider whether the little vibrators might be worth money to certain people. Perhaps it would be smart to buy a couple cases of the things, sell them under the counter.

Mothers would likely prove eager for the ability to provide at-home therapeutic treatment for the scalps of their husbands and children.

The picture was murky, but Chester sensed a market with genuine potential out there. Surely the Hand Held Electric Scalp Vibrator was a solid prospect to market to the ladies of the house. Gifts, whatnot.

2

Roundup, Montana
Population 1,500

Twenty-two year-old Andrew James Carmichael stood across from the house he'd carefully selected and conjured up the image of a guy looking for his dog. He then projected the idea outward to the world, which usually bought him at least a minute of look-around time before anybody started to get curious. The small neighborhood was quiet, blocks from Main Street. He strained his eyes and ears for any sign of life inside the targeted house. Nothing so far.

He ordinarily staked out a house for a solid hour before attempting a break-in, and it was precisely this level of caution that had kept him at large during the six months since his escape. But already that morning the temperature had dropped so far that it was becoming alarming for a guy who had to break into places to get somewhere warm to sleep.

His run from the law out of Oklahoma had left him with nothing but the clothing on his back and the stolen car that broke down and stranded him in this backwater town. His coat was thick enough for ordinary winter weather, as were his pointy-toed shit kickers, but an arctic front had settled over the region. It felt as if all the heat had somehow left the planet and the deep cold of outer space gripped him. The bite in the air was so sharp and hard it made him want to scream and punch at nothing.

With every breath he inhaled a cloud of razor blades. No more waiting, then. The house was big enough to have lots of stuff inside, warmer clothes at least. No signs of a dog.

There appeared to be no kids living there, maybe a single person or a couple, away for the day. He tossed down his cigarette, irritated by the strange fact that cigarette smoke was hot but did nothing to keep the smoker warm, then ground it underfoot.

Andy's intuition told him he wouldn't have to resort to the .32 caliber Smith & Wesson tucked into the back of his waist band. He hadn't been forced to use it in Montana yet, partially due to his elevated caution there. From the moment he arrived in that creepy town of working stiffs, something had been telling him to keep everything on the down low, to wait until he could make one perfect score with enough money to travel a long distance and then grab a solid car worth stealing. Now he had no choice but to begin, no matter how large or small a score might be.

He played the doggie act for maximum effect, as always: *I'm just a guy with the lost dog, folks, looking all around, checking under cars. See how my face is creased with worry?*

One thing Andy understood about himself was his ability to project illusions the way a radiator puts out heat. He didn't know why this form of dark magic worked for him, but most of the time it did. He knew the trick was in believing your own lie. Project it out there and then walk inside of it with determination. Never look back.

"Spot!" Andy called out. "Spotty! Come on boy! Supper time!" He projected the act while he continued to move all the way across the street, through the yard of the house next door, and into the back yard of his target home.

He dropped the dog-calling to avoid actively attracting attention, but continued looking all around just in case anyone happened to spot him. If so, they wouldn't see Andy Carmichael, they would only see the lie. *Where oh where can my Spotty be?*

And then he was at the back door. He could see that it opened into the kitchen. Dutch door, wood on the bottom half, French glass panes on the top half. Andy turned his back to the door and scanned in all directions for nosy bastards before making a show out of coughing once, loud and hard, at the same instant that he rammed his elbow backward and through the nearest glass pane. It shattered under the blow and hit the floor inside. He winced. The sound could prove to be a problem if anybody was inside after all.

If someone's in there, they must have noticed. He covered that possibility by hurrying away again and into the yard of the house next door in a pretense of having spotted his beloved dog vanishing around the corner. That took him out of the line of sight in case anyone was inside the target house and peeked outside.

He huddled behind a bush and covered himself with a veil of worry, projecting more thoughts of Spotty the mythical dog. *Come on, boy—where are you?*

When nobody appeared, he made his way back to the door and reached through the broken window pane to discover that the door wasn't locked anyway. He shrugged, turned the knob, and walked in.

Luck was with him—a quick scan of the rooms confirmed that the occupants were gone, apparently an older couple. Their living situation looked solid, the kind of thing it takes years to put together. As usual Andy found greater satisfaction in violating the personal space of people who lived "on the square," as the warden called it.

He was in and out of the place in less than five minutes. In another five he was walking smoothly down the sidewalk of Roundup's little downtown area, vanishing among the town's young working men who looked pretty much like Andy but definitely were not. It was a good score this time. He'd made off with a decent haul: thicker jacket, warm gloves, better winter boots that actually fit, plus forty dollars in cash, a man's elaborate ring, and a gold lapel pin.

The ring was molded in the familiar "Compass and Square" shape of the Freemasons' symbol with a scroll reading *Unity Lodge 71, Roundup.* Andy recognized it from a similar ring worn by his former warden. He never got close enough to that one to see what its scroll said, probably the name of the warden's local lodge.

Back in the joint, there had been no opportunity to learn much about the so-called Freemasons except that they were sometimes just called "Masons." He didn't know why that was. Ever since he first saw the symbol on the warden's ring, he associated the organization with people in authority – some kind of a club filled with squares who used their ultra-secret methods for keeping the whole world on the square. Great idea, except that they were the only ones who got to say what "square" meant.

He had only grabbed the ring as a reflex without considering its resale value. The attraction was from imagining himself a part of some secretive group. Now he walked along feeling like a real-life spy with the Masonic lapel pin stuck to his shirt collar, marking him as part of a secret group of People Who Know Things. He liked the feeling enough to know he would be wanting more of it in the future. It put so much spring in his step he practically bounced down the sidewalk.

It was suddenly clear to him that this easy score might be a sign that his luck was changing for the better. He dared to think it might finally be safe for him to move on, maybe head north, make his way into Canada. He had never been there, but the other inmates had assured him the women in Canada would go for him. He also had it on good authority that Canadians were mostly simple church-goers, working types, easy pickings for a fast thinker like Andy Carmichael.

Fast thinking, after all, had kept him free so far. He considered himself to have been graced with criminal brilliance in about the same way a man might be graced with a beautiful singing voice. It had flashed inside him once again when his stolen car broke down, bringing him the inspiration to leave it with a mechanic who would agree to put it on his back-burner priority list.

He told the guy he was in town on a job and wouldn't need to drive, so there was no rush—could the guy maybe have it ready in ten days or so? He used the I'm-your-friend smile to make sure he bought it. Of course Andy fully intended to abandon the car there, but the beauty of ruse was that it gave him up to a couple of weeks before the police found out about it. That two-week period would keep the hot car and its incriminating license plates off of the streets for free.

After that, there was nothing left to do but roam around, lie low, and hide under what Andy liked to think of as his False Face. He was a skilled non-worker, possessed of training taken during his youthful spells of incarceration with adult male populations who forcibly educated him in many useful things. Not all of them were related to the secrets for placating human monsters with bizarre sex acts; some had practical value on the street.

The acquired art of the False Face was chief among them. It was the secret source of his escapee status and a principal tool in remaining at large among the functioning humans of Roundup, Montana.

Andy roamed secure in the knowledge that whenever he put the False Face to work, folks never knew what hit them: a guy so polite and pleasant that nobody could take offense with him. If the danger level was high and the False Face was not enough, Andy's reliable response was to add his Harmless Goofball character, grinning ear-to-ear over anything and everything. He was happy to play the fool, projecting the picture of a young man too simple-minded and agreeable to pose any danger. Dirty clothing? A rumpled appearance? Not a problem in a rough town where the working men were as dirty as the vagabonds. Fitting in was effortless, as long as he kept quiet, stole nothing but trivial amounts unlikely to be missed, and never allowed anybody to strike up a conversation. As far as he was concerned, you couldn't put a price on a talent like his. It had saved him from going back to jail more than once when sheer force or mere intellect would have failed him.

Now while he left his freshly robbed house behind, he made it a point to move down the sidewalk projecting the image of a tired guy who has just worked a long shift among the cattle ranchers, coal miners, and oil rig roughnecks.

If he looked unfamiliar to anyone, well, it would be natural for them to assume he was in town on a short-term job. It helped him project an illusion when he actually thought the words, so he ran it through his head, over and over: *"I'm just here to work that new job outside town, then move on."* He didn't have to know why it worked for him to successfully employ it, just like he didn't have to know how to build a car to drive one.

In this fashion, he could get away with all kinds of things. *The secret is to make sure nobody sees you!* A flash of satisfaction gushed through him every time he reminded himself of that. He loved to experience his own wisdom.

But when the late winter temperatures dropped farther within the past few days, he was forced to start breaking into homes that were empty during the daytime, just to have somewhere to get inside and warm up, raid the ice box, maybe pocket a bit of cash, a watch—just enough to show for the effort but not so much as to set off general alarm. A good day of thievery was when he could take things people would hardly notice at first, things they might even believe they somehow misplaced.

The problem on this day was mainly the insane cold of the weather front, much worse than anything he had felt in Montana up to that point. He tried to remember why heading north seemed like such a good idea when he was back in Oklahoma. But that memory involved unpleasant images of those Bible-thumping hypocrites he hospitalized in Midwest City. The memory gave him the definite sense that he ought to leave all that alone.

Yes, there had been that one lucky break in his flight from Oklahoma authorities by picking up a car in an easy steal, but the apparent trend vanished when he was forced to shoot a bum for gas money. So as usual, the past didn't hold any answers for him. Nothing good for him ever lay in the past.

Now on the crowded side of too late, Andy recalled the advice of the few criminals who ever willingly offered him guidance: *crime works better when the weather is sunny and mild*. He couldn't help but agree with the sentiment but the thought left him feeling hollow. Someone else's line was less satisfying to him than the feeling of thinking up his own stuff. Originality mattered greatly to Andy. He considered it the most important aspect of his way of life.

3

Coffee Shop Spy

F.B.I. Confidential Informant of Known Reliability Number 7 sat in a back booth of the Roundup Café and nursed her third cup of coffee while she waited for "Jerry the Red" O'Connell to show up so she could wrap her peepers around him and take all the right notes. She was acting on the Bureau's information that her subject was most likely to come to that place around that time. FBI confidence in her subject's arrival was based on the disappearing act his girlfriend had been kind enough to perform after agents arrived at her little house and brought up uncomfortable moments from her known history.

To Number 7's pleasant surprise, she found herself savoring the sense of being part of the world of spies and espionage. Fifty miles away and one day earlier, the loudest of the agents at the FBI field office had managed to terrify her into thinking they were sending her out on this case to get shot or something, if not by some perpetrator then by the feds themselves. Worse, he described in vivid detail the dreadful things the Bureau planned to do if she refused to cooperate.

And yet now that she was actually there, the afternoon was somehow entertaining as hell. She had rushed to the Café on short notice on the heels of a last-minute call from the field office over in Billings and a thin file that showed up in her mailbox.

At the Roundup Cafe, she only experienced a few minutes of doubt before the Assigned Target came sauntering through the door, just like magic. The Bureau boys told her this was called "following from the front." It struck Number 7 that she loved following from the front when the Assigned Target launched into a lecture even before his food arrived, randomly picking other patrons to preach at, exactly as predicted inside his case file. It was like having a crystal ball.

Number 7 found it almost sexually spooky, how much the Bureau knew about things. In that instant she understood the satisfaction of using someone's vulnerabilities to make them your unknowing puppet. Her spinal column vibrated in resonance with every other member of the power elite. To her great surprise she reveled in the sensation of stepping onto a grand and important stage, joining in with the other performers in their terribly important play.

She also noted that her Assigned Target's file described a tendency to sweat heavily, and once again she felt a rush of satisfaction when the indoor air went to work on him and his forehead began to bead up. She sat back and allowed the subject to prattle on while she made it a point to show no interest and to do nothing that might draw his attention. It was a rare occasion when she had cause to appreciate her ability to sit completely unnoticed by any man in the room.

Still she savored the sensation of being in an exciting dramatic production, a mystery play of danger and intrigue. She couldn't help but wonder what sorts of favors she might be able to do for her friends and perhaps against her enemies if she ever got into this line of work full-time.

This Jerry O'Connell fellow turned out to be the very model of the short, chubby, balding man in his forties described in the file. On top of that he appeared to be wearing the same tired business suit as the one in his file photo. The date in the picture placed the image at nearly two years old. His file said he didn't drive anymore, for health reasons. She wondered if he walked to the café from the bus station.

He seemed to know several of the other diners in the lunch crowd and called out to them by name from his stool at the counter. Most of them answered back, but always with a simple "Hi, Jerry" in a tone that didn't encourage conversation. He raised his voice to include everybody in the room.

"Well, I tell ya, folks, hospitality could be better in Roundup. I just rode the Greyhound express all the way from Great Falls to see a friend here, instead I find a note on the door telling me "something came up." No phone call. No warning. And here I am in town on a one-way bus ticket. Where are the manners? Nearly froze my fanny making it over here on foot."

He looked around as if expecting someone to offer him something. Everybody in the place suddenly appeared to have other things attracting their attention.

So, thought Number 7, this was their man. Some guy used to be in Congress or something, secret Communist. As far as she was concerned, he didn't look like much. Still, she maintained a dutiful surveillance and reminded herself to only use the corners of her eyes. Nobody at the F.B.I. told her to do that. She invented the move herself.

O'Connell then called out to the owners while they huddled in the back booth. Number 7 already knew all about Donnie and Claudette Thornton, mid-thirties, high school sweethearts. They had run the Roundup Café for the past ten years.

"So Donnie! Claudette! As we used to say back in Jersey, whattaya got that's good here?" O'Connell laughed along with himself.

The Thorntons briefly turned to O'Connell with a matching pair of wan smiles. Number 7 nearly laughed out loud at their lack of enthusiasm for the guy.

"Hey there, Jerry. We're on our way out for the day, but Jeanette back there does a great job. Everything she makes is good."

"Hi Jerry," Mrs. Thornton added with a little wave.

"Aw yah, you kids have a good time, go home early, leave it to the working staff to run the business while you enjoy your profits on their labors." He toasted them with his coffee cup and gave a phony royal bow.

"Jerry..." said Donnie Thornton in a tired warning tone. He glanced around at the other customers, who were already pointedly ignoring

O'Connell. "No political speeches today. Nobody's running for any-thing right now."

O'Connell laughed again. "Guilty! Guilty!" he called across the room. "My apologies to all. People say I can't have a conversation without making it political, but I'm not here to antagonize."

Everyone else in the place seemed to know enough about O'Connell to automatically dodge his preachy opinions. Maybe some had discovered the same thing the file said of him—that the only two endings O'Connell allowed to a debate were for his opponents to admit to their mistakes or be dismissed with a sneer.

The booth next to the owners opened up, so Number 7 casually moved into it as if she just wanted some room to spread out. She set down her coffee cup and placed the Bureau's file with the blank back cover facing upward. She was careful to never look at the owners while she eavesdropped. It became much easier to hear the two of them after O'Connell's lunch arrived and he finally shut up long enough to eat something.

The owners caught her attention right away. Their conversation had nothing to do with her assignment, but this business of snooping was really turning out to be a natural fit.

"We should get out of here before he starts talking again," Donnie muttered to his wife.

Overhearing the whispered comment made Number 7's spy experience even more real. She focused on her peripheral vision and noticed that Donnie kept his face blank for the sake of the customers but that he added a loving stroke to Claudette's cheek with his fingers. His wife warmed to the touch and leaned into him. The sight of it sent a cloud of warm sparkles through Number 7's nethers.

"I don't care about him," Claudette murmured. "I just want to know if you feel sure this time."

He squeezed an arm around her shoulders and replied with a nod. "Jimmy's been gone nearly three years. We aren't honoring him anymore by not having another child."

"But I want to know if you're sure or if you're doing this to humor me."

"Yes I'm sure I want to try having another child because I don't want our house to be empty anymore. And yes, I'm probably humoring you a little. If there's anything else I can do to make you smile that big, I don't know what it is."

Claudette beamed so hard in response that Number 7 could nearly feel the shine coming off of her, "Then I know a man who is about to have a very interesting afternoon."

She said it so softly that Number 7 really had to strain to eavesdrop. She found it impossible not to envy them, married sixteen years and still in love like that.

But the mood shattered when the front door banged open and a young man in a heavy coat stomped in. He kicked the door shut and stood fanning his arms around his torso to beat away the cold.

"Whew!" He called out in a good-natured tone. "Feels like we're importing winter from Russia!" The guy looked around as if waiting for someone to acknowledge, then went on.

"Anybody heading up toward the border? I've got a job waiting up there but no car."

Everybody seemed to suddenly develop a stronger interest in their meals.

"Anybody?" he continued. "Any Masons in here?" He held up one hand and showed off a large ring and gave up a friendly smile. "If so, you've got a fellow traveler here needing a ride."

That comment seemed to wake up O'Connell in a big way. He grinned and called over to the new arrival, "Fellow Traveler, you say?"

The new guy laughed. "Well, I don't mean that like a 'Fellow Traveler' communist or something. I just meant if you're traveling, I'm looking to travel, too."

"Oh you have some grudge against the Communist Party?"

"Who doesn't?" the young man asked, looking puzzled.

"Perhaps the members of the local *Progressive movement*? Perhaps any *Democrat* with a brain and a heart? Somebody who wants real change in this world and not politics as usual?"

Everybody was watching the young guy, now, who clearly had no idea what he had just stepped in. But he just held up his hands in surrender and smiled. "Hey, hey, I'm not a political guy, I'm just a fellow needs a ride, that's all."

"Oh, you're a political guy all right, pal. We're *all* political guys whether we want to be or not! Because the fat cats are going to keep on raping and plundering all of us until we get *political* enough to stop them! Look at the menu, one whole dollar for a lousy 'Deluxe' burger and a fountain drink? How long does a worker have to toil to earn that money? For one sandwich? How would it be if all *you* got at the end of every working day was dinner and a place to sleep, just enough so you could do it all over again the next day and the next—and all the while there you are, doing nothing but getting older?"

The young guy exhaled heavily with a sound like "Bwwuuuhhh..." and then just shook his head and ignored O'Connell in favor of stopping at each booth and briefly checking to see if he could score a ride there. The Thorntons took the interlude as their cue to leave.

Number 7 watched them get up and head toward the door with their arms tenderly around each other. She imagined smelling sex on the two of them and was beset with the urge to say something indicating she knew what they were up to, off to make a baby.

The temptation process ignited. Number 7 wondered why in the hell she shouldn't say something, anyway. After all, the entire town knew about the Thornton's loss of a young son to some kind of disease, and how it nearly killed both of them. At the time, nobody had held out much hope for the couple or their mutual business. But the pair weathered that storm together. Why not congratulate them, out loud in front of everybody about having the courage to try it again?

Of course it would also reveal her new power of knowledge. But was that so terrible? Was it terrible at all?

Was it not, in fact, a *bon-bon* of private delight melting on her grateful tongue? Was it not like getting away with a tiny robbery, a crime too small for anyone to see except for the ones getting robbed, and damn them into Hell for happiness she would never have believed if she had not seen it herself, happiness that ridiculed the entire state of her life simply by existing in her presence, happiness that took her new thrill of spy work and reduced it to the level of ridiculousness she now plainly realized. Her false *amore* of undercover glory dissolved and reformed as garbage wadded into her mouth and left there to mock her.

Number 7 felt herself losing the battle of self-control. A nice, loud remark tossed at the couple would not only satisfy her urge to trumpet her secret power, but the violation would feel sexual in itself. She stood up in her booth and prepared to speak—until the young guy beat her to it.

"Madame?" He called to Claudette just as she and her husband reached the front door. When she turned to him, he made a grand gesture of picking up her leather gloves from the floor.

Claudette's face lit up. "Oh! Thank you! I didn't even see them fall!" The young man handed the gloves to her with a grand gesture, then turned to the other diners as if to say, *See? I'm a good guy. How about a ride?*

The couple thanked him and made their way on out the door, disappearing among the freezing winds on their way to a warm encounter no one else knew about except Number 7. Her bitterness intensified now that the opportunity to get one over on them was gone. She was left with nothing else to do but turn her attention back to the Target Subject.

Again, as if taking his cues from his own FBI file, O'Connell piped up in his loudest voice yet. "You Freemasons are behind half of the backroom business shenanigans that increase the burdens on honest working people."

He was looking straight at the young guy who wanted a ride while he announced to the room, "This is one of them, folks, the overlords who keep you down in the same way the Masonic *cult* has always done!"

What happened next was strange enough for Number 7 to make a note of it in her file. The young man, for just one second, looked like he was about to storm O'Connell and throttle him. She had no doubt he could kill the older man with his bare hands. Instead, the hitchhiker stared at the floor and took a deep breath. Then he looked back up with a smile that was so bland Number 7 found it scarier than the rage it had replaced.

"Mister," the young man spoke up in the most polite tone you could imagine, "have you ever seen one of the fat cats who ride on the backs of workers who had to ask for the kindness of a lift because his car broke down?"

O'Connell laughed at that is if he genuinely appreciated the point. "Well said, fellow traveler! I guess even the Masons can slip up and let in an honest man now and then!"

But then O'Connell turned to the other customers and added with a wink, "Of course that doesn't mean you're one of them! Ha-ha-ha! No, but really. Have a seat. I'll buy you a cup of this watered-down coffee, brought to you by your *campesinos* in *Meh-hee-ko* for the benefit of chumps like us, eh?"

O'Connell gestured toward the door. "Of course the people who profit from it have already left for the day. *Eh*, folks?"

Number 7 also made a note of the fact that the young man reacted with a silly smile directed to everyone in the room and then extended one arm toward O'Connell.

"Ladies and gentlemen..." The younger man announced. After a dramatic pause he added, "He's all yours."

The handsome hitchhiker stepped out the door and was gone. *Just like that,* Number 7 wrote in the file, forgetting that the guy was not part of her mission.

Jerry O'Connell never missed a beat. He continued his lecture about evil capitalist business owners for the edification of the suckers who couldn't run until they paid their checks.

4

Day Of The Mason

Andy hustled up Main Street to the corner of Highway 12 and stuck out his thumb, still steaming over the bullshit attempts by the arrogant fat guy to publicly humiliate him *for no reason*. It flabbergasted him that any grown man would want to spend his time that way, acting the part of a buffoon and lecturing strangers. As if the fat guy had some direct line on the truth that everybody else missed out on. Back in the café Andy had searched for a calm reaction to the provocation, despite the sweet feel of his .32 caliber Smith & Wesson pressed against the small of his back like a lover's daring hand. He privately offered his act of restraint in the café to the Universe in hopes of snagging a quick ride down the highway.

But the post-lunch hour traffic was light. Of the few cars that passed, none even slowed down. He wondered how they could do that to a fellow human being. Were they telling themselves it really wasn't that cold, that he was not in any danger or anything like that? Because how could any son of a bitch just keep driving by and leave a man to the elements? How could they not realize the damned elements were taking on killer properties?

He figured the rancher-types must be a bunch of suspicious bastards—not sympathetic to a guy without his own transportation. Sure, he had that forty dollars he swiped from the Freemason's house, but if he spent it now on a bus ticket, he'd be broke again at his destination. No. The thing to do was try to reserve his little grub stake strictly for emergency use.

It struck him, *once temperatures drop well below freezing, no amount of winter clothing will keep you going for long.* Without shelter, a well-stolen parka only postpones the inevitable loss of body heat. There was nothing left to do but dance in the frigid air and keep his circulation going while he concentrated on projecting the image of the sort of guy *nobody* would want to leave out there in the cold.

He decided to stay in one spot and just try his luck there instead of venturing on outside town, walking backward alongside the Highway and hitching on the way. *Find you in the spring with your thumb still stuck out.*

It was clear to him that Life or Fate or Something was messing around with him in a serious manner, but he had no idea what to do about it. The only response he could form had to do with blowing town in a hurry and hoping things turned around after he landed somewhere safe far away. He'd been lucky enough to stay low since fleeing Oklahoma, but he knew cops like to share information and it was only a matter of time before the story of his exploits moved north. The made the clear choice a run for the Canadian border and a long cool-down spell. They mostly spoke the English language up there and that was all he needed to know to get started.

He masked his growing rage over being ignored by keeping an empty smile plastered on his face. Meanwhile each passing car fanned him with a blast of frigid air and hurtled off down the highway. A couple of them passed by far close for sanity and one of them even mock-shot Andy with his fingertip. What the hell was the matter with such people? It suddenly became the most important thing in Andy Carmichael's life to get the hell out of Dodge, which in this case was Roundup, Montana.

He had more than enough skill to get himself another car, but Andy still felt that strong instinctive message about keeping his head down until he was away from that town. Every day, he walked past decent vehicles that he could have driven away in a matter of seconds, keys or not. Most car doors were left unlocked, which helped, but didn't really matter. He could also open any locked car and climb right behind the wheel, using a thin wooden strip with a hooked end carved from a piece of kindling wood.

Thus it wasn't resourcefulness that held Andy back in Roundup. The little town was the county seat and the Sheriff was known to be especially tough on crime. Andy had eavesdropped on a number of conversations among the normals that spouted references to the sheriff's diligence.

Andy's feeling of dread about it remained so strong that he figured he was either developing some new mental power or there actually was something haunted about the place—something dangerous and easily fatal for him.

Getting shot at by those Bible thumpers down in Oklahoma had increased his tendency to be cautious. By the time he arrived in Roundup to begin with, he was on a streak of luck so foul it drove him out of Oklahoma, nonstop, all the way up there.

He hadn't wanted to stop in a two-bit place like Roundup fucking Montana, but true to the curse or whatever it was, his nearly-new stolen car broke down exactly at the town border. Right next to the sign, *"Welcome to Roundup! With a big cutout of a cowboy twirling a lariat in a giant circle and inside the giant circle were the words, "Bring your round-up to Roundup—see why all the other round-ups rounded-up here!"* The slogan struck Andy as so offensively stupid that he took the time to use a burned match head to draw a very tiny penis on the cowboy.

He thought about how funny it would be to actually go to the trouble of returning to Oklahoma just to track down the stolen car's owner and kill him for letting his vehicle fall into such bad condition. An involuntary giggle snorted out of him at the thought of tying up the guy and spelling it all out.

Here's why you're about to die, idiot. You let your car get so run down that it broke out from under me in some one-horse town in the middle of Montana! It's not that far away for a car that's been kept up.

But you didn't care a thing about what could happen to a guy like <u>me</u> if I was depending on your car to get me someplace, <u>did</u> you?

Really do it right—treat that sad sack to the same kind of lecture the bald guy dished out to Andy back in the café. Hell, maybe even shoot him every few sentences to emphasize important points. Andy visualized the scene so clearly it was like remembering a very special Christmas.

He sighed and reluctantly allowed the fond fantasy to go, knowing that today was the day for Andy Carmichael to change his luck. That much at least, he thought, should not be too hard because *the whole secret about luck is that luck always changes.* Andy felt a flash of satisfaction at being the kind of guy who recognized a fundamental truth like that.

■ ■ ■

"Donnie, isn't that the guy who was back at the cafe looking for a ride?" Claudette Thornton pointed out the front windshield at the lone figure some fifty yards ahead, jumping up and down on his toes at the side of the road and holding out his thumb.

"The fake Mason?"

"Oh, maybe he's from another lodge."

"I watched him shake hands with the guy near the door. He's no Mason."

"Come on. We should stop. Slow down up here."

Donnie faced a dilemma. He recognized that Claudette's generosity was partly because they were in this beautiful bubble of love and hope radiated by their decision. Donnie could see Claudette was full of that spirit. Right then she just wanted to mother everybody. That was part of why he loved her as fiercely as he did, but he also knew she tended to forget that not everyone shared her generous motives. Donny always claimed the duty of making sure his partner's kindness was scattered on good soil.

On the other hand, he had also waited for years to come to grips with trying for another baby and if he quashed her loving impulses at that moment he feared watching her turn cold again. That sort of cold-ness was worse than anything a weather front could bring in, and she could keep it up for days.

He had one card to play. "Uh, honey, we have a pretty special afternoon planned. Maybe we—"

She stopped him with a hand high on his thigh and spoke in a tone of warm honey that left him powerless. "Shush, now. This is going to be a blessed day for us. When you have so much love, it's only right to share it with someone in need. If we don't, it's as if we're ungrateful."

He sighed just as they passed the hitchhiker, then applied the brakes. While the car slowed he looked into her eyes and softly told her, "I'm not ungrateful, Claudette."

She smiled the same smile that had sent him head over heels in love with her back when they were still in school. As soon as the car stopped she quickly kissed him and replied, "Neither of us is, honey."

They both turned to watch the hitchhiker come loping toward them. The fellow's youthful face was covered with a smile of relief and delight. He looked completely harmless.

■ ■ ■

Andy's False Face got him safely into the car and through the introduc-tions to Johnny and Claudia or something. They warned him that they only lived a mile or so past the cemetery outside town on Highway 12, but Andy was savvy enough to put out the idiot grin and assure them that every little bit was a help to him.

It was the husband's fault that things went bad. They might as well have run straight off a cliff. All because the driver was a pushy bastard who seemed to feel the need to twist corkscrew questions into Andy over the issue of one Masonic ring and a lousy lapel pin.

The ring did it. Andy clearly saw that. From the first moment his own strategic error occurred to him, nausea snaked through his intestines. Not that it would have changed anything necessarily, but the gut snake seemed to want Andy to be honest with himself about his responsibility for failing to drop the Freemason pose as soon as he got in the car.

If he had climbed in without showing the ring or the pin and said nothing at all about Masons, maybe the tough-guy driver might not have said anything about it. But Andy had failed in that regard, and that was that. He wasn't a man to shy away from admitting his short-comings.

He had tried to keep up a lie without doing his homework, and that move was strictly for amateurs. It surely wasn't for a guy with serious incarceration time under his belt and up his ass. If he had played it cool, maybe things would have worked out and he could have just shot them each quickly in the head and they would never know what hit them. Bingo—you're gone.

But apparently Fate decided Andy hadn't been getting the shaft hard enough lately, because the driver of the car turned out to be a Mason himself. The guy took way too much pleasure in pointing out half a dozen ways Andy failed to establish himself from one brother Mason to another.

Mr. Real Mason also seemed to take extra amounts of delight in humiliating Andy in front of his beautiful wife Claudia or whoever she was.

Now Andy glanced at her without intending to and he winced at the sight. Her vacant eyes stared in his general direction with that look people get after they realize you are about to kill them and then you do it anyway. Andy realized he was responsible for putting that expression on her face, but he still hated the beautiful woman for allowing herself to look so ugly. He had seen dead people who didn't look completely foolish. It was possible.

Oh, but when he had first climbed into that warm car and the smell of the man's overcoat mixed with the female aroma of his wife, Andy had immediately breathed in a holy mix of her body odor and some sort of faint perfume. She had just finished an egg salad sandwich back in the café and still had the familiar eggy smell on her breath. Within a few seconds of climbing in he was overwhelmed by the urge to leap over the seat and bury his tongue in her mouth. He had to look away from her while they picked up speed. Andy's whole body ached with envy over everything that lousy driver had in his life.

All the guy needed to do was drive the car like he was serious about it and he could have died clean. But no. He had to mock Andy for his fakery.

And in that moment, Andy's sudden passion for the Missus and her charms had seamlessly blended with his raging envy for the life of a man of substance. The contempt heaped onto Andy by the driver was the real clincher, with the guy looking the same way the big boys always did back in the joint when they declared ownership on him.

The sneer did it. In the next moment, Andy fell into that old state when he genuinely didn't care if he lived to see the next minute or not. He was overwhelmed with the desire to return the contempt tenfold. With no warning at all, he threw himself forward against the driver's seat and hooked his left arm all the way around the guy's neck, then squeezed it closed while he leaned his full body weight toward the floor, pulling the man backward over his seat.

With the driver flailing in shock and outrage, the wife screamed and, bless her heart, tried to break Andy's grip on her husband's neck. But Andy's true point of advantage lay not merely in his indifference to death but also in knowing that a crash would go easiest on him, braced there against the back of the driver's seat the way he was.

Ten seconds or less was enough for the blackout chokehold to work, and he felt Ronnie or whatever the name was go limp just a few seconds before the car ran off the road and rolled to a harmless stop in tall grass. When the Missus tried to jump out and break for it, Andy was able to let go of the unconscious husband and pull her back in by her shirt. He threw the same grip on her with his right arm and closed it off with his left, gave it the ten second hold and felt her drop limp against him—it was the only feeling he preferred to having sex.

After he hopped up front and drove the car far enough off the road to get privacy, Andy realized in review that his mistake lay in allowing them to wake up. He should have known better and he derided himself for missing that one. But in the heat of the moment, it had not been enough for him to merely kill them. Not after the man's attempt to embarrass Andy for no reason, right there in front of a gorgeous wife any man would want to run home to every night of his life. Andy would. He would know just how to treat her right. It was unbearable to be humiliated in front of her.

So instead of listening to his own criminal brilliance he settled for allowing them to wake up once he tied their hands and feet with strips of hubby's shirt. Her blouse was useful in making good blindfold pieces, but he left off the gags because he wanted to hear the man plead. This part, he also realized afterward, was also an error.

He had no need to hear their pitiful conversation when they realized they were about to die. Who did the husband think he was, carrying on like that? Asking her to forgive him, saying he should have done his duty and driven her home, regardless. She just said she loved him, over and over, and she was in the process of thanking him for being her husband when Andy had to stop it from both of them. One, two, quick, quick. No shit. Enough of that.

The car, however, was a solid black three-hole Buick Super, only a year old, with excellent rubber on the tires and a full tank of gas. Andy discovered that the Thornberrys or whoever they were turned out to be generous right up to the end.

He pointed the car back toward town to brazenly pass on through and then hold the road west until he picked up a wide highway going north to Canada. There, he had been told, people would believe just about anything you told them if you were nice about it.

5

"Jerry The Red"

Sheriff Preston was relieved that the task of transporting Jerry O'Connell from the Roundup Café to the home of Byron and Ruth Sherman only took a few minutes. Even that small amount of time in the company of "Jerry The Red" was on a par with having hemorrhoids sand blasted. Fortunately, the Shermans' place was easy to find. The couple published The Worker's Monthly – "Common Sense With A Conscience!" and were known to pretty much everybody in that small town.

Preston was frustrated and appalled. It should have been a beautiful afternoon. But instead his freshly released, newly outfitted highway cruiser, which required an open highway to test its rocket-like strength for the first time, was drafted into the service of babysitting some clown with a big mouth.

The car was already last year's top model of the heavy duty Ford sedans, delivered to the County as the be-all and end-all of police cars, factory equipped with a "police package" consisting of everything the auto company considered useful to crime-fighting work: twin sirens, wired-in cherry lights, heavy glass interior partition. They even removed the door handles in the passenger compartment and covered the holes with shiny round chrome plates.

And still it took an entire year to squirrel away enough County money to finish the job right. Today's release of the car from the County shop was a long sought victory of public funding. The geniuses in the shop not only figured out how to install a massive engine, but they also designed and manufactured a set of custom disk brakes that were years ahead of the marketplace. The new brakes complimented the vehicle's ferocious acceleration power with the surprising ability to stop it, planting rubber so hard that if you didn't hold on tight to the wheel you'd get your chest jammed into it.

But it was the new engine that truly transformed the vehicle. Although the boys at the motor company built a product sufficient to the traffic needs of a cowboy lawman chasing drunks through the snow drifts and rain storms, Wade Preston had his own ideas about how to finish the job. Since he was the guy who charged with preventing the roads from turning into killing grounds, he considered the real solution to his needs to lie in raw engine power.

Wade Preston felt personally deprived. The fool was no longer wrecking the peace of mind of the customers in the Roundup Café, but he was creating *coitus interruptus* of the new cruiser's maiden voyage.

As of this day, the Sheriff of Musselshell County was driving a cruiser powered by a mammoth straight-8 engine that produced enough power to push the heavy vehicle up the side of a glacier. The inline pistons developed more thrust than any V-8 engine on the road, period.

The unfortunate tendency of the straight-8 pistons to fall out of rhythm at high speeds and explode through the engine wall was offset by the irresistible sensation of invincibility delivered through the engine torque. The sensation overflowed the heart muscle and dribbled onto the groin, pooled in the lap, and emerged as a hard-on for highway speeders. Half rocket ship, half sedan, it was sure to change the whole highway game.

Yeah sure, Preston couldn't help but think, *come speeding through Musselshell County like we all drive tractors out here and nobody gives a rat's ass.* He felt his own heavy foot ready for action. He was eager to present the first roadside customer with a ears pre-deafened to any and all bullshit excuses.

And yet, and yet, and yet, on the very day he took delivery of the vehicle that at last gave him the power to actually perform the duties charged to him and catch the rampaging bastards before they could speed over the next rise and disappear onto a side road, here was this doughy little carbuncle of a man presenting the challenge of getting him out of the County with as little fanfare as possible. Problem being that for "Jerry the Red" O'Connell, a confrontation (and who knows, maybe an interview with a reporter?) was just the ticket for the old rabble rouser, something he went around looking for in the first place.

So Sheriff Preston figured to let the bastard go have his heart attack back in Cascade County, where he belonged. Old Jerry got himself expelled from Congress by his own Democratic party, too left wing even for them. He now he ran around the state preaching against capitalism instead of working and appeared to be constantly in need of survival money. He was known to have a wife at home, and he told people stories about becoming a recent lawyer back in Great Falls. Preston couldn't picture the guy actually passing the bar; he had to wonder who O'Connell bribed to get his license.

But for the last month or so, O'Connell had been appearing in Roundup a once or twice a week, claiming to be "inspecting working conditions on behalf of employees." Preston was mildly amused by the loud-mouth's failure to realize half the town already knew the real purpose of his appearances, and it had far less to do with righting capitalist wrongs and much more to do with moistening his wick with a local girl named Rebecca Corday. Preston ran a couple of checks on her after spotting them together the first time. Ten years younger (obvious), homely but stacked like a rock trail marker (very obvious), lacking in personal taste (immediately obvious, being with O'Connell). She was, overall, a giant red flag as a believable match for a chubby, bald, broke, married man who lived in another town and couldn't drive to see her because he had a heart condition.

Sheriff Preston didn't care about any of it. Upon reflection, he found the little worm the perfect subject for the inaugural passenger's ride, locked up in the sealed rear compartment of the brand new souped-up car. The right place for him, as long as he just had to ruin Preston's afternoon.

Preston tilted his head so O'Connell couldn't see him from his perch, then grinned at the thought of showing him the police file on his new squeeze. Let the sap know about that little sweetheart's past record at strip–mining married men and selling them her silence.

But then the Sheriff's stomach twisted with the painful knowledge that he could do no such thing. He hung by the neck from the same laws he enforced every day, and though he had surely dreamed of retribution at times during his ten years on the job, he never acted out his rage, no matter how much appeal retaliation may have held. Now those bygone days of the Vigilante movement and their cryptic motto of *3-7-77* were like a siren song, begging him to crack the ex-Congressman's head with his nightstick and roll him out of the car someplace way off in the grasslands.

But no, those clearer days were gone. Most of the time, the world was better for it. And that was only right. It was human progress. *Just not this time.*

He appreciated rare opportunities for on-the-job humor, so when the cruiser was nearly in front of the Shermans' modest home, Preston simultaneously blipped the siren, flashed the cherry, and stomped hard on the brakes.

This threw his passenger forward and into the thick glass partition, causing him to bang his forehead against it. The siren and lights assured the attention of anybody in the area. Many would peek out their windows and see their Sheriff delivering some guy to the Sherman household, bringing trouble in. There would be discussions over dinner.

Preston calculated that most of the neighbors likely hated the Shermans already over the neighborhood's frequent visits from cars full of rabid anti-communists shouting invective. The brief siren blasts would shoot a cold rush of concern into the arteries of everyone within earshot. After that, all he had to do was drive off and give them time to marinate in the knowledge of that disruptive influence in their neighborhood, their town, their state. A little indirect action could be just the thing to remind the Shermans of their local status as anti-American rabble rousers.

O'Connell continued howling like a child and cursing over his little bump to the forehead, already whining about police brutality. That kind of self-pitying talk got thrown at Preston from time to time, and it always felt like tooth pain. He gave the man a look that implied he would suffer a bad death if he didn't shut up, then turned off the engine and spun all the way around to his passenger.

"Only reason you aren't in handcuffs is I don't feel like dealing with them. I'm lazy today so you're lucky."

"I beg you pardon?" O'Connell gasped, using a polished tone of fake outrage that the Sheriff had heard before. "I appreciate your kindness in giving me a ride, Sheriff, but I'm *hardly* a perpetrator!"

"What you are is a man who disturbs the peace in my county on a regular basis. And before we get to your story of working for 'noble causes,' let me just make sure you realize that I know the who, the what, and the where, of you sticking your cock into, shall we say, a certain local resident misguided enough to grant you the opportunity."

"Hey! Hey! Hey, Sheriff! I only asked for—"

"You didn't get a ride from me because you *asked*; you got a ride because people at the Café are tired of listening to you and wanted you gone. They're sick of the disturbances you cause."

"The system needs to be disturbed, Sheriff! And I'm sorry if that hurt's your feelings or something."

"You got a ride from me to this place so I don't have to haul you to the county line and drop you there, mister. Now I agreed with Mrs. Sherman on the phone to deliver you to them, but only because it lets me get back to my real work, see? It's not for you. I'm holding her to her promise to drive you to the county line or give you bus money, but to see you get out of here and proceed on your way. And damn it, don't come back here broke anymore."

Preston started to get out, then stopped and again turned back to O'Connell. "What the hell are you doing running around with no car, no bus fare or anything, anyway? You come here on a one-way bus ticket. What did you think would happen if you got stuck?"

"I *was* stuck! I got stood up by, by, my appointment. But as you see, the Shermans are willing to help me. That's what people do when the almighty dollar doesn't dictate the choices they—"

"I could run you in for vagrancy, you know, but I'm not putting you up for the night at county expense! If you want to bunk somewhere, find a friend or pay for it!" Preston got out of the car, opened the rear door, and pulled O'Connell out.

"Hey! Gently if you don't mind! I'm not under arrest!"

"You're close enough. Now walk to the front door under your own power or I'll drag you."

Preston pulled O'Connell onto the front porch and knocked at the door. He was gratified that it opened right away, by Mrs. Ruth Sherman, thirty-five, face sharp as a hatchet. Preston realized she must have been watching them from behind the curtains.

"Here he is, Mrs. Sherman."

"Sheriff, was it necessary to alert the neighborhood like that?"

"Yes."

"Hi, Ruth"

"Yeah. Hello, Jerry. Seriously, Sheriff, we have enough trouble with the neighbors already without—"

"I'm holding you to your promise to get this guy to the county line. And O'Connell, if you show up in my county during the next week I'm arresting you for vagrancy." He glanced at Ruth Sherman, "You want to pay his bail once he's in custody?"

"Hell no. We don't have any extra money."

"I guess that settles it then, Jerry—you're on your way home." He glared at O'Connell for emphasis, then nodded to Ruth Sherman, turned around and strode across the yard to the souped-up cruiser without looking back.

6

Montana's Only Working Conscience

Ruth looked at Jerry and sighed. "Well, I guess you ought to come on inside."

"Thanks, Ruth," Jerry beamed. "I knew I could count on the Shermans!"

She shook her head and moved aside to let him in. "Yeah, you could count on one of us, anyway." She glanced back inside at her husband. "I'm afraid if you want to bring Byron on board you're going to have to sell him yourself."

Moments later, Jerry cooled his heels alone in their living room while Ruth and Byron carried out a whispered argument out in the kitchen.

"Couldn't you have told me before you did this?" Byron demanded. His forced whisper made him sound like he was choking.

"No. I knew you'd refuse."

"I'd say so!" Byron peered around the corner at the dumpy man twiddling his thumbs on their worn sofa, then turned back to his wife. "That bastard brings trouble everywhere he goes!"

"He's also the most valuable ally the progressive movement has in Montana because he knows just enough law to make himself brave. He'll stand up to anybody! I mean, he doesn't care who! Sooner or later he'll get his comeuppance, but until then, if we're going to beat out the likes of Bushmaster Mining..." She straightened her skirt and forced a smile, then started toward the living room while she whispered back to him, "We need useful idiots."

Ruth threw Byron that saucy grin that always melted any resistance on his part. She left him poised on the brink of wondering whether tonight might be one of those rare nights when she might actually let daddy pretend mommy was a hooker.

■ ■ ■

Andy slipped across the border at Sweetgrass, Montana, firmly concealed behind his False Face. He penetrated the border as easy as blowing smoke through a nylon stocking.

When he topped off the performance with a dose of Harmless Goofball, the Mounties in the little guard hut even threw in travel directions to help him proceed on up Highway 4. By the time he hit the gas he was nearly ready to ask if local people were known to lock their doors, maybe get some information on who had the money in those parts.

He picked up a couple of sandwiches at one of the border hotel restaurants, then jumped back in the hot Buick and took off. He needed to be thoroughly dissolved into the Canadian background before the cops back down in Montana put up out the alarm.

Andy's overall plan was the same as it had been since the day he escaped the road crew: remain at large and follow his quest for adventure. Part of the joy of being free from the restrictions of prison life was the power to stop people from messing around with you. In prison, you had to just take it. Out in the wilds, you had a whole range of choices on how to go about shutting them up. The quickest remained his handy-dandy .32 Smith & Wesson short barrel, but until that morning he had kept his cool with it concealed in the small of his back.

He drove at the top of the speed limit for the next half hour, waiting for life to changeup on him. His luck had been so up and down that day, he couldn't believe he would just pass into Canada and that would be the end of his troubles. He could tell life had him trapped in some sort of crazy change-of-luck pattern, but couldn't make sense of it.

He was able to keep things pretty quiet back in Roundup by lying low, but that auto mechanic was going to run the plates on the hot car sooner or later. Clearly, it was time to be gone, and yet the instant he got out into the world, everything started going off track. Everybody seemed to exist for the purpose of putting up obstacles to him. If it wasn't for all the other people out there, Andy was pretty sure he would be doing all right.

Instead the first half hour of his trip to Canada was spent immersed in dread and confusion. Questions haunted him: how could he watch out for the next big drop in his luck? Could he somehow head it off and keep it from happening in the first place? He sensed it was coming. He sensed it as the feel of deep ground vibration from the approaching footsteps of a giant predator, steadily advancing.

He steered the Buick around a sharp bend in the highway and just when the road straightened out once again, the next change in Andy's luck manifested directly ahead of him, right there at the side of the road. Two of them: males in their late teens, standing with their thumbs out, just as he had been doing earlier that same day. He glanced ahead. The road was empty, and nobody was in his rearview mirror. The empty road explained why they were waving and smiling at him, trying to dazzle him into stopping with the excitement on their hopeful faces.

The spectacle they put on made Andy laugh out loud. It felt wonderful, his first laugh in hours. A sense of relaxation washed through him in a warm wave, loosening tight muscles. It brought him a clear message, namely that his next Luck Changers stood right there before him, by way of Divine delivery. It was fate, and Andy prided himself on being bright enough to know only fools ignore such a call.

The hitchhiking jerks were so dumb about the correct way to thumb a ride, they actually carried hockey sticks, clearly not considering that people might worry about such things potentially used as weapons. When he got close enough to see that each one of them also had a campfire hatchet strapped to his belt, he laughed again, right out loud. Andy was instantly charmed by their naivety. He felt something close to love.

He hit the brakes and pulled to the right, watching the two idiots jump up and down when they realized he was stopping for them. They ran toward the hot Buick with their hockey sticks up in the air and their hatchets actually *flapping* at their waists, God love them. Clearly, two skulls of solid bone were approaching, oblivious to the one-in-a-million chance that had just befallen them with an actual ride in this arctic weather in spite of their hatchets and long sticks. They had the appearance of a couple of rowdy fellows, no doubt full of drinking songs and foul intentions for the ladies. Not a single introspective thought between them. Lovable dead heads, good-hearted simple-tons, they appeared to be just the sort of distraction Andy needed at this difficult hour.

7

To Break, To Enter

Jerry tended to wave his wine glass while he talked, making Ruth nervous about her carpet. So far she had kept her concerns to herself while she and Byron received their lecture from Jerry, hoping he would get to the point of his visit.

"What you two need to understand is that your magazine has an obligation to follow the dictates of the Communist Party headquarters in Great Falls! Your publication is the only outlet they have in this part of the state."

"Jerry," Byron said while he wiped his eyes in a tired gesture, "The Worker's Monthly is a progressive magazine, but we do *not* represent the Communist Party. Never have."

"That's just it!" Jerry beamed, fully warmed to the topic, "You don't have to! Don't you see? If you're genuinely progressive, then the entire Communist movement already represents *you*! Don't you see? *Automatically!*"

"That might be debatable," Byron tersely replied.

Ruth decided it was time to cut to the chase. "Jerry, when you called from the café and asked us for help with your, ah, situation there, you were quite specific that you needed to discuss something confidential with us."

Jerry gave up his most charming laugh, the one that usually worked wonders. "This is it!"

"What is?"

"This! Us! Talking like this! Hell, I couldn't meet you at the café and talk like this! This has to be done in private!"

"No, Jerry," Byron jumped in, "We had no need to meet with you to be told to toe the Party line. Just because we're against companies that abuse their workers—"

"Byron," Ruth warned.

"No, I mean it, Ruth! And Jerry, it looks to me like you didn't have any reason to meet with us. This could have been done over the phone."

Jerry assumed the role of a righteous man unjustly wounded. "Damn it, Byron! That's not true!"

"Byron," Ruth warned again.

Byron slapped his hand on the table in impatience. "Don't 'Byron' me, Ruth! And Jerry, I've got this sneaky suspicion your visit to Roundup didn't have anything to do with us. I mean what're you doing here?"

Ruth shook her head and looked away.

"Unfair, Byron!" Jerry exclaimed. "I'm the victim, here. I reached out to you! I trusted you as the only people around here who don't judge a man by the money in his pocket. Sure, I got abandoned here today, but it's hardly my doing if certain people not only can't keep an appointment, but couldn't even have the courtesy to call ahead, instead of letting me find out from a note on the front door."

"What, somebody in Roundup?" Ruth asked.

"Let's just say I spent money I can't afford for a one-way bus ticket just to oversee these particular employee complaints, and I was brought in even though my heart condition is known and I can't drive and I was depending on them to send me back home. *That's* what I was doing in town today, and I was only at the Café because I needed to find a lift back to Great Falls after I got stood up. With complete disrespect!"

Ruth found herself beginning to share her husband's frustration. "Jerry what does this have to do with us having to promise the Sheriff we would either see you back home or across the county line?"

"I'm telling you that wouldn't have been necessary at all, except for that hitchhiker! People were frustrated by him, mad at *him*, not me! It's just that *he* just left first, so they took it out on me! Hell, I wasn't the one waving around a Freemason's ring and wearing their lapel pin, saying you know, 'Give a Mason a ride,' and all. People were made suspicious by his conduct! I even heard somebody said he wasn't a real Mason 'cause he didn't know the right signs, whatever they are."

At that point Jerry performed a rare mid-course check and slowed down at the sight of the alarm on Byron's face. He pressed on like a man walking in chest-deep water, "I mean Byron, *you'd* have known, I guess. Right? You're a longtime Mason. Right?"

Ruth's hand went up to her mouth while Byron jumped up, knocking his chair backward, and grabbed Jerry by the upper arm. "Come here and look at this," he said, pulling Jerry hard enough to make it clear that there was no refusing him.

He towed Jerry into the rear of the kitchen where the door led to the back yard and pointed at a section of newspaper taped over a missing glass pane in the backdoor.

"See that? We had a break-in here sometime this morning after we left to see the printer over in Billings, and before we got back this afternoon. Strange thing. Hardly touched anything around here, not that there's a lot, but there are things he could have stolen to sell."

"It was a man?"

"I don't hear much about female break-in artists."

"All right, so what makes you think somebody came in? Something missing?"

"I wasn't sure, at first. I have this big Masonic ring and a matching lapel pin, but I don't wear them anymore."

"Wait. They're gone?"

"Well, now I guess so. Actually I thought I misplaced them and figured I'd come across them around here."

"Well, there you are! Maybe you will!"

Byron glanced at Ruth to see if she approved of him going ahead and telling Jerry the rest. The gesture was an honorary offering to her, intended to pay for going this far without her permission. He was relieved when his placation worked well enough that she played along and gave him a quick nod. If he was in real trouble she would have just gone cold and refused to see him. She had such skill at it that she could remain blind to him for hours.

"Here's the thing. My new winter coat is definitely missing and my best pair of snow boots is gone, too. They were in the front closet when I left this morning. Hell I almost wore 'em, but I changed my mind!"

Jerry's expression paled. "That guy had on a huge coat. Heavy boots, too."

Ruth interrupted, "Wait a minute, By. How do you know it was him?"

"Are you kidding?" Byron responded. "In a town of fifteen hundred? It was him."

"Did he get any money?" asked Jerry.

Byron nodded. "Four hundred dollars, cash." Byron nodded when Jerry whistled at the amount. "We'll have to get reimbursed on the magazine's insurance."

"The work doesn't pay us enough to carry our own," Ruth quickly added.

"I understand perfectly," Jerry replied with a wink. He shook his head at Byron. "And the bastard was showing them *your* ring. Think of that! I challenged him about it, though. I think that's why he ran out, 'cause I told him he was no Mason."

"Well what kind of idiot takes chances like that for those few little things he took out of here?" Ruth fumed.

"Maybe a guy who wasn't here to rob you in the first place?" Jerry replied. "You two have a lot of enemies. What if some group like Bushmaster Mining or the Cattlemen's Association sent someone after you? Maybe he just grabbed a few things for his trouble since he was already here."

Ruth blew up at that one. "Oh that is *enough*! You cannot come into our home and put an idea like that into the air. Don't you think we lose enough sleep already?"

Byron interrupted, "Okay stop it, you two. I know what happened now! I know! And I tell you what, this was one of the itinerant workers on his way out of town. He was looking for an easy score. The guy was careless because he knew he *wasn't coming back here*, see? He's across the state line already, I'll bet you! So relax!"

He knitted his hands behind his neck and leaned back. "Guy could be all the way to Canada by now! Even as we speak!"

8

Everything With A Capital "E"

Andy pumped the brakes gently on the steep and slippery downhill side of the mountain, squinting through snow flurries that were just beginning to swirl. He was careful to keep his voice down while he cursed the rotten luck that continued to plague him. He fought with the need to talk to himself out loud instead of just in his head, but every time the pair in the trunk heard his voice, one or both tried to respond as if he was addressing them.

Andy was forced several times to execute a series of persuasion maneuvers, jamming the brakes hard and then stomping on the accelerator, over and over until they took the hint and shut up. This time they started up the noise on their own, in spite of his efforts to avoid setting them off.

But his options were much more limited, now that traffic was forming under the harsh weather. With other cars visible, he didn't dare hit his trunk passengers with the old stop-and-go, funny as it was to shake them around.

It took all his willpower to ignore their racket. He chewed his teeth on the knowledge that the miserable pair of beer farts cheated him just as badly as the former driver of his car tried to do. In both cases, there he was, trying to do nothing more than put distance between himself and Roundup, Montana. And he had been so careful. All for nothing.

Escaping town wasn't enough, escaping the state wasn't enough, escaping the country wasn't enough. He was currently at least an hour's drive north of the border, and still there had been absolutely no change in his luck. Nothing.

Events that he would have bet his life were going to turn out a certain way kept right on turning out another way altogether. He had no sense of control over any of it. The question haunting him was simply why. He had nursed high hopes that the Oklahoma situation would be his worst mistake following his escape, but still one slip kept right on leading to another.

"God-damned guh-hucks!" he shouted, suddenly not caring if he roused them or not. "Beaver-eating tree choppers! And I mean *actual* beaver, too!" He stomped the brakes extra hard for emphasis, but this time he only did it once and covered the move by simultaneously projecting the idea that he was trying to avoid hitting wildlife—just in case anybody else out on the road happened to be looking. He felt certain he could get away with one hard brake stomp and not look too suspicious. It just might be enough to shut the boys up again.

Goddamn it! He had really been looking forward to the company of two good-hearted simpletons from the local woods. Two kids dumb enough to *voluntarily* stand in the arctic air and bet their asses on catching a ride in spite of their tall sticks and the large cutting instruments. No one was going to stop for them, but nevertheless Andy did. He gladly took on the role of their angel.

And then what did his good intentions bring back to him? Two local morons who made it crystal clear they were part of the invisible plan working against him, set in motion by the Freemasons. Right from the first moment.

They introduced themselves like good fellows as soon as they hopped in, shivering and grateful as hell. The first one gave his name as Roger or Roland or something, and the second one—looking straight at Andy and speaking right out loud—said, "Hi! I'm Mason!"

The dead giveaway was that the kid announced his name like he was just the proudest thing on the planet to be named "Mason." This was a stupid mistake for Andy's pursuers to make. The excessive emphasis on the name clearly revealed the sort of ironic humor the Freemasons were trying to employ while they roped him in.

But why? Andy couldn't fathom what a secret organization made up of people in powerful positions wanted with him.

Could he have started it that morning, with that little home burglary? Surely, whoever owned the coat and boots and ring and pin and the cash realized that it all was taken by a fellow who really needed a hand. Besides, the guy had other coats, probably a bunch of them. If such a man had half a heart, he even might feel proud to have helped out a less fortunate individual. Thus the forty dollars became Andy's reasonable fee for providing a sense of self-righteousness to a man who, until then, was just another guy with too many coats.

But now as the snow flurries thickened and the road became treacherous underneath the wheels, Andy began to regret habitually keeping his .32 Caliber Smith & Wesson tucked into the small of his back. That had been his true mistake, right there.

He realized it now. It was far too easy to reach the weapon in a hasty moment of panic, which wouldn't happen if it was locked in the trunk. Of course there wasn't much point in owning a gun for self-protection if a man couldn't get to it. *Hell,* he reminded himself, *guys going pheasant hunting lock their gun in the trunk. But guys looking to stay alive keep the thing handy.* Nevertheless, as he was so recently reminded, accidents do happen.

A lump welled in his throat. They were just boys, really. They seemed so terrified when he yanked out the gun and shot Mason, seated directly behind him, square in the knee. Suddenly Andy had two screaming little girls on his hands and it was only by threatening to shoot again that he persuaded the second one to squeeze off his buddy's wound and slow the bleeding. It was a chore to have to then get them both climbed back there into the trunk, what with blood all over the place.

Now the question of finishing them off was built in. What else was he supposed to do with these Freemason spooks following him around, working for a hidden organization so mysterious that he had heard people say they were behind everything that mattered, and that was Everything with a capital "E." All of it.

Let them go, so they could report back to their superiors on him? Why not shoot himself in the head and get on with it?

The car rolled hard over a chunk of ice and one of the trunk passengers yelped a couple of times. Andy felt the last of his sympathy drain from his heart. Those noises were enough to seal the fate of both young men.

What to do? He hated to pollute Canada so soon and get the Mounties looking for him. He didn't dare to leave these Masonic spies out in the open, the way he had with the couple in Montana. But the ground had to be frozen solid, probably several feet down. He sure as hell wasn't going to dig a grave for two with a sharpened stick or even with a shovel, and he wasn't about to spend money on a shovel. Gas and sandwiches were already eating into that forty dollars fast enough.

9

New Burns From An Old Flame

By the time Donnie and Claudette Thornton were found and the call went out, Sheriff Preston was just pulling back into the station after several highly satisfying hours out on the highway searching for the legendary Lead Foot and then running him down like a jet fighter going after a biplane. The souped-up cruiser proved to be a complete sweetheart, everything he hoped for, a kiss on the mouth from your best girl.

But the moment he walked into the station, two badly shaken boys inside changed everything. The young ranch hands reported that they were out driving alongside their fence line, looking for a couple of wandering cattle, when they "stopped to water a tree" at a turnaround spot just off the road. When they pulled over, their headlights came across a dead man and woman sprawled among the small grove standing there. The woman was mostly naked but the man was fully clothed. It was obvious even at a distance that both had been violently killed.

Ten minutes later Preston was out at the scene in a small grove of scrub trees, just a few miles down from the cemetery. His two deputies were close behind in the second county car, but he parked and went ahead on foot by flashlight. He only had to take a few steps before the beam found them.

The soft yellow light was enough to deliver a sight that caused Preston to recoil and sent his heart slamming inside of his chest. He heard the sounds of his deputy vehicle approaching, bringing power-ful lights. He was glad for their company in this terrible moment, but he hated the thought of these two particular victims under the harsh artificial lights of a crime scene.

Donnie and Claudette Thornton were much more than friends to Wade Preston. The two men had managed to accomplish that rare feat of fighting over a girl and yet ending up with all three remaining friends. All it took was for Preston to face the fact that his best pitch wasn't going to be enough to win her. At first he hated Donnie with such red rage that his revenge fantasies frightened him. But all three had grown up in that town and none felt the desire to leave, so he sim-ply kept on loving Claudette even after he lost her to Donnie Thornton, and because he loved her he never said a word to cross her husband.

The final twist of the blade was that Donnie Thornton turned out to be a kind man who held no grudges and welcomed Preston into friendship with the couple. Each encounter was excruciating for him, but it kept him in her presence. It was a way to remain on the receiving end of her charming tenderness and her dazzling smiles.

For him, every trip to the Roundup Café was a private challenge. Still he always managed to keep himself proper in their company and they kept the welcome mat out for him. It was a perpetual source of humility for Wade Preston because he had to admit in the privacy of his heart that he would never have done that for Thornton. He would have told the guy that while the three of them would remain civil in public, he would absolutely shoot him on sight if he found him sneak-ing around his wife. And then he would have kept Claudette, whom he had loved with a full heart from the day they met, all to himself.

The years since then had convinced Wade Preston that his life was not one that produced magical things. But he remembered every detail about meeting young Claudette Stiles before her name became Thornton, right down to the song playing on the radio: Harry Babbit and Gloria Wood doing "On a Slow Boat To China." He could still hear Kay Kyser's fabulous orchestra and clearly recalled the lyric floating in the air while he took in her beauty for the first time. *"Honey, I'd love to get you On a Slow Boat to China, all to myself (with nobody else) yes, all to myself alone."*

Some old form of envy sent a sick wave through him while he stood stunned by the sight of Donnie's swollen tongue between blackened lips. In addition to the strangulation, part of the victim's face was blown away by what could have either been the killing shot or just some form of post-mortem rage.

Preston heard his men approaching and had to swallow the urge to turn and shout them away. It was terrible to allow Claudette to be seen the way she was, there on the ground. It felt somehow sacrilegious to leave her that way instead of holding the others back until he could cover her with a blanket and at least protect her from further shame.

But he recognized the impulse as useless and didn't follow it. Instead he turned his flashlight away to give her another moment of respect before the brighter beams of two more lights found the scene. Moments later, when the lights played across her, both deputies took a step backward at the sight and swore in shock and outrage.

For a moment all three men stood transfixed and tried to make the images in front of them come together in their heads. Donnie lay closest to them, no drag marks around him, looking as if he'd been rolled out of a vehicle. He was fully dressed. But his wife lay a few yards away with her clothing ripped to shreds. The few torn fragments left on her did nothing to preserve her dignity.

The pair were abandoned in a small grove of trees next to a small pond used by the ranch for a watering hole. The deputies were able to drive right up to it—an easy dump site for a killer in a hurry. It might have been perpetrated by two or more males, but Preston already certain in his gut that this was the handiwork of a single individual.

The things done to Claudette Thornton were evils a perpetrator would surely savor in privacy while enjoying supreme dominance over the victim. Three would be the ultimate crowd. The loss of personal control necessary for a perpetrator to carry out such acts would naturally work best without the presence of judging eyes, or a pesky partner wanting to share.

It was also immediately apparent that this wasn't the crime scene. Everything that happened to the couple took place somewhere else, maybe inside their car. They were left there by someone who was in a hurry but remained mindful of possible traffic. Be quick and go, drop the bodies and run.

Preston had been twenty years old when he the army hit him with a 4-f, but twenty-one when he ran unopposed for Sheriff of Musselshell County, and considered himself to have changed from a boy to a man during his years as a lawman. Evil in its extreme forms didn't particularly surprise him anymore, but it was wrenching for him to know that a monster would do this to a woman like Claudette Thornton, a woman filled with loving kindness. He realized in that terrible moment that she still owned more of his heart than had been willing to admit. His mind filled with bloody thoughts about secretly killing the perpetrator in some kind of especially cruel and prolonged manner.

Instead, as Sheriff, he took control of the scene and began to go through the motions of putting out all the right radio calls, bringing in the coroner and the detectives. But his truer self remained invisible, hungering for personal revenge. In that darkened grove of trees, he instantly understood and appreciated Montana's history as home of the Vigilantes. In a case of obvious guilt, their form of justice was quick and clean.

He was aware that their old call sign was *3-7-77*, which they painted on the house of criminals as a warning to leave town, though he had never seen it used. During the heyday of the vigilantes, its meaning was understood by most of the short-lived population: a standard grave measures *3 feet wide, 7 feet long, and 77 inches deep*. Back then plenty of people knew about digging graves.

But to Preston, the idea the standard grave used for an ordinary human being was far too good for whoever did this thing. He sensed that the sneering evil of this crime was not only committed against these two innocents but against the whole town, against everyone in his county—up to and including the Sheriff charged with protecting the people. The weight of that was enough to drive him into the ground.

None of that changed the fact that he simply could not allow his grief over Claudette to ruin his effectiveness as Sheriff. The best way to show her respect at that moment was to process this crime scene as carefully as could be done, then go apprehend the bastard behind it.

He stared across the dump site, at the two sad sets of remains. This, in his county, his home town, on his watch. He swallowed a brew of emotions that went down like molten lead.

Preston knew full well that his artificial eye was a favorite topic among the bar-joke crowd. And in spite of that easy point of social ridicule, he had found that after a while, the very fact that a man is willing to withstand his indignities over time gives him back a measure of respect.

That had come to be the case with Preston and his single eyeball until this new agent of criminality, unlike anything he had come across in his years as Sheriff, showed up here to chew through his personal life and professional reputation, leaving the pieces strewn around just as casual as you please. Preston knew the jokes would be out in force.

In that moment, he was as close as he had ever come to throwing his badge on the ground and taking the vigilante route. Every muscle in his body tightened with the need to spring into action. Find the man, and it was certainly a man who did this, and then throw the procedural book straight out the window. Use every county, state, and federal resource at his disposal while simultaneously following not a single one of their rules.

The man who did this thing needed to be captured alive and reduced to a condition worse than both of his victims put together. More important, he should then "escape into the mountains" while being transported back to County Jail. Let it be a lasting local mystery as to how the perpetrator could possibly have gotten away and then disappeared with such skill. Former military? Specially trained? Who could say?

Poets would tell it. Or maybe those Tin Pan Alley songwriters who put his favorite ballads on the air could write a song all about the magical escape of the Roundup Killer. That would be fine with Wade Preston because there would not be a single line about the killer being packed into an unmarked hole way, way up in the mountains.

Let the world speculate about how the killer got away. The legends and songs about his escape would have nothing to say about the corpse of a well-killed perpetrator, wadded into a hole upside down, pointing face first at the new home of the body's former owner.

These and other images Wade Preston kept to himself.

10

Go Greyhound

Byron and Ruth Sherman stood in the Greyhound parking lot and watched the bus for Great Falls depart in a whirlwind of diesel smoke. At the rear window, Jerry O'Connell pressed his grinning face to the glass and waved like a kid going off to camp.

The brand new interstate highway system would make the bus ride smooth and easy, but Byron would have greatly preferred to strap Jerry O'Connell to the underside of a cargo truck and let him kiss the bumps in the road for amusement. Instead he simply turned away from the sight of the bus and put his arm around Ruth's shoulder while he walked her back toward their car.

"Please," he muttered, "no more visits from that guy."

She smiled and put her arm around him while they walked, but her reply was firm. "Useful idiots, By. Useful idiots."

Byron choked on that one. "How is he 'useful'? The man can't seem to take care of himself. All he can do is pick arguments!"

They were still a few yards from their car when a familiar pickup truck came roaring into the lot and pulled to a rough stop. Several man were piled into the back, in spite of the stiffening cold. They all carried rifles and shotguns.

The driver was a local rowdy who frequently made his disgust for their magazine clear. Now he leaned out the window and yelled, "Hey Sherman, if you've got a gun you better grab it and get over to the

Sheriff's office! If you don't, maybe you can just watch and then *write* about it!"

Byron would have expected the other men to yuk right along, but none of them cracked a smile. In the next instant he realized he was looking at a lynch mob. The realization struck him like the sound of a gong, a single deep note that he felt throughout his bones. It rattled the truth into him; somebody had given those men a reason to let their inner demons out. He imagined the smell of sulfur.

"What's going on?" he called to them in his best not-looking-for-trouble voice.

They stared back at him until he thought they were just going to ignore him and that he should perhaps continue walking with Ruth. Then the driver responded in a voice so quiet it approached normal volume. "Well, it's the Thorntons from over at the café. Both of them. Both dead. Killed outright!"

"What?" Ruth cried. "No! We saw them this afternoon!"

"Well *this evening* they were found out on Route 12. Shot in cold blood. Bad things done to Mrs. Thornton too, word is. Go home and get a firearm! The Sheriff's forming up tracking teams!"

Someone in the back of the truck pounded on the roof to get them all going again. The driver hit the gas and the guys in back hung on for life while the truck roared off toward the Sheriff's station over at City Hall.

"My god." Byron turned to Ruth and saw her face tighten. He felt certain they were thinking the same thing; "Ruthie, we need to ask whether this might be connected with whoever broke into our place. Don't we?"

Ruth couldn't look at him. She began to walk in little circles and seemed to speak to the ground. "I have this bad feeling in my stomach, By. This very bad feeling. I'm sick inside, I tell you."

"We should call Sheriff Preston." He started for their car.

"Wait!" she grabbed his arm and pulled him back around to face her. "Wait, wait, wait! I mean, wait a minute. Just think about this. What if we're wrong? No, do *not* smile like that! *What if*? That kind of conclusion-jumping is exactly what reactionary bastards do. We won't go down that road!"

"Because...?"

"Because we're better than that! Somebody has to be! What the hell does <u>The Worker's Monthly</u> have a motto like *Common Sense With A Conscience*, if we don't stand up first for the little guy? For the guy getting stomped by organized power!"

"You're talking about the thief who robbed us."

"How about if we describe him as the desperate soul who took *equally desperate* means to provide himself with nothing more than the most basic comforts of life!"

Byron sighed and rubbed the back of his neck. "And a little jewelry. Hoo-boy, Ruth. Listen, if he killed the Thorntons—"

"*What*? Killed? Why are you using that word? We have nothing to do with bigots; let's not use their language."

"I don't think it's using anybody's language to say—"

"That desperate soul is *innocent* until proven guilty!"

She turned and scanned outside the window. "And wherever he is right now, we can bet that somebody as desperate as he was, breaking into a home in broad daylight that way, he's got it worse than we do by a long shot. We are *not* going to add to his burden before we know the facts!"

Ruth's ability to explode with sincere passion on behalf of the plight of a stranger was an ongoing source of pride for Byron, even on days like today. He loved her with unrestrained devotion and stood in awe of the size of her heart. He sometimes thought she was being outright crazy, but time and experience had taught him that even when she seemed crazy she often turned out to be right. She just got there by a pathway he couldn't imagine on his own.

He simultaneously carried the silent fear that his wife suffered lapses of judgment that put her viewpoint on a par with the exotic fishes in their salt-water tank. The tank itself was a monument to her fluctuations, since ordinarily Ruth was a dedicated anti-materialist. Personal needs and sometimes passing fancies were attended at her insistence as necessary points of indulgence. He could still hear her sweet soprano voice and unabashed warbling, "you have to live a little bit if you're gonna give a shit," as Ruth loved to sing of an evening.

But there in the parking lot she simply spun on her heel and walked off toward their car by herself. She seemed four inches taller, using that ramrod straight posture she reserved for formal occasions or, in certain cases, personal situations in which Byron knew he would hope in vain for intimate wifely considerations. In spite of his earlier optimism, the day was no longer set to end well at home.

11

Just Another Gang

Once darkness set in, the true isolation of the road began to weigh on Andy. Old voices of self-doubt worked overtime, reminding him that it was a complete game changer to have uncovered the existence of these two new pursuers and the Freemasons' desperate level of trickery.

As demoralizing as it was to be confronted with such a potent new threat, he consoled himself with the idea that at least now he knew about them and he could take steps to protect himself. So the Freemasons supposedly carried all sorts of "secret knowledge," did they? Andy snorted at the thought and reminded himself that he had a few secrets of his own. Those other guys might be powerful, but they had severely underestimated how well he learned his forcible lessons back in the joint.

Masons, Freemasons, they were just another gang. And the main weakness of every gang is always their own gang structure and rules that make them predictable in a number of ways. Each of those ways is a point of vulnerability: recruits, weapons, supplies, and best of all, innocent family members.

One of the universal truths of Andy's incarcerated life was that inmates doing hard time stay alive by remembering that anyone who exhibits predictable behavior can be turned into a victim. In the out-side world, there was a strong added bonus in that the predictable ones can be victimized from a distance with relative personal safety for the perpetrator.

So Andy realized that although he was up against one of the most powerful secret organizations in the world, they had already given up the advantage of surprise by sending incompetent emissaries to snag at him from the side of the road. He drove along through the night carefully turning that idea under a mental jeweler's loop.

From time to time he stomped the brakes while he considered his best move. The braking action worked well enough to shut up the one making all the noise, but it only lasted a few minutes each time.

He pushed farther north and the evening grew late, while traffic eventually thinned to nothing. By the time he spotted the perfect exit, his stolen Buick was the only car on the road. He could have easily missed it: a thin dirt road that branched off the highway and disappeared into a vast stand of giant conifers and shrouded undergrowth.

He hit the brakes harder than he needed to do for the turn, just to remind everybody who was in charge, then drove back into the black shadows of the woods and parked. It took half an hour to force both passengers out, get them over to a nice thick tree, seated on the ground, and tied to the trunk.

He knew the one guy was likely gone already, but he made the other one drag him along and tied them both for good measure. He could have been alive yet and he would give the loud one some company while they all worked their way through this pickle. Andy had never heard anything about Freemasons being immortal or having the power to raise from the dead, so he figured once you had them tied up they had to be as killable as the next guy.

Handling those knots with freezing fingers was surprisingly aggravating, adding to the distress presented by these two hit men or whatever they were supposed to be. It struck Andy that this was what he got for not following his own rule about never picking up hitchhikers. There were reasons for rules and when rules got violated, bad things tended to happen. It pained him to know that he had managed to bring this on himself but still couldn't begin to explain how any of it happened.

"For Christ's sake!" he shouted at the whole world. "Shit! God-damn it!" He kept *trying* to lie low and be more or less good but the stinking Universe simply would not allow it.

Once he had the pair of spies well tied and the stage was properly set, he finally bent down close to the two hockey-playing wood chop-pers and spoke just loud enough for them to hear—or loud enough for one of them to hear, anyway. It was a private message strictly between the three of them or maybe just the two of them. Nobody more than ten feet away would have been able to hear it.

After all, if these two could show up in his life the way they did, jumping up and down at the side of the road and luring him so perfectly, who could say where others might appear? He had been warned that modern Freemasons could use secret powers handed down through the centuries from the ancient Order, but nobody had ever told him what that was supposed to actually mean.

What sort of things could they do? How many secrets did they have at their disposal? A wave of dread washed over him. No doubt there were all sorts of nasty invisible snares they could catch him up in, or maybe surround him with spies who could blend perfectly into the background population. Enemies who could get in close to him while nobody suspected them.

Andy realized accurate information was essential in such an hour, but the harsh cold was unforgiving. It was time to get things going. He looked back down at the two Freemason spies, his incompetent would-be executioners. The one who still had his eyes open was the winner, by default. He was simply going to have to talk, spill all the information required of him, and that was all she wrote. Andy got out his hunting knife.

12

Songs Of Twin Sirens

Sheriff Preston sent the fourth and final search team off on foot, evenly spaced and moving across their appointed territory carrying one signal flare for each four-man group. Nearly a hundred volunteers had materialized at the station once his two part-time Deputies started working the phones. Some of the volunteers came from outside the county. All of them felt connected to the victims and arrived hungry for vengeance. Now with the process underway, he climbed back into his cruiser to begin making the rounds between teams, wishing there was something else to do.

His newly equipped version of last year's Ford offered a military grade two-way radio, quite unlike the stellar piece of shit installed by the well intended factory. This one was capable of catching good signals way out in the back country. So even though he was currently parked amid tall hills, the dispatch was perfectly clear when one of his part-time Deputies piped up.

"Sheriff?"

He thumb-keyed the microphone. "Go ahead, Lloyd."

"I called the Royal Mounties like you wanted. Told 'em we might have a felon fleeing in their direction, and, you know, I told them about the Thorntons, and anyway, the fella on the phone started acting like he just caught the bouquet at a wedding, you know? And I asked him what was up and he said to wait and made me hold on for their head guy from the Alberta district. I'm sorry I forgot to write down that fellow's name."

"Okay, you forgot his name. What did he tell you?"

"That's the thing. He says they just, that same hour, come across the bodies of two young men, killed. About an hour's drive north from the border headed up toward Calgary. One of them was tortured and it sounded like what you told us about Mrs. Thornton and all. This sounds like our guy, so much I could hardly pick up the radio to call you, I was so nervous. Little embarrassed about forgetting to get the name, too. Know what I mean?"

"Right, Lloyd. Listen. I just set up a full-scale search operation and the temperature is down to ten or twelve degrees out here. So if the volunteers are all wasting their time I need to get these folks back to their homes. What makes you think this is our guy?"

"Bodies left right on the highway. And they were put there on purpose, he says. Like what was done to the Thorntons, but really obvious this time. Right out in the open where they had to get found in a hurry. You would think the perpetrator would be worried about trying to escape. That doesn't seem to be the case."

"Just the two males?"

"Well, so they said."

Preston calculated the distance to the border, assuming the killer took Highway 12 west to, say, Helena. He could turn north and be in Canada in something like 400 miles. Maybe eight hours of driving in slippery weather, then another hour north of the border. The potential timeline worked.

"Lloyd, we're they robbed?"

"Oh! Nope. No robbery. Still had cash and wallets on them. Very bad rope burns on the one guy, however. The tortured guy."

"Uh-huh. Thanks for remembering that insignificant little detail, Lloyd."

"Come on, Sheriff, we're practically volunteers here! I'm doing the best I can! How about if you got the county to pay for some deputy training?"

"Nothing left in the budget for that." Preston decided to change the subject. "So this perpetrator did things so terrible that the victim tore up his skin trying to get away."

"So they said," Lloyd replied, clearly stung.

"Straighten up, Lloyd."

"*What*, Sheriff?"

"You sound like somebody stole your cookies. Now we've got ourselves a true-life monster on the loose, so stay with me here. You ever hear anybody say there's no such thing as a coincidence?"

"Well yeah, I've heard that. But what does it—"

"People who say that are full of shit, that's what. I see coincidences all the time in this line of work, and just in case this is another goddamned *coincidence*, I'm not pulling our people back in and maybe letting the guy get away out here. I need details. What are we looking at here? So you get Mr. What's-his-name up in Canada back on the horn and patch him through to me."

He thought for a second, then added, "But in case our boy's gone international, go ahead and call the FBI over in Billings. And Lloyd?"

"Yes Sheriff?"

Preston noted that Lloyd's tone was better. "Soon as you get through to the feds, you better patch them through to me as well. Don't try to handle it yourself. I don't want anybody coming back later and saying we didn't blow all the right whistles on this case, understand?"

"Whistles?"

"Just patch them through to me if you get to them before I come back into the office." He suddenly felt that the idea of running from group to group was essentially a time-waster. He had a strong urge to be at the station when the calls came in. "Check that. I'm on the way now," he said, and signed off.

Preston sped back to the station at a flat-out Code 3 with the light bar flashing and the new twin sirens cranked to full power. He knew it was unacceptable to roll down the windows and scream his rage and frustration into the night, so he let the souped-up cruiser do it for him. The twin sirens sang a cruel opera to the darkness.

13

The Golden Walk

Andy spent the last of his cash on a tank of gas and hit the eastbound road to Quebec. There wasn't enough dough left over for any decent food to quell the hunger pangs, so he settled for a large bag of chocolate cookies. The bag was half empty now and the contents had quieted his hunger, but the excess sugar was hitting him hard.

He fully appreciated the need to avoid large doses of sugar because of its effect on his nerves and had known about it since boyhood. But what, he wondered, was he supposed to do? He didn't dare shoplift better food. He knew once anybody starts down the road of stealing just to eat, they will set the law of averages into motion and essentially put in a reservation at the nearest county jail.

On days like this he couldn't help but wonder if he had really wanted to escape incarceration on the day he ran, or if the goal of freedom simply became a glittering mirage to a captive young man, luring him into a lethal desert.

True, freedom was a fine thing. To walk any distance without turning corners and to stare up at an open sky felt wondrous, as if his bone marrow drank in beautiful silence where there was once there was the nonstop flow of orders from overseers and streams of torment from the tough guys.

But in the outside world the daily struggle to survive was such a full-time effort there was no time to do anything with his so called "freedom" anyway. He was haunted by the sense that he somehow been tricked into escaping, that he had made himself a fool.

As far as he could see it, the cost of "freedom" for him was to either constantly rob and burgle his daily sustenance while the odds of capture rose with every new crime, or attempt to work at a job that would condemn him to constant abrasion from those who would be his overseers.

Of course such overseer types always pretended that their infectious intent didn't exist, fearing with good reason that if the truth were acknowledged it might cost them their power. But Andy's curse was that he possessed the mysterious ability to see through all of that phony crap, in a world clogged by would-be wardens and actual cowards.

As a prisoner, his climb to accumulate the "points" required to earn the Golden Walk had been so brutal that he only survived it by lapsing into the Harmless Goofball and staying there, every time.

The warden's mandatory goal was for the inmate to complete two dozen trips to the warden's office without a *single* failure to bring their leader to ejaculation while also doing the same for himself. One lost erection between either of them, and the inmate's point score dropped all the way back down to zero, no matter how high it had climbed at that point.

Scuttlebutt said the typical sucker made it all the way to twenty-two or even twenty-three "dates with the Warden," only to find himself kneeling and staring at a dangling wanger—followed by a rough trip back to his cell. The chosen ones agreed that this was how the warden clung to his favorites while keeping the system going. And the system was necessary for creating that all-important aura of hope.

Hope, after all, was how they got you. Hope was the load-bearing wall for the warden's entire operation. And what the chosen ones quickly learned about themselves, if they didn't already know, was that there was nothing the warden's sick brain could conjure that they would not endure in return for the tiniest ray of hope, all in pursuit of that magical number of twenty-four and the prized Golden Walk.

For all these reasons it came as a shock to Andy when he somehow broke the invisible barrier and accumulated the illusive goal of twenty-four successful oral and anal sex sessions. He felt like one of those ladies on the radio who get crowned "Queen For A Day."

Suddenly, he was a man who had earned himself the Golden Walk and impossible as it seemed, the warden didn't appear to mind. The only explanation Andy could think of was that the warden might consider him used up and just wanted him gone. Andy's reservoir of experience with the tough guys told him some men were just that way. Once they used a person for sex a few times, they got to where they couldn't stand the sight of a former object of passion.

When Andy's big payday arrived, it turned out that the so-called Golden Walk didn't consist of much. It was little more than a momentary turning of his overseer's head at a pre-arranged time and place, while Andy was allowed to break for it with the promise of a five minute head start. After those five minutes elapsed, the pursuers would be close on his heels.

The catch? If his pursuers caught him, the Golden Walk carried a built-in guarantee of his execution "while escaping." This policy was the backup parachute for the warden's secrecy, since he hardly intended to allow the knowledge of his little game to leak out. The Golden Walk was the warden's sickest joke of all.

Word on the yard was, three of the guards once threatened the warden with public exposure. They immediately found themselves at gunpoint, marched to a holding cell, and locked inside with six of the institution's largest and most gravely demented individuals.

Nobody out in the yard knew the whole story, but the following day the three guards were carried out of that cell in pieces. All traces of their genitalia were missing, a remarkable accomplishment for six inmates who possessed no cutting tools.

The warden made it a point to frequently remind the chosen ones of the story. Andy noticed afterward that nobody expressed any difficulty with the warden's little private club or with the many novel activities and entertainments that went on there.

Then as he drove along the realization hit him so hard that his body jolted in the seat and the car swerved in response: his mistake in dealing with those fake hockey players loomed up in front of him. How could he have missed it? He neglected to show his two captives what the warden had clearly shown him, because he failed to offer them some source of hope. They would have been a lot more cooperative getting into the trunk if they were hoping for something specific. He shook his head. All that dragged out struggle for nothing.

Later, once he had them tied up to the killing tree, Andy realized he ought to have given the conscious one something to strive for, in addition to stopping the pain. If he had offered the Freemason hit man a shot at escape, he felt certain that he could have obtained the necessary information with a lot less blood and screaming from the guy. Yes the fool deserved it, but the unnecessary experience was damned unpleasant for Andy.

He turned off the country music playing on the stolen Buick Super's excellent radio, then spent a silent minute or two driving along and hating himself for forgetting that thing about offering the boys hope. Such a mistake was beneath him.

Nevertheless, the things he learned from the dying young man were more than enough to chill Andy inside about the mysterious Freemasons. Every twist of the knife embedded between the young man's ribs brought out more of the group's secrets.

He forced himself to listen to it all because those Masonic people were known throughout the world to have an endless capacity for secret plots. The only defense against them was to know how they operated. But it astounded him to think the Masonic Order would go this level of trouble simply to track down a guy who stole a god-for-saken ring and a lapel pin. What would they do over something that mattered?

Maybe if you kissed one of their girlfriends they came to your neck of the woods and burned down your whole neighborhood. Hell, up until this very day, Andy had been prepared to reserve judgment about the Freemasons. He even acknowledged the unfortunate fact that his experience at the warden's hands *may have* unfairly soured him on the whole lot of them. And yet here they had sent two morons to kill him, not only believing he deserved to die but adding insult to it by sending a couple of incompetent boobs to do the job.

They clearly hadn't counted on Andy turning the tables and learning so many of the things they kept secret. That, he knew, had raised the game to a whole new level.

Chief among the secret things he learned was the revelation about their top-secret Smoke Code. A bafflingly complicated system of signaling with smoke columns. It took Andy nearly an hour out in that freezing cold night air to pull all the details out of the captive.

The method was so brilliantly disguised that it safely existed within plain sight wherever it was used. At first Andy wondered if the young man might be lying, just to try to please him and get him to stop the torture. After all, the idea of a "Smoke Code" seemed so primitive and stupid that he laughed in spite of his annoyance.

But the true brilliance of it had quickly struck him; the secret of its successful concealment was that it had no need of encryption into some genius-generated cipher. Why, the very fact that it was so primitive and stupid had kept it safely hidden down through the centuries. Right there in plain sight, the whole time.

So, Andy thought, let the rest of the world try to intercept Masonic messages by performing fancy magnetic sweeps or with dogs trained to sniff out opposing opinions. Meanwhile right outside their windows, the vertical length of any smoke plume, its thickness, its color, was employed in messages capable of carrying specific meanings. These meanings could be understood by all Freemasons whose rank was high enough to entitle them to the code key to the ancient secret Smoke Code—which Andy had obtained with a knife and a little effort.

The kid's loyalty to his cult or whatever it was proved to be pathetic. He was more than willing to give Andy each specific smoke column length, thickness, color, and its corresponding meaning. Andy had no time to master the actual Smoke Code Key and it did seem as if the kid contradicted himself several times, but at least he now knew such a thing existed. He would never look at a smoke plume the same way again.

The interrogation got muddled up in the details of how to measure the length of any given smoke column while observing from varying distances and angles. But at that point the kid began to cough up so much blood that Andy got tied of trying to make out what he was saying. No matter how valuable the information might be, there was only so much wheezing and gurgling crap he was willing to listen to.

The other kid, the one who forced Andy to shoot him following his very bad joke about being named "Mason," had pretty much bled out by that point. Fortunately he was tied so close to his accomplice that when he went into his death twitches his body kept bumping up against the other guy. It automatically prodded the conscious one for details, with Andy expending so little effort that all he had to do was promise not to twist the knife again in order to get all the answers he needed.

The bastard's story was enough to alarm anybody. Andy felt his former tolerance of Freemasonry erode with every piece of new information. By the time he finished emptying out the kid, his position regarding the Masonic Order had changed from one of suspicious tolerance to something more like a set of cross-hairs on a bombardier's scope.

Because the bastards were out to control everything, just as he had always heard they were, only more so. They wanted all of it. "Everything" with a capital "E."

They could do this using secret signals carried on puffs of smoke, in a system a hundred times more complex than anything ever used by natives out on the plains. The color and shade of the smoke plumes could be chemically controlled with natural substances, and could even be used, confessed the hit man, to express ironic humor. The Freemasons appeared to spend a lot of their time mocking people with puffs of smoke. It only took a couple of twists of the knife before the hit man broke down and swore to it all.

Back in the joint, if that level of disrespect had been randomly flashed around the way those Freemasons were doing, it would likely bring down a bad death. And for such an offender, even the release of death would only be permitted following a disastrous number of shattered bones and some solid pleas for mercy that would be long in coming.

Of course Andy killed both operatives, but it wasn't done out of cruelty on his part. The simple fact was that there could be no safe way to show mercy to such an enemy; it was no different than the folly of releasing prisoners of war, only to have them return to battle and shoot you. If the Masons elected to launch secret attacks against him, they might have at least sent qualified people. These two failed and it should have been expected. How could they not? They were directed by cowards hovering back in the shadows, who so underestimated Andy that they sent boys openly carrying hatchets that they proved unable to use in defending their own lives.

All that remained was the nagging question of who else might be out there. The world was full of cops, and now that he had killed in two countries, the world was full of Mounties on the north side of the border and the FBI to the south.

After today, who could say how many Freemasons were also getting in line to make a run at him as well? Andy remembered murmured rumors about those Masonic bastards being spread all over the world, anywhere money was to be found. There was supposed to be no getting away from them.

For the first time since the disaster in Oklahoma, Andy felt that terrible sensation of being unable to get enough breath into his lungs. The feeling imitated drowning and was tinged with icy panic. It made him want to claw at the air.

He mentally speed-searched his memory for any usable wisdom to help him in this hour, wisdom gained from the adult male inmates with their fatherly shower room rapes and venomous survival lessons. Those demon teachers possessed powerful tools for living that Andy had learned to put to work. Muddled in with their mix of cruelty and cunning there was occasionally a way out, a path around, a tunnel beneath.

But the invisible noose around his neck seemed to become even tighter—another one of his mistakes leaped up in front of him. "Son of a *bitch*!" he screamed, pounding the steering wheel. "No!"

Now that he was sixty miles away from the highway dump site and there was no way on earth he could do anything about the situation, it hit him like the windshield hits the bug; he should have left a sign openly blaming the Masonic Order. Carve it on their foreheads if he had to. Paint it on both of their shirts with any colored fluid available. A lesson: These *two hit men from a secret international order are dead as a result of their own evil intentions!*

That would have forced the Freemasons to come out in public, if for no other reason than to issue denials. Such a thing might even be enough to start people thinking about who really runs things in this messed-up world. It might get them to see that they should to quit worrying about a guy like Andy Carmichael, who really only wanted to find somewhere he could exist without constant friction from over-seers. It might convince them to go after things that really matter in this life, instead.

But he had left his defiant statement without a signature, or even a clear message. Now all the Freemasons had to do in order to beat him was sit quiet. How could the local authorities see the spider web of conspiracy that enveloped him now, merely by looking at evidence from two simple murder scenes? Not even murder scenes, really. More like dumpsites.

Andy's stock of street wisdom was full of holes on this issue. He rolled down the window and tossed his gun into the thick underbrush lining the road, but when he looked inside of himself for any source of guidance about his next move, he continued to come up with nothing.

He had never been the subject of a manhunt, having always been caught at the scene of his latest petty crime. His repeat offender status was what that got him put away among the monsters, not the severity of his crimes. Of course, he admitted to himself, that was until Oklahoma City. By then he was an escapee on the run, and it was

Andy's firm conviction that when a fellow's hand is forced, he ought not be penalized for certain unfortunate resortions.

He was precisely at that point in his thought train, just as he powered the stolen Buick Super around a wide bend in the highway, when Andy realized he had neglected to take into account that the police up in Canada might also have radio dispatchers to organize manhunts over huge distances. And that there was no way he could outdrive a radio wave.

Six RCMP vehicles formed a blockade across the roadway. A couple of dozen Mounties were lined up behind the cars, guns drawn, red jackets showing the only color in his headlights. He felt certain of their number: four to a car, six cars: *Twenty-four.* The pretty police lights twinkled away like an invitation to a party—which he realized it was, when his eyes registered the rifles pointed at his windshield and the attack dogs straining at the leash.

The criminal in him knew the jig was up. The only consolation was that he had been wise enough to get rid of the weapon only a few seconds before rounding the bend and encountering his pursuers. Typical of Andy's luck, it was a fortunate break followed by a hammer blow.

He remained relaxed enough about it to allow the rest of him to wonder—was this grouping of twenty-four yet another message from the Freemasons? After all, the same number twenty-four had freed him from the clutches of his warden. Who was also a Freemason.

It was too much to figure out on the fly. Andy took his foot off of the accelerator moved it toward the brake pedal and gave it one good last stomp, just to show those knuckleheads what he thought of their show of force.

14

The Vanishing Cigarette

Royal Canadian Mounted Police Officer Morley Sinclair watched the American killer's car hurtling toward him. He felt a burst of disappointment when his commanding officer called for the sharpshooters to stand down. "No shot!" his sergeant bellowed. "Hold your fire!"

Officer Sinclair relaxed his finger on the trigger of his Winchester 270 caliber rifle in response to the order, but it hurt him to hear it after the kind of build-up they'd all received with the description of the two murdered young fellows—two youths on their way home from an amateur hockey game, for crying out loud. Shot like dogs, one of them tortured. There was also the communication from the States about how the same kind of thing occurred only one day earlier, down in Montana. He cringed at the thought of giving this sort of creature any show of restraint.

The few minutes he had just spent huddled and waiting for the American to arrive left Sinclair dripping with sweat and knotted with tension. Now instead of a nice, clean shoot, there would be attorneys and a trial and privileges for the inmate. So while the part of him that was trained and professional responded as ordered, his mere human side clenched hard and tight and screamed for a release that only the rifle's recoil could give him.

It helped matters not at all when the American driver stopped his car by slamming on the brakes and cranking his steering wheel hard to the right, throwing the car into a leftward spin that turned it perpendicular to the roadway and stopped it ten feet away, with the driver's profile directly in front of them. Not since Officer Sinclair's schoolyard days had he been struck with such force by a juvenile piece of mockery.

And then again, in the very next moment, it turned out that all was not lost and things immediately became interesting again. Because the American driver remained inside the car and ignored the orders being bellowed by the sergeant, telling him to get out with his hands in the air.

Sinclair slipped his finger back onto the trigger, just in case the driver emerged with a weapon. He focused close-up with his Weaver K-4 scope and saw the move: the right hand dipping down to the driver's seat and coming back up, daring them to shoot him in fear he was picking up a gun. But the hand reappeared holding not a weapon but a fresh cigarette. Still in complete defiance of the orders being screamed at him, the American's hand vanished once again, then reappeared as he struck a match and held it up to light his fag. Classic American contempt, straight out of a Hollywood movie.

Meanwhile the rifle needed firing and the chambered bullet wanted to be gone. Before Sinclair realized what he'd done, he put the cross-hairs of the K-4 scope squarely upon that magnified cigarette and blew it from the American's cocky lips with such perfect placement of the projectile that the cigarette simply disappeared and left the smoker untouched.

This shocked the American into some sort of temporary paralysis, making for an uneventful arrest moments later. The fool was cuffed up and on his way to Calgary Jail in minutes.

Officer Sinclair was later fined two weeks' salary and ordered to spend the rest of the month on temporary desk duty, mostly as a precaution to avoid setting off any editorial campaigns in the news against the RCMP over the certainly excellent though perhaps unnecessary sniper shot. Sinclair didn't mind it in the least. He considered the loss in pay a fair trade for his new legendary status around the force.

■ ■ ■

Andy wasn't surprised by the naked hostility of the Mounties. Who could say how many of them were in on the Freemason conspiracy? They appeared to know all about his treatment of the two Masonic hit men, although it was also apparent to him that they knew nothing of the men's membership in the Order or in their deadly purpose. The only skill Andy possessed for dealing with his captors was to fall back on his jail yard experience at surviving the tough guys.

The first blow came from the Mountie who shoved him into the squad car after his arrest. It was a hard right cross to the side of his head that caught him cold, and with his cuffed hands unable to help him brace himself against the vehicle, he fell straight into the back seat. He immediately curled up his legs the way he'd learned to do to ward off the next blows, but it stopped with that. The Mountie checked around to be sure nobody had seen, then just went ahead and hauled him all the way to the Calgary Jail without speaking a word.

The real treatment began as soon as he was alone in the holding cell. One big Mountie came in by himself and closed the door. He was an older guy, probably nearing retirement. The expression on his face convinced Andy to keep quiet.

"I'm Officer Morley Sinclair. I'm the one shot that ciggie outta your mouth." That was all he said before throwing a jab straight into Andy's nose so hard it knocked him backward onto the holding cell cot, with blood spurting and his head on fire.

Andy curled up just as he had before, but once again the attack ended at that point. Officer What's-his-name walked out and slammed the door behind himself.

Andy lay back with his head tilted to get the flow of blood under control. He knew there would eventually be a way to turn this treatment to his advantage, if he could live through the next couple of days.

Another Mountie came in and shut the door, took one look at Andy laying on the cot holding his bloodied face and responded by throwing a hard kick into his ribs, then turned and left without a word. After that, Andy figured they must have been standing in line out in the hallway.

He lost count of how many there were, stepping in and inflicting a single blow, then walking back out. A couple introduced themselves like the sharpshooter did, wanting to make their attack as personal as possible.

Andy knew how to take a beating. And since it appeared this one wasn't going to include forcible rape, he knew he had them by the balls. He went completely limp an instant before each blow hit him, absorbing much of the energy without damage. His rich experience as an inmate blessed him with the ability to disassociate from his sensations enough to endure pain that would ordinarily be unbearable.

By the time they seemed to taper off, his head was swollen twice its size, his face was a purple mash, and most of his ribs felt like they were broken. He took it all without screaming for mercy or begging them to stop or even asking them why they were doing it. He knew, they knew, and he knew they knew he knew, all the way down to the fine details.

He decided to stay on the floor in case more of them showed up. That way he only had to endure the blows themselves, but not additional impacts with the concrete.

After a few minutes of silence he dared to roll onto his side, then his stomach. He pulled his feet underneath himself and crawled up onto the cot to take stock of his condition.

The good news was that his arms and legs weren't broken and his major joints were all working. The third time he hit the floor following a particularly well thrown punch, he thought the impact had dislocated his left shoulder and felt the first touch of real fear. But he discovered in getting to his feet that he was still able to move his left arm and even take some weight on it. He thought his nose might be broken, but this would be the fourth time so he didn't feel much concern over it. Give him a couple days of rest and he would be able to walk, perhaps to run, maybe even to fight back if the time came that he could dare to protect himself from these goons without getting shot for his trouble.

His sense of being able to endure the treatment of his captors helped dispel the terrible cloud of depression that descended at the moment he rounded that bend and saw all those Mounties.

He focused on resigning himself as quickly as possible, to take some of the pain out of his return to the joint. As much as he hated the idea of going back to prison, his ability to survive his uniformed attackers at least confirmed his mastery of the art of taking a beating. He was much better at it now that he had been as a boy, and as an inmate once again, it could make all the difference for him.

A small point of consolation occurred to him while he lay on the cot and stared at the unpainted metal ceiling. If they didn't kill him right out, he could probably survive long enough to be executed with dignity and die with his name in the papers like a movie star.

He found the prospect much more cheerful than the thought of growing old in the criminal life, inside or outside of prison.

15

The Comeback Kid

It was late in the following afternoon when Sheriff Wade Preston arrived in Calgary after long hours of powering through a raging Canadian snow storm in the souped-up Ford police cruiser. He still wore the same uniform he had on the day before and he knew he smelled like a wrestler. He had barely slept and didn't remember eating anything that day.

At a time like this the loneliness of his bachelorhood was eased by the fact that there was no one at home being abandoned while he went after the man who had ruined everything about life in their town. For Preston, at least, nothing was ever going to be the same. His only family was an older brother living up in Helena, but he was married with kids and they didn't see each much anymore.

Preston and his two part-time deputies, Lowell and Bikowski, barely took time to piss. Even then, if he'd been alone in the car he would have used an empty jug and stopped for nothing but fuel.

Lowell rode in the passenger seat with Bikowski in the back. The men took their cue from Preston and spoke little during the long ride. Sometimes he played the radio when a decent station was within range. Other than that there were few other sounds but the hum of the tires, for hours at a time.

Wade Preston never ran for Sheriff expecting to deal with monstrous levels of evil. The deputies weren't trained for it at all, since their training funds had been consistently diverted to pay for the enormously improved highway cruiser. Up until Preston walked into the Thornton murder scene, his law enforcement career had consisted of domestic disputes, bar fights, robberies, drunken drivers, and highway accidents that could be gruesome but seldom had more of a story than bad judgment.

He never started out a workday expecting to come across creatures so depraved as to revel in the horror and suffering of their victims the way this perpetrator had obviously done. From the moment Preston's flashlight played across the Thorntons' bodies, especially that of brutalized Claudette Thornton, he began searching his experience for anything that would help him function in the impotent urgency of the aftermath: the cleanup, the hunt, the capture, the punishment.

These were all the things that did nothing to bring back stolen lives, their hopes and dreams, their love of each other and of their families. The parade of the aftermath did nothing to wash away the sewage left by one who had not yet paid any price at all, yet.

His heart felt as if the muscle was torn by the sight of two good and decent people destroyed. Their murders would have enraged him even if Claudette Thornton had not been a woman who represented everything good about her gender, in his mind.

So much for the superiority of so-called modern society, he thought. Mostly what we know how to do is clean up. Prevention, that's the part that keeps you up at night.

And so he made the long drive up to Calgary with his arms and shoulders tight and burning, his teeth clenched. The terrible thoughts filling his mind disturbed and shamed him, but he couldn't do anything to shut off the flow. He was consumed by the need to get this perpetrator, this Andrew Carmichael, out of Canadian hands and alone in the woods. He ruminated on ways to get the deputies to play along, feeling certain they wouldn't mind slaughtering the bastard but wondering if they would be able to keep quiet about it.

Preston knew that up in the Northwest Territories the Inuit people had a name for individuals who were hollow inside and who lacked a conscience: *Kunlangeto.* He considered the Inuit forward-looking in that regard, because their preferred method for dealing with a *Kunlangeto* was to invite that person to go hunting far out on the ice and then push them off into the frozen sea and abandon them there.

By the time Preston and his men reached Calgary it was already sunset. His muscles ached, and after all the terrible fantasies his imagination inflicted upon him over the course of the drive, he sported a headache that felt like it would split his face.

The deputies didn't look like they were feeling a lot better themselves. while they didn't have his history with Claudette Thornton, both deputies had known the Thorntons for years. The evil done to the couple delivered a deep shock. All of the survivors were scalded by this.

Preston guided his two men through the formalities of introductions with the local Mounties. Ten years of elected office enabled him to move through the proprieties of the encounter without having to think about it.

He made it a point to show respect by moving around the station introducing himself and shaking hands, starting with their sergeant on duty and including a brief conversation with a sharpshooter—who, he was later told, shot a cigarette right out of the killer's mouth. He gave the sharpshooter a big smile of approval and clapped his hand on the man's shoulder with plenty of the other men standing around, to show professional courtesy by bestowing status on the officer. It was an opening salvo of wheel grease from a determined man hungry to get his hands on the perpetrator and escape with him.

The Canadians respected the fact that Preston's county had suffered the first of this killer's known crimes, and he was equally astonished and relieved to learn the Alberta authorities didn't plan to contest Carmichael's extradition back to the States.

Just like that. They were willing to let the Americans handle it because executions were met with more resistance in Canada. So Preston and his men were going to get Carmichael into their custody and there wasn't going to be any muss about it at all.

Preston tried not to show his elation. He didn't dare jinx it by asking if their decision also had anything to do with defraying the cost of prosecution onto the Americans. As far as he was concerned, it was only fair to leave the cleanup duty to the States. Carmichael was American made.

Preston pulled out every political instinct and adjusted his artificial eye to be certain it was aligned, and then smiled his way through fatigue so strong it made his legs felt as if they were made of lead. *Our wonderful neighbors to the North.* He repeated it to himself several times, using his old habit of mental programming. It was useful in situations requiring the pressing of flesh, the winks, the nods, the appreciative bursts of genuine laughter, the recruitment of fellow conspirators in the delicious act of giving him want he wanted.

Experience had taught him that if he tuned his inner attitude by this method it helped him persuade people. His gift was that he could allow other people to see that he believed what he was saying by looking into his eyes, whether they were both working eyeballs or not.

Just get your hands on him he admonished himself. *Say anything that will get him into the car and back to the States.*

He promised himself that if Fortune really had smiled on them and they got Carmichael back this easily, then he would take full advantage of it. No amount of fatigue would permit them to stop until they made another drive all the way back down south across the border. Only then could they afford to stop at a motel, chain Carmichael to a radiator and get some reasonable shuteye before deciding how to proceed.

Sheer fatigue numbed him to the sheaf of forms that had to be filled out in triplicate before access to the prisoner could be grated. Preston lost track of time in the process, but before he could lose his temper and create a problem in accomplishing their mission, the clearance process was over at last.

A guard escorted Preston and his deputies down a long hallway until they stopped outside the cell holding Carmichael. He turned the key in the cell lock without opening the door, then stepped aside and opened the exit door to the outside. The wind blew straight in and instantly chilled the area. Instead of closing the outer door, the guard left it open and walked away without a word. He disappeared into the night.

Preston understood. He was ready to agree with just about any expression of contempt the Mounties wanted to heap onto him for coming from the same country that gave rise to a man like Andrew Carmichael.

16

The Smoke Code

Andy's jail yard skills kicked in again when the cell door flew open and the men wearing American police uniforms walked in. The big one with the Sheriff's badge slipped and let his face show surprise before he shut down the expression. It was enough to let Andy know the sight of his ruined face and torn clothing shocked the new guys and therefore posed a potential for sympathy that might play to his advantage later. He filed away the detail while the Sheriff introduced himself and his deputies.

Nobody offered him any explanation, they just started hooking up his hands and feet with manacles they brought in themselves, then shuffle-walked him out of the cell and all the way to the building's exit, into the howling wind. They moved quickly toward a waiting Sheriff's car.

Hooked up to the car on a tow bar was the stolen Buick Super. "Oops!" The sight hit Andy so hard that he spoke out loud and had to cover by pretending to stub his toe. The cop car was marked with the insignia of the Sheriff of Musselshell County, Montana, and Andy knew the county seat was in the town of Roundup. A cold rush of fear ran through him. Layers of meaning struck him at the same moment. Because this meant the Canadians weren't going to hold him, which made no sense at all because the Masons would never allow him to be taken away from them after he killed their operatives. Therefore if the Order didn't care about letting him go, it could only mean he was going to remain under Freemason control whether he was in Canada or down in the States.

He automatically slipped into the Harmless Goofball mode and began to attempt to mix his own bizarre behavior with the pity he had seen on their faces when they walked into his cell. He giggled while they hustled him into the back of the car and one of the deputies climbed in next to him. He giggled again when the Sheriff and the other one got into the front and started up the engine. He laughed out loud when the car began to move, towing its load as easy as could be, and he kept his best foolish grin plastered wide on his face when the Sheriff punched the gas so hard that it pressed Andy back into the seat.

"Wheee!" Andy cried out like a kid starting off on an exciting roller coaster. Inner angels guided him now, toxic fathers and brothers returned as living memories from the maximum security wing. They collectively withdrew their penises from Andy's openings long enough to drill him with wisdom: *When they've got you cold, change up on 'em. Keep changing up on 'em. Turn left every time they're willing to swear you'll turn right.*

Throughout the five hour ride back to the States, Andy kept up a stream of chatter, even when they ordered him to shut up. He sensed it was important to get the information about the Freemasons established right at the beginning. Lay the groundwork, make sure it had to show up in the arrest report. Experience assured him that arrest reports were public documents. He wondered how their damned secret Order thought they could keep their communication secrets hidden from everybody after he was done talking. You bastards should have killed me while you had the chance, he thought.

By the time the squad car hit the southbound highway, Andy was already beginning his plan to get the word out about the secret Order of the Freemasons. "Anybody here from Unity Lodge 71?" He asked with his best harmless grin, turning in his seat enough to show his ring finger and wiggle it at them.

But in the next instant the Sheriff hit the brakes so hard the car skidded to a stop in the middle of the highway. Without a word, he turned all the way around and grabbed Andy's handcuffs, pulled them toward him and then ripped the ring off of his finger so hard that Andy yelped in spite of himself. The Sheriff had leaned in close enough to take note of the lapel pin, which he then also ripped off of Andy's shirt. He pocketed both little items, then turned back around and started off once more. Neither of his two goons said a word.

Andy pretended not to notice the layer of skin peeled off of his finger and instead threw out his best Harmless Goofball giggle. They wouldn't expect that kind of reaction from him, and as long as he could keep them confused he could keep them off balance. Sometimes the monsters in the joint could be held at bay for a while if he acted crazy enough and laughed when he was supposed to scream. After all these years, he still wasn't sure why it worked, but the reason seemed to have something to do with reminding people about their own demons.

Maybe, he thought, that was what happened with the warden. His eyes took in the back of the Sheriff's head. Nice ears, the big man had, not the kind that stick out or those little rat ears some guys had. He wondered, in an offhand sort of way, if it was possible to earn a Golden Walk away from the Sheriff's custody. Would his magic number also be twenty-four? The big man did appear awfully touchy about the whole ring issue. *"And come to think of it,"* Andy's inner prison yard angels reminded him, *"he never said he wasn't a Mason."*

The Sheriff and his deputies sat like stone statues trying to ignore him, but every once in awhile he could tell that his words struck a nerve. It began with his opening line. "Too bad it's dark. We could look for smoke plumes. Little ones, big ones, makes no difference. I know it's important to you guys to keep everything under tight control, and so the Smoke Code key would be just the thing to help us read the signals. Right?"

All three turned away and pointedly ignored him. It convinced him he was onto something. Masons, all three of them, more than likely.

"I hear Masons have to swear not to rat each other out." He realized as soon as he said it that he shouldn't be saying that he "heard" about what they do, since he was trying to come off like one of them. He decided not to call attention to it by correcting himself and instead just ploughed ahead.

"So if I'm not a real Mason, *how come* I know that, gents? Why the hell would I know that you can communicate with any high-level Freemason in the world using a secret universal language, and the meanings are all based on the height of columns of smoke? Or the colors? ... What, nobody got any smart answers for that? Hee-hee-hee! Did it just get hot in here? ... And if I'm no Mason, how come I know that you can control the color of your smoke using special chemical mixtures, and each shade has its own meaning, too? Of course I'm not at a high enough level to know all the secrets, so mistakes can happen. You know: 'Hey, is that a brush fire outside town or did we just get orders to kill everybody who doesn't belong to the Lodge?' Ha-ha!"

Andy wasn't getting much reaction, although he realized that he could expect them to be trained in keeping secrets. They just gave him the old shut-up-and-stare routine. Okay, he had all kinds of buttons left to press. It was going to be a long ride.

"So that couple back in Roundup? The dead ones? What, they didn't give you a clue? I'm sure you know that guy was a Mason, since you guys are obviously Masons, too. I mean, where's the loyalty here? The male half of the couple was threatening to spread the word around about the secret signal system. I tried to talk him out of it, tried to reason with him. Then his wife joined in."

That one got the Sheriff's attention. Andy saw his eyes come up in the rearview mirror and zero in on him.

"That's right, the wife! I couldn't believe it! She started laughing and saying they were both going to get rich by selling the Smoke Code to some big magazine! Maybe put it all out there on radio and television! Somebody had to shut them up! Hell, you guys ought to be thanking me for it and dropping me off this side of the border!"

Andy saw in that instant that he had taken things too far. The eyes in the rearview mirror flashed with rage so bright, it was just like staring up at some of the psychotics back in the joint who liked to linger over their rape victims before letting them go. Even then, in the worst of situations, Andy always knew they weren't really angry at him. It was just that he had this unfortunate tendency to draw the demon out of other people. He had always thought of the trait as the undesirable side of his criminal gifts.

So when the car once again fanned to a stop in the middle of the empty rural highway and the Sheriff and both of his deputies began to all beat Andy with their fists, swinging with impassioned blows that were fairly easy to ward off by hunching over and taking them on his back, it didn't really come as any surprise. He had been helping people reach their popping point since boyhood and by this point he knew all the signs.

He silently predicted they wouldn't break any bones or open any arteries. He could stomach whatever else they decided to throw at him. He felt his old jail yard angels distract him from his fear by sending him memories of beatings far worse. *After all,* he heard himself say to himself, I survived them, didn't I?

Part Two

Canned Dastard

* 1951, Deader Winter *

17

3-7-77

Plenty of people living in the region had a tough time containing their rage. The old Vigilante symbol of *3-7-77* began to appear in scrawled graffiti around town. The sight was especially odd for a region where the rights of private property were deeply respected. Local people just didn't deface other people's fences, barns, or store fronts with scrawled messages.

That changed after Andrew James Carmichael came into their lives. The silent rage inside the quiet homes came leaking out. People took a step back from each other, wondering how much they really knew about people they thought they knew. The primal need to retaliate against somebody or something overrode the old ways of respecting another's property.

Feelings ran so hard among the townspeople that The Weekly Roundup, which was the town's only paper and ordinarily came out on Mondays, put out a special Friday edition at the Sheriff's request. It called upon the public to remain orderly and to allow the justice system to work, now that the known perpetrator of these senseless crimes was safely in custody and would murder no more.

Byron Shafer spotted the special edition displayed in a coin-operated newspaper vending box in front of the drug store while he was on his way out with some Bromo Seltzer and a box of rummy dark cigarillos, enjoying the fact that they gave him the look of the kind of *campesino* who polishes his weapon by firelight. The happy thought was ruined for him when the paper's moronic headline grabbed his attention through the little display window on the box. It was so poorly written he would have recognized the paper's local origins even with the masthead covered: *"Sheriff Calls For Public Calm!"*

Byron sighed and shook his head. "What kind of idiot uses an exclamation point to call for 'public calm'?"

The machine only operated on nickels for the five-cent paper, but Byron knew how to trigger the release with a penny. He dropped on in the coin slot and gave the machine a good smack on the bottom just as the penny landed inside. For some reason it always worked on that particular box. He had picked up the move from some kid he spotted using it to empty the box and then sell the papers on the corner. He found the kid's enterprising nature hilarious, but the sheriff and the capitalist newspaper owners strongly discouraged such theft. With the boy now off in the state work home, the move was Byron's sole intellectual property.

As far as he was concerned, every time he got away with that little trick, his own publication of The Monthly Worker struck a four-cent victory against the evil Weekly Roundup, voice box of the oppressors. The so-called "Special Edition" had things so screwed up that they actually claimed the perpetrator was already being *sentenced* at the courthouse on Saturday evening at seven o'clock.

Byron did a quick calculation and verified that this timeline, if true, had to be referring to that very evening. This was surely another misprint, he mused. Such a thing wasn't possible. Wasn't there a little matter of a murder trial and a proven case to be established first?

He scanned the article again with utter disdain. The so-called villain's capture was reported to have occurred only after he made an unsuccessful run for it and then fought his captors like a wild man. The whole piece was predictably rendered in crime-writing prose suitable for wrapping fish. Much worse for Byron was the absence of the word "alleged" anywhere in the article.

He scanned the piece again, slower, and still couldn't find any use of the "alleged" or any similar qualifier coming from the fingerless hack who concocted it. Not a word about reasonable doubt.

His heart tightened in his chest along with his old habit of grinding his teeth—in spite of those six visits to a hypnotist over in Billings—because this was not only a clear case of jury poisoning, it was done with such blatant arrogance that it defied belief. The town's "newspaper" had jumped out into the public mind with an engraved image of a pre-convicted killer.

Byron ran his finger over the phrase: "a murderer whose guilt is not to be doubted." The whole piece smelled of a railroad job, and thanks to this country rag that wasn't even worth the penny he stole it for.

Terrible images flooded his imagination: government kill-systems disguised as courts employed in service of the big money business interests. In Montana, those forces had to involve operations like the powerful Bushmaster Mining Company, a host of gigantic cattle ranches, and a rural forest of oil rigs, some of which were pumping away right outside town.

Go up against their owners, he reminded himself, *and see how fast the local press kicks off the process of poisoning your name. Find yourself advertised far and wide as a fool.*

Byron's stomach tightened with the realization that this article was one more example of the processes employed by the region's power mongers in silencing the kind of vital dissent that defined his life and work. He thought about using a phone booth to call Ruth with this news, but remembered that the one on the street corner had been out of order for months. It occurred to him that he could get back home and tell her himself as soon as he could locate a working phone.

Within half an hour he had already swung by the courthouse and verified that there was actually a "sentencing hearing" on the docket for seven that evening. The desk sergeant failed to appreciate the important little detail of going ahead and bothering with a trial for a man so obviously guilty. Byron expected the sergeant to chide him with *Haven't you seen the paper?*—but the guy was too clever to reveal himself.

And then Byron was back at home, pacing in their living room while Ruth held the phone and tried to get a word in edgewise with Jerry O'Connell, up in Great Falls. "Jerry! Jerry, hold on a sec... Jerry wait. *Wait*! No you're way ahead of us. It's too soon for you to come here."

"Do *not* have him come here!"

"Byron says you shouldn't come. No! No listen, we didn't call you to bring you down here, we just need for you to let the every Party member in Montana know about this case."

Byron snatched the receiver and added, "A solitary working man with no friends in the area has been arrested for serious murders and the press is already convicting him! This could be important for the People's cause!"

Ruth angrily grabbed it back and added, "Listen Jerry, we can't prove Bushmaster Mining is behind this but we sure as hell have to ask ourselves if they might be, don't we? I mean, given their history around here? You have to wonder, who did this guy piss off?"

"Make sure he doesn't come here," Byron whispered.

"Yes, for now at least. Just let them know; I'm sure they'll track the story. Byron and I are going to the hearing this evening. It can't be a sentencing, so that part of it must just be bad info. I'm sure it's just a plea hearing. But there's no doubt they're holding it after hours like this because they don't plan to waste any time in putting him down like a dog. You better hope he's guilty! *What*? No, wait!"

Ruth covered the mouthpiece and whispered to Byron, "He wants to defend him."

"Don't even joke about it."

"Jerry, he might have a lawyer. Just *wait* until we get back tonight! I'll let you know what happens."

"Make him stay home."

"Stay home by your phone, will you Jerry? No! No I said we'll call you! Jerry? Jerry..." She let out a sigh and hung up the phone, then turned to her husband.

"He hung up."

"What for? You told him we'd call."

"He says he's going to find somebody to drive him down tonight."

"Shit! Shit! No!"

"You heard me try to stop him. What can we do?"

"I'll tell you what we *can't* do," Byron fumed. "We can't let him stay here. We'll never get rid of him! If he's involved in the trial, he'll have a full-time excuse to see his girlfriend across town."

"So that's it, then." Ruth looked straight at him. "We're agreed?"

"Hell yes, we agreed. No Jerry here."

"No Jerry."

"Good. It's time to get over to the courthouse."

Ruth smiled. "I'll get my notepad."

Now that was more like it: shake off the crazy energy and get back to work. Byron loved going on a job with his wife. It always felt like moving out with the troops in a combat operation. The more dangerous the mission the better. It only intensified his sense of appreciation for having a partner who filled in his blanks as well as Ruth always did. And hey, if their magazine got a major anti-corruption series out of the case, why then that one-cent edition of the town's newspaper would be the most fruitful petty theft Byron had ever committed.

■ ■ ■

Andy couldn't help but giggle while he watched Judge Ryan Coolidge bang his gavel over and over, trying to reestablish order. For some unexplainable reason, the old newspaperman who identified himself as Byron Sherman was all wound up on Andy's behalf. He had to concentrate hard on his Harmless Goofball act, just to avoid laughing out loud.

"Sit down, Mr. Sherman," the judge shouted. "You're out of order!"

"Your Honor!" Byron matched the judge's volume, "*Look* at that goofy smile on his face!" He pointed straight at Andy. "He obviously doesn't appreciate or understand what's going on!"

The Judge pounded his gavel again. "You are not an officer of the court, sir! You do not represent him or anybody else here!"

"My paper represents the workers of the world, and this looks like one of them to me!"

"Bailiff, escort Mr. Sherman from the room."

"You know I won't be silent about this!" Byron protested while the deputy took his arm and walked him to the door. "You realize I'm going to write about this!"

"Oh, yes," his Honor agreed while they all watched Byron Sherman disappear. "We all realize that." A chuckle ran through the small crowd of court observers.

Andy showed them a smirk of his own. He knew nobody had expected him to waive his right to an attorney, or especially to waive his right to a trial. But the judo masters back in the joint had taught him a move he learned well. What they did when an opponent got them in a death grip was, they just went limp. No resistance whatsoever. The change-up seldom failed to rattle the aggressor for just an instant, which would break the strength of their grip long enough to allow for a counter-move. And that counter-move could very well be the thing that saved you.

The toxic yogi masters inside the joint repeatedly filled him with the message: *the trick is to ignore your survival instinct. You have to stick your head in the lion's mouth, then grab its balls and squeeze.*

The court authorities fought him, of course, but he had them cold. That big sheriff had even called in two separate shrinks *and* a priest to take turns interviewing him, all trying to prove he was too crazy to be allowed to represent himself. The shrinks left baffled and as for the priest, Andy wasn't even Catholic. The old Jesuit had known many of the town authorities since their childhood days and needed access to do research for a book.

Andy spoke to all of them in a clear, quiet, and polite voice that never waivered. He knew none of them would be able to say he wasn't responsible for his actions. There was no way to prevent him from going "in propria persona" and acting as his own counsel.

The monsters of the cell block taught him by example: *when the heat is on you and you've got no idea what to do, take the craziest route you can, but act like you know exactly what you're doing.* Sometimes just shaking things up that much could open new escape routes.

And who among them had been prepared for Andy to waive all his rights? Plead guilty? Agree to be sentenced right then and there? Nobody.

People could call him stupid all they wanted, but he could wrap practically anybody around his little finger with his crazy faces and goofy behaviors. It was a powerful way to keep them from getting a bead on who he really was or what he might do next.

From somewhere deep inside the Harmless Goofball, Andy peered out at the gaggle of official attendees for his sentencing hearing and listened to the judge tell him he was to be hanged by the neck until he was dead. Andy's intuition told him not to react with any shock at the sentence.

Insist you're not crazy while you convince them you are. It was more of a sixth sense than a plan, but his intuition about it was strong. He giggled several times while they led him back to his cell.

With the formalities out of the way, the first thing Andy noticed about being under a death sentence was the way it seemed to satisfy the guards and everybody well enough to quit shoving him around and looking for excuses to beat on him. A little pity was fine with him. If the image of his carcass slowly twisting in the wind placated them well enough to make them leave him alone, then Andy considered his finely tuned criminal intuition to be taking him in the right direction.

His transfer to state prison wouldn't take place until Monday morning, so he was led back to his holding cell. He heard the sheriff specify that since Andy was a walking dead man they would house him alone at all times. He ignored the remarks. Later, after lights out, in spite of everything he was glad to be on a decent cot in a warm cell, swaddled in a blanket of darkness. His personal comfort had not been so well attended since he made his break for it six months earlier.

A placid feeling enveloped him. It reminded him of the mental state imparted by good whiskey. Memories might stalk him, but he remained immune to their fangs.

18

The Rise Of Jerry The Red

By the time Jerry O'Connell arrived back in Roundup for the second time that week, he was primed and ready for the fight of his life. Byron and Ruth Sherman were going to help him, too. They just didn't know it yet. Jerry accepted the idea that it was his mission to bring them aboard.

He knew he needed all his strength for the task but for him, physical strength was in short supply. He had reached the age of forty-two already suffering palpitations and wondering how long his heart would hold out. His doughy body was made for physical troubles, and his lifelong high tension levels and massive appetite resulted in his bloated and fragile state. Somewhere in his bones, he knew that he needed to be underway with whatever life's work he hoped to leave behind.

Back before his own party dropped him from his congressional seat, citing his so-called disruptive behavior, he tried hard to explain his essential motivations to their hierarchy. It was a futile effort on his part, as if they didn't even believe his background of experience. This seemed especially strange to him because so much of his story had played out in open public.

When he was elected to congress at the age of twenty-seven, he was already a firebrand. His viewpoint was forged in the crucible of his father's early death, deep in an unsafe mine. Throughout his childhood in Butte, Montana, he had watched the mine workers being shoved around like loose dirt by the tyrannical mine owners.

Jerry O'Connell was a short and homely boy, socially awkward. Even so, long before he was grown he realized that he had a talent for public speaking that belied his tongue-tied persona in private settings. He learned that pretty girls whom he could never summon the courage to approach were easily swayed by his political discourse, and as long as he avoided anything personal, Jerry had a good time speaking to people who otherwise wouldn't bother with him.

Early baldness did nothing for his social abilities. He was still a young adult when he realized his physical attractiveness, such as it ever was, had already begun to desert him. Thus it was not his physical qualities but his fiery ranting self that seduced his first wife, Alvina, and later his second wife, Mazie, as well as any other lonely women who needed something warm to bring home in privacy and who were able to close their eyes in the darkness and perhaps imagine that his impassioned monologues came from one of those handsome announcers who spoke on the radio and not a guy like him.

In the Montana State Legislature, he thrilled the Communist Party with his anti-capitalist speeches, but the Democrats who actually elected him recoiled from his relentless contrarian stance on practically everything. Party leaders noted with dismay that he appeared to lack any political sense regarding how and when to pick his battles.

That was then. Now, fifteen years later, his anti-establishment zeal had hardened into that of a man who had received very little encouragement as an individual but who had scratched and scraped his way to the modest life of political gadfly whose only modus operandi was a sustained attack.

■ ■ ■

Back up in Great Falls, FBI Confidential Informant of Known Reliability, Number 5, sat in the freezing sub-basement tending to the wiretap on Jerry O'Connell and wondering how his predecessor, FBI Confidential Informant of Known Reliability, Number 3, had managed to survive the midnight shift. *No wonder the guy got himself out of it*, he thought with disgust. It was so cold down there that he could feel the pittance of warmth radiating from the suitcase-sized tape recorder. He leaned closer to it and felt the tiny glow on his face. It teased him but it did him no good.

With tape rolling and the headphones in place, Number 5 listened in accordance with his new directive from J. Edgar. Once the phone call had come through from the Shermans alerting O'Connell to the situation with that madman killer down in Roundup, the Boss decided that he wanted the Bureau to know anything they could find out about O'Connell's involvement for that cause.

There was no way the pinko was going to fire up the Communist Party troops for an attack on American jurisprudence while the FBI stood silent. Number 5 was even hungrier than Number 7 to find out something good and send it up the line to the Boss. Get himself the hell out of there.

So he immediately marked the rolling tape with a spot of ink and took copious notes while Jerry worked the phones. The guy employed unabashed begging and emotional pleas for help as if he was asking them to save the world by firing up their Comrades to a protest campaign against the death sentence. The anti-death penalty crowd had their poster image to rally them now, even if it was only some murderer who got himself chased all the way up to Canada. With the perpetrator back in Montana, the authorities planned to hang him in the town square with a portable gallows borrowed from the hobbyist who made it over in Billings.

The Boss was particularly upset by murderers who managed to get away with their crimes in court. Any challenge to the execution of this one was going to be a personal affront to the Boss.

Number 5 shuddered at the thought and this time the cold had nothing to do with it. He had already seen enough of FBI backroom conduct that the last thing he ever wanted to do was to be the guy who made a personal assault on the sensibilities of J. Edgar Hoover, which was exactly what the ex-congressman on the tapped phone line was in the process of doing.

■ ■ ■

Jerry dropped his small valise on the living room floor and stared at Ruth and Byron in shock. "You can't be serious! Sentenced to hang— *with no trial*?" He nearly screamed the last words.

Byron unhappily eyed Jerry's valise while he nodded in agreement. "He insisted on representing himself, then he pled guilty and demanded to go straight to sentencing."

"I don't believe that!" he exploded.

"We were there, Jerry," Ruth assured him. "As lousy as it all sounds, he was given every opportunity under the law. This young man appears to have cut himself off at the legs on purpose. We don't know why, unless he's not mentally sound."

"Well there you are!" Jerry shouted. "You'd *have* to be nuts to do something like that. Hell, his performance in court ought to be enough to win him a sanity hearing, right there!"

"Maybe," Byron acknowledged. "Problem is, these folks are hungry for vengeance and this kid played right into their hands."

Jerry sat and put his head in his hands. "I can't believe this is happening," he sighed. "Thank God I came on down," he leveled a murderous glance at Byron, sparing Ruth for the moment. "Instead of listening to you two."

Ruth's color drained in anticipation of the response she knew was coming, and Byron was right on time with it. "Now you wait just a second, Jerry!" he shouted. "You couldn't have done anything about it if you had been there."

"Do you *not* realize I have been admitted to the practice of law? The Communist Party lists me as their main resource for party members who get themselves tangled up with the authorities."

"Yeah, I heard you got your shingle but I also understand you never went to law school and you've never tried a case!"

"Hey I get results for our people!"

"Have you gotten anybody released yet?" Ruth quietly asked.

"Doesn't matter. In this state you can get a law license if an attorney sponsors you and you pass the bar exam. Which I did. Besides, I graduated from Southwestern University Law School."

"With a law degree?"

"Believe me, I learned what they had to teach me. I never could have passed the Bar if I hadn't."

Byron bit his tongue to avoid asking how much it cost to bribe the panel. "Jerry," he said with a tired sigh, "I respect the fact that you feel our concern and share our passion over this travesty, but—"

Ruth interrupted and finished for him, "Don't you think this case deserves a top notch attorney to go up against the establishment on this?"

"Sure it does," Jerry nodded. "And they're going to have to work for the court's minimum wage, too. You think that guy will? How many men with a license to practice law *aren't* capitalist bastards, eh? Whereas I would expect to work for the standard public defender fee paid by the state."

"Jerry!" Byron nearly shouted it. "It's too late to get yourself declared the Public Defender on this thing. Don't you get it? He's cooked. They're done with him! It's all over but the hanging. Our job is to make sure the public is aware of the horrors of a system that puts a man to death and does it on a crazed confession that was probably beaten out of him. Who knows what they did to him to get him to declare himself as his own damned attorney?"

"Jesus," Jerry said, shaking his head.

"Jerry, what Byron's trying to tell you is that we're both impressed that you would come all the way down here like this—"

"Out of personal concern!" Jerry added.

"Out of personal concern, to be sure, but Byron and I were both in the courtroom tonight. Carmichael's only hope is a top-notch volunteer lawyer with extensive capital case experience and knowledge of the appeals process."

"Do you have all that, Jerry?" Byron harshly asked, with another wary glance at the O'Connell's valise. "We know the answer to that. So please. Just use your contacts in the Party and have them spread the word *fast*. There's got to be a like-minded Party member out there who has legal qualifications to take on this case and who also appreciates the opportunity this would be to their professional standing if they can—"

"I get it, Byron! You don't think I can do this and you want me to hand it off."

"Jerry for Christ's sake they beat the shit out of that kid. He looks like they hit him in the fact with a board! He behaves as if he's brain damaged and we don't know how long he's been that way. It could have been done by the Mounties or even right here in Roundup."

Ruth continued, "Plus we have scuttlebutt that says the FBI is pushing this case and that Bushmaster Mining wants to show a get-tough stance to outsiders. Some gesture to make local workers feel like they give a shit."

Byron added, "There's more. Andrew kept mentioning the Free-masons at the hearing. He thinks they're out to silence him."

"You're on a first name basis?"

"No, it's just easy to have a fatherly stance toward a guy in his position."

"So you think he's innocent?"

"Who cares? This case stinks even if he's not. And the things he was shouting about the Freemasons had a ring of truth to them."

"Freemasons?" O'Connell sneered. "Please. Why would they give a damn? Is Carmichael a Mason?"

"The local Masonic Order says no." Byron looked him straight in the eyes. "This guy actually says he learned secret codes from those two boys up in Canada. Some kind of elaborate smoke signal code that's so complex you need a code key to decipher it. And he claims they have to silence him now because outsiders are forbidden to know how Freema-sons communicate."

"Secret Masonic communication codes..." O'Connell chuckled. "It's brilliant. I can use that on an insanity plea."

"Unless he's telling the truth."

O'Connell laughed. "If he's telling the truth I'll take the information to the local Order and tell them I want the them to pay for his defense, or I'll release the 'secret' codes myself! Ha!"

"Jerry," Ruth added. "If the codes are real then they're things the Freemasons have protected for centuries. You can't help but wonder how far they'll go to do that."

"Hey," Byron said, "did you know that during part of the initiation ceremony for new Freemasons they have to swear that they'll cover up the misdeeds of any other Mason? Even crimes. And if they don't, the other Masons can kill them. They're like the Mafia."

"What? I never heard that." O'Connell asked.

"Yeah well it's true," Ruth interjected. "And not only that but Bushmaster Mining has a high ratio of Freemasons on their management staff. So this kid may be crazy, but he isn't stupid. Hell, he might actually be in all this trouble because he stumbled across something big he's not supposed to know."

"Bushmaster will do anything to trick their workers into thinking they care about them and hold off union protests," Byron added. "So please. Let me drive you back to the bus station and buy you a ticket. Go home and get somebody from the Party who has the qualifications to—"

"Hey!" Jerry shouted. It shocked them both into silence. He dropped his voice to a plaintive tone. "I don't think either of you appreciates the fact that this case is the thing I've waited for. And I mean waited for years. I've waited for a chance to go head to head with the established forces in this state, hell in this *country*. If you ask me, this isn't about one framed convict anymore. As if that wouldn't be bad enough in itself. This is about a fundamental clash between the old forces of corrupt capitalism and a whole new way of seeing the world. We're getting close to a People's Socialist Utopia in this country if we can just get the greedy bastards out of the way!"

Ruth felt a sinking feeling in her stomach while she watched Jerry move his valise next to the sofa and open the lid. "Nope," he said with resolution. "We have to challenge this thing on every single level we can. I'll just bunk here on the sofa for the night."

"Jerry," Byron began in a whine of protest, but Jerry cut him off.

"Don't worry, you two. I'll be sure the Party knows you spearheaded this operation and that you're behind me on this. I can steer a lot of support to your magazine. I can get Party organizations to advertise in your publication! New subscribers! An expanded readership!"

Ruth flashed an expression at Byron that he immediately understood; O'Connell had just iterated their primary concerns in maintaining their magazine. As painful as it was to acknowledge it, they needed his sources of capital to continue functioning. Most of the Montana public failed to see the light regarding utopian ideals for humanity, and needed to be educated. But to do that, the message could be strongly reinforced if couched inside something they already wanted to read about. Say, an interesting murder trial.

Ruth and Byron had already agreed there was a perfect platform here for enunciating the plight of the country's enslaved workers. It had the potential to be precisely the bully pulpit they needed to let The People know that the case at hand ran far deeper than one inmate's brutal treatment by the authorities. Both Shermans knew public attention, properly stoked, could be magically transmuted to massive political action.

Their struggling magazine had never done more than barely sustain them, but now they joyfully faced the potential for earning serious money in the heartfelt task of casting light on the deficiencies of the American system. The lure of personal wealth had little hold on Ruth or Byron. They envisioned the money as fuel for driving their magazine to announce a vital message of sorely needed revolution. The purpose was nothing less than that of restoring decent sensibilities regarding America's beleaguered workers.

But the uncertainty of a loose cannon like Jerry O'Connell put a precarious slant on the whole picture. If they didn't come up with a way to ease him away from the case and prevent him from gaining influence over the it, there was a good chance he would pave Carmichael's way to the gallows. Ruth and Byron both knew with cold certainty that in such a case they would become the living symbols of a highly unpopular lost cause.

19

The Hairy Eyeball Returns

By five o'clock the following evening, the fancy lighted barber pole at Chester's Barbershop was already turned off. He was about to lock up when the entry bells jangled, and he looked up in surprise to see Sheriff Preston lean in the doorway.

"Got time to finish up the haircut? You know, since we got interrupted before?"

"Sheriff! Of course! Come in! Come in." Chester set aside his broom and escorted Preston to the big chair.

Preston walked in and lowered himself into the chair as if he weighed a ton. "City Hall's full of reporters from Great Falls, Helena, Billings, you name it."

Chester twisted the lock and hurried back to his late customer. He snapped up his sharpest scissors and reached for a comb with those ultra-thin teeth that offer pull resistance to balding wisps and make a man feel like he's got more hair than he really does. "We've all been following the news. What a thing! And how strange to think that the last time you were in here, your biggest problem was just some nuisance call from the café!"

He whipped the barber sheet into the air and let it glide down over the Sheriff, then fastened it at the neck. "And now everything is all about the Thorntons."

He glanced down and noticed the Sheriff didn't look at him but just stared toward the wall. "...Um, were they still there at the café when you arrived?"

Preston let out a heavy sigh. "Nope. No. They were not. They'd just left, in fact. I never saw them alive that day."

Chester riffled through Preston's hair above the back of the Sheriff's neck and winced at the sight of the uneven gash he had left there during their last visit. The man didn't need more haircutting as much as he needed a couple of weeks for things to grow back. Still, an important customer had requested assistance and professional ethics prevented Chester from refusing.

The Sheriff looked deeply fatigued, as if he hadn't slept since the last time he was there. Chester wasn't surprised when his experienced hands felt the slight forward droop to Preston's head. The poor civil servant was dropping off to sleep within seconds of hitting the chair. Chester kept the scissors busily clicking away at the neck hairs while he sneaked a peek at the Sheriff's eyes.

Both lids were drooping over both eyes, the good one as well as the fake. From that angle Chester couldn't tell a thing about the artificial eye, but the phrase *The Hairy Eyeball!* involuntarily ran through his head. He snorted so hard that he had to spin around and fake a sneeze, but he threw in a few extra clicks with the scissors to cover the move. He was back to the task a moment later.

After that the old familiar sound track took over the barbershop while both men fell silent and the scissors did the talking. Ordinarily Chester loved such moments when the talkers finally stopped running their mouths and he could do his work in peace without entertaining them. The thin metallic voices of the scissors and their snickity rhythm reminded him of the voices on French radio stations beaming down out of Canada. He sometimes left one playing in the shop just to enjoy the fact that he couldn't understand them and therefore didn't have to be subjected to their constant manipulations and outright lies.

It was Chester's opinion that such moments were the real reason he stuck with his profession and put in the long hours. A man with a wife and kids had a hard time finding peaceful moments.

This one was brief. He sensed motion outside the front door a second before a hand pounded hard enough to rattle it in the door-frame. A voice called in.

"Sheriff? Is that you in there? It's Stan Winkleblech with the Montana Daily News out of Helena!"

"Shit!" Preston was instantly wide awake. He turned to Chester and put his finger to his lips.

"Sheriff?" Winkleblech continued, "I waited in your office like you asked me to. I must say I am disappointed that you ducked out on me, sir!" Winkleblech had his face pressed to the door glass.

"You're in there, Sheriff! I can see your legs there! You are standing in the way of the people's right to know. Now I have six other reporters with me from papers all over the state, and there are people in this town who think I ought to just break on in and *make* you talk to the public about this!"

At that Chester tossed his scissors and comb onto the mirrored counter. He stormed to the door and yelled through the glass. "Damn it! Not in *my* shop! You can just go right ahead and print in your papers that Sheriff Preston will have safe haven in Chester's Barbershop on Main Street in Roundup for *as long as he wants*!"

"Get away from the door," Winkleblech yelled back, "or I'll misspell your name and give out the wrong address!"

Chester immediately turned back to Sheriff Preston. "Sorry," he shrugged with a rueful smile and stepped back from the door.

"Jesus. Get out of the way, Chester," Preston nudged the barber aside and stepped to the door, opened it, and stepped outside. Several flash cameras went off in succession.

Chester closed the door behind him and relocked it, then pulled down the blinds and turned off the interior lights. Nobody outside the shop could see him now. He folded his arms tightly against his chest and silently remarked to himself that as much as he resented having others threaten to break into his shop, he had certainly not kept it in business for so long without learning when to shut the hell up.

■ ■ ■

Preston tried to focus on the gaggle of reporters clustered around the barbershop entrance but blue spots filled his vision. He hoped they were done with the flash photos. For a moment all he could do was stand reeling with his legs close to buckling. His body felt weak and hollow. Some combination of standing up too fast and going for days without allowing himself to rest was catching up to him hard. He could no longer ignore it.

He waited for his night vision to kick in and was glad that this wasn't an armed conflict. The nearest streetlight didn't reach this far and Chester had turned off the exterior lights. He detested how vulnerable he felt in that moment.

"Sheriff?" Winkleblech swam up through the blue dots. Preston knew the voice even though his vision hadn't resolved.

"Sheriff, you all right? Okay boys, let's give him some room!" The other men were decent enough or clever enough to keep it quiet and not swarm him.

As for Winkleblech, Preston had always tried to cut him a little extra slack when the old ink-stain needed information from the sheriff's office because the man went through life named Winkleblech. Now Preston could only look in the direction where he figured old Wink's face ought to be and covered his weakness by glancing around at the silhouettes of the other reporters as if he could clearly see them.

At least the wave of dizziness passed and he was able to speak in his on-duty voice. "Gentlemen, I came over here tonight because I'm way behind on my sitting down. You know what I know. This whole thing went out of my hands the moment we turned him over to the court."

"But Sheriff," Winkleblech began, "I really think you could tell the folks—"

"I don't know anything more than you do!" Preston hollered. When old Wink fell to a respectful silence, he went on.

"I can't say that I read all your papers, gentlemen, but I've seen enough of the coverage on this case to get an idea of the slant you've been giving this, and I think there's a problem here.

"We kept the worst details of the crime scene out of the news, and since we got a confession and a guilty plea, that means a lot of the facts you fellows would ordinarily expect to pick over have been kept away from you.

"Well I'm here to tell you right now the same thing I would tell anybody else about this case, and that is you can be thankful as hell you'll never know the worst of it. It you say the public has some kind of right to know that garbage, I suppose I have to agree. But if you tell me you have any personal interest in the details, then I say you're sick all the way down into your bones!

"Is there anything left in the public's mind that will hesitate at acquiring the worst information about human conduct they can find? Isn't there any sense left among you guys who form public opinion that just because you can know something doesn't mean you should?"

"Sheriff," Wink demurred, "I don't think—"

"I knew the Thorntons well and I knew them for years. So did a lot of the people around here. We don't see two victims, we see two people we happened to be friends, two people who were as much as part of this landscape as anybody. And we understand there is something foul and disrespectful coming from us toward those good people when we roll in the horror of their last minutes like dogs rolling in shit.

"And yes, please print the word "shit" gentlemen, because I believe the people deserve the truth and the truth is that I said it. And if you find or if your editors find that the sensibilities of your good reading public might be offended by the word "shit"—which I once again I ask you to quote—then I assume you will also put it to your readers that there is some small bit irony in the fact that a single word about a common bodily function is abhorrent to the dear, general public, but intimate knowledge of the terror and agony two of our finest citizens is not only acceptable to the public but is something to be wished."

During the long pause that followed no one said a word. Nobody moved. Preston could feel that he had landed a punch squarely on the jaws of these professional voyeurs.

A moment later, he felt one of the men inch close to him. Preston didn't recognize this one. Some new guy with a big flash camera shuffled up to him. The man moved closer until his face was almost directly under Preston's, then broke into a delighted smile.

"Hey this guy's got one eye out of whack! It's tracking off the other way!" The reporter leaned back and broke into such a gale of laughter that he looked mad. Preston expected the others to take a step back, but instead they began to chuckle and then guffaw right along with the loudmouth. It was strange because the new guy might have been surprised by Preston's condition but every other man there had known for years.

He reached up and felt his ceramic eye and realized it was stuck looking to the right. Ordinarily he was sensitive to the feel of his orbital muscles and would have noticed right away. Chalk another one up to sheer exhaustion, he thought. He needed to get home, disable the phone line, and lock the doors and windows. Preston mused that if he got lucky, one of them would try to break in for an exclusive interview and he could finally afford to... he stopped himself at that point.

20

Flight Of The Pigeons

Andy felt the first waves of panic begin to sweep through him when he got within a few hours of being transported up to the state prison outside Deer Lodge. The weight of the thing was beginning to press down hard on his spirits. He had maintained discipline since the moment of his arrest and remained inside the Harmless Goofball even when they were beating on him, but it just didn't seem to have done him much good this time. He even kept an eye out for a glimmer of interest from his guards and would have been quite willing to employ his polished skill set in that regard for a little consideration. But no.

Three separate guards had been by his cell since the sentencing hearing to voluntarily describe the state prison to him and make sure he realized that they were sending word ahead about him so that nobody up there would have any doubt about who they were dealing with. One went so far as to call Andy out about his Harmless Goofball, saying "Go ahead and try that smiley bullshit up there and see how far it gets you! Every one of those guys is going to know you could have just as easily been out there killing their innocent families for no good reason, instead of the Thorntons."

This particular guard seemed to have skills of his own when it came to driving the knifepoint home with nothing more than a few words and a grotesquely false smile. "Condemned men get their personal dignity ruined so bad, it gets to where the thing they love most is the chance to feel superior to somebody, *anybody*, and I mean they want to feel superior over anything at all, doesn't matter what. Ha! Are they ever gonna *love* feeling superior to you, once they find out you're a random killer of helpless victims!"

The guard leaned in to whisper to him, as if this was all some wonderful secret, "They're gonna want to know just how tough a guy like you really is."

And then there was the guard's smile, which he stretched beyond its limit. "You bet they'll make it point to find out, heh-heh-heh."

For Andy, all these hours later, the taunt was still a fresh burn. Despite his experience at the incarcerated life, none of his formerly effective jailhouse behaviors were working for him. He couldn't seem to influence anybody to the slightest degree.

That was most frightening of all. Without the ability to soften the time behind bars by winning special privileges and loosening the bonds in little ways, he would be reduced to existence as nothing more than a run of the mill long term convict. Everything in his life, every detail, would be standard issue. He would, for all practical purposes, disappear into the background and just wait there for death to find him.

It was as if somebody had gone and changed up the rules on him. True, his prior crimes never included brutal murders, and these Montana people didn't even seem to know anything about the whole Oklahoma City fiasco. But they still had it in for Andy Carmichael, and the prevue of the prison life ahead for him was infinitely more grim than it was before.

That deep sense of unease started converting to bone-deep panic when he realized nothing was working the way it used to. His every instinct had told him there would be a magic moment somewhere in the mix—a moment of opportunity such as few but Andy might recognize—and that he would be able to exploit that moment to ease his situation, maybe even use it to escape again. Instead there had been nothing. Grim stares from uniformed robots.

The adrenalin of capture had given way to the despair of throwing himself on the court, and now even the miserable comfort of self-pity was deserting him. In its place there remained only an icy tightening of his major muscle groups and a clenching of his sphincter with which any death row inmate would be familiar.

Andy recognized that was what they were doing to him, of course. He could play the Harmless Goofball all day long and still never fail to notice that they had only offered him their "deal" of sparing his life in return for his plea because they intended to use the prison population to dispose of him. It was painfully reminiscent of the way his old warden employed his worst prisoners in disposing of his troublesome guards. Andy took to clenching his teeth until his jaw muscles throbbed.

He ought to have kept quiet. When was he going to learn to keep his mouth shut? And why did it always have to be so easy to see where he went wrong after it was too late to do anything about it? Hindsight forced him to ask himself whether or not he ever should have mentioned anything about the Freemasons and especially if it had been a mistake to tell them he knew about their Smoke Code.

No. He could see now that he played that hand too soon. It was desperate thinking. He made a mental note to desist with all desperate thinking. This sort of thing was always the result.

The obvious problem now loomed in front of him even though it had eluded him at the time. It was simple; there was no way of knowing who *else* was a part of the loyal Order of Freemasons or whatever they called themselves. The way he saw it, anybody who loved having power over other people was a candidate for membership in the Masonic cult.

So now by talking about what he knew, right there in open court, he had drawn a target onto his own back for the Freemasons and it was just as big as the one the cops planned to pin on him once they got him up to state prison.

It was impossible to determine if the worst danger came from the inmates who would be set to attack or eliminate him, or the Freemasons implanted among the authorities themselves. The ones who had strong motives for keeping their secret methods away from inquiring public eyes.

The cell was a cave of despair. It's silent power drained him of all his strength and of the ability to feel hope. He could recall once seeing a magazine with a picture of an ancient elephant with some other name frozen solid in an iceberg. The big animal had been stuck in there for a million years or something and had not decayed at all. It still had food in its mouth, for crying out loud, as if some huge, warm-blooded thing somehow got frozen in one second. However it happened, the same force now had swept through Andy's life. He was frozen too, helpless in his iceberg of a life sentence.

He sat down on his cot and slowly brought his chest down to his knees, then hung his head down between them and closed his eyes. He could feel his heartbeat trying to speed up, so he took deep breaths and kept his head low. He had no idea how long he stayed in that position. Time had taken on a new meaning.

After a long time or maybe it was only a short time, keys jingled like Santa bells and the big steel door clanged open. The guard with the keys ignored Andy but stood aside to let some guy walk into the cell. It took a moment for Andy's eyes to register the man's features, then it struck him: the guy from the café! The Asshole! This was the one who started it all!

But why was he there? Was he some kind of unofficial executioner? Weren't they even going to wait until he got to state prison before they had him killed? Andy jumped to his feet and raised on arm to block the blows he expected. But instead the man just took a quick step back and laughed.

"Whoa! Ha-ha! Relax, relax! Feeling jumpy, eh? No shame in that, I would be too. My name is Jerry O'Connell, former state congressional representative, licensed attorney-at-law. And buddy, whether you know it or not, right now I am your best friend."

Andy just stared at him, trying to digest this turn of events.

O'Connell didn't wait for him to respond. "Your guilty plea was made under duress and I'll get it thrown out. You need an actual trial, and if we can move the venue we'll do that too. You, my friend, have rights, and I'm here to see that you get them."

The man stuck out his hand to Andy like an old friend would do. "There is no fee to be paid by you, of course."

And that was when Andy's darkness lifted enough for him to realize what was happening. The magical moment he had been searching for arrived after all. It came along with such perfection that he could hardly restrain himself from jumping up and down and kicking the walls for joy. But his finely tuned criminal instincts knew better than to display such behavior when the Lone Ranger had just walked into his life. Instead he simply painted his face with a silly grin, then reached forward and shook hands with his new attorney.

■ ■ ■

Circulation doubled in that first month over at The Weekly Roundup. By the time Ruth and Byron got the next edition of their monthly magazine into print, all The Worker's Monthly could do was add commentary to the case. The news was already used up.

But Ruth Sherman considered the facts of the news to merely be the gateway to the story. The weight of the story rested in how the facts were interpreted, and it was in the shaping of opinion where Ruth Sherman shined. She began with a long analysis of the powers displayed by the region's business and capital forces in securing a death sentence for a stranger who happened to look guilty but was given no chance to defend his innocence. She ignored his personal demands to skip a trial.

The issue was a fitting receptacle for Ruth's lifetime of second class treatment by the men of the world over her combination of sharp-tongued intelligence and homely features, and of her treatment by the women of the world who had shunned Ruth for her politics. She had grown up in a pleasant working class home, so she could not fathom why so many other Montana citizens failed to grasp the importance of the socialist state simply because their own lives were also comfortable.

Passionless people were always a mystery to Ruth, but she burned with enough of it to share with all her readers. All the more so when she poured her heart and sole into the cause of a scandal put forward by the power elite upon a helpless individual working man, an itinerant who desired nothing more than the sort of work opportunities that abounded in Montana. What, Ruth implored her readers to tell her, were the consequences going to be for all the business people in the region if they stood back and allowed this perpetration of injustice upon a lone working man, friendless among them?

Ruth cried hard enough in the writing of it that she felt certain it would be a hit with the readers, especially the females. She had always been able to count on the feminine socialist energy of the readership to resonate best with the sensitivities she expressed. Ruth considered her best chance for advancing enlightenment to be that of reaching the nurturing tendencies of society's socialist females through their natural concern for the young ones.

Her stand was simple; the only tyranny to be tolerated from the government was that which makes the world a better place with its benevolent leadership. Every line in her editorials assured the readers that this case of Andrew James Carmichael had nothing benevolent about it.

Ruth was so wrapped up in her next opinion piece that she didn't notice when Byron came home until she heard him flop down on the living room sofa with a heavy sigh. She stepped into the room to check on him and immediately saw trouble in his eyes.

"Well, Ruth, Clerk of Court confirms it. Jerry convinced Carmichael to let him represent him."

"Oh, no. Byron what's the matter with him? He'll be in over his head and sink the whole effort!"

"Preaching to the choir, kid. They both just went in front of the judge to stop his transfer to prison while they challenge his confession, his entire guilty plea." Byron stood and looked down at the sofa, where Jerry had slept the night before.

"I tell you, Ruth. We have to get this guy out of here or he's gonna live on that couch for the rest of the year."

"Suits me. Let him go stay at his girlfriend's house, as long as his wife doesn't mind."

Byron laughed at the picture she conjured. "So, then. You going to be the one to tell him?"

"What? Get serious! I'm not telling him, you tell him."

"I can tell him but you know he won't listen. He just goes pathetic on me. You, however, can make him feel guilty enough to do it."

"About having a girlfriend?"

"No, that won't work. Make him guilty *because* what he's doing hurts your conscience since he involved your home!"

"...Oo."

"Eh?"

"Ooo. That's right."

"Of course!"

"What can he say?"

"Not a thing! Sayonara! That's it!"

"I Won't judge him, I'll make it about me!"

"Yes! And then you're bulletproof. Just tell him as a married woman, you can't let him stay another night and facilitate this deception of his wife with the local girl. One night was bad enough, but that was on the spur of the moment. He's got to be on his own."

"Wow. You've sure got the moves down pat. I'm going to have to keep that in mind about you."

"Hey, I'd do it myself, but this is a job that needs a woman's touch."

Ruth could have thrown a wisecrack back at him but she realized he was probably right and so she kept quiet about it.

21

Rude Awakenings

Mazie O'Connell managed to ignore her gnawing suspicions about Jerry's behavior during those first few months. Nevertheless the atmosphere in their home continued to sour into a strangely familiar one. Being Jerry's second wife and formerly the girlfriend with whom he cheated on his first wife, Mazie's own skills at deception prevented her from missing the sudden uptick in occasions when Jerry had to work late in his tiny office, or even make those odd trips out of town.

One day, two days at a time, his "rescue missions" were always made under duress and in service of honest workers he described as exploited by the capitalist pigs of the region. When autumn rolled around the pigs appeared to really go active. They remained active straight through the Thanksgiving and Christmas holidays, leaving Jerry to rant and rave each time he packed his suitcase yet again and disappeared in a flurry of epithets about the Robber Barons of the Montana mining and drilling industries. In spite of the fact that he had few cases at work and their income was only a trickle, he somehow found the means for almost constant travel on a *pro bono* basis.

When he missed their fourteenth anniversary and didn't remember to call home, Mazie's suspicions stopped gnawing and smacked her over the head. Awareness bloomed. Not only had he used the same deceptions to disguise his movements back when she was the one he cheated with, but Mazie had conspired to help him do it. The only difference was that back then his first wife Alvina was the one standing where Mazie now found herself.

Thus, in addition to the FBI Confidential Informants of Known Reliability who sat in secrecy in the freezing sub-basement of the building next door, Mazie O'Connell became a frequent third party to Jerry's calls by quietly listening in on the extension phone upstairs. The clincher for Mazie was also the deadly component to the whole scenario, in that Jerry would stand downstairs in their kitchen and whisper his nasty conversations with his latest new skirt. Whispering to hide his words from Mazie, while she sat with her hand covering the mouthpiece and heard every syllable no matter how quietly spoken.

Despite all that, the realization came to her slowly. It was not the realization that the tables had turned on her but that the desperately cheap household budget available to her for maintaining their home was as small as it was partly due to whatever amount of money her husband was spending on his private recreational activities. Jerry's terrible health and constant chest pain had caused her to mistakenly conclude that the reason he lacked sexual interest in her was because his heart condition had somehow robbed his sex drive.

Therefore his feverish whispered conversations and the sexual encounters with this new girl not only mocked her marital status, it mocked every one of Mazie's careful trips to the grocery store with a fistful of coupons and books of carefully saved S&H Green Stamps, all in service of scrounging up enough food to keep the meals coming for a husband with a bad heart who ate like a barnyard pig when he was at home and blew their family cash on other women when he was away.

When she thought about it, every soup she stretched with tap water, every time she swept with a broom because they couldn't afford a vacuum, every aspect of her meager life had actually been the voice of experience trying to give her a lesson by showing her exactly what her husband's faithlessness was costing her.

Everything about the man she once admired so deeply that she had cheerfully stolen him away from his wife seemed to have disappeared. Left behind was this shell of a husband who gave her no more sustenance than she might get from hugging a cardboard cutout of a man.

Slowly, moving so gently it would not make a sound, she placed the phone receiver back in the cradle and left Jerry to pull on his pecker down in the kitchen while he worked the phone with the new kid over in Roundup. Mazie padded into the den and opened up the file box to check Jerry's life insurance, just to be certain the premiums were paid up and that she was still the beneficiary.

After all, his weight was excessive, his heart was bad, and he was holding up the strain of a double life. How long could that ticker last?

■ ■ ■

The courtroom was full of radio reporters and newsprint journalists. It seemed as if everybody in that part of the country had heard about Andy's case and the attempt to unravel his death penalty.

Andy watched the judge's every move and felt certain the old guy was buying the story. All of it. Impossible as it seemed, there was no mistaking that he was actually nodding along in agreement while The Lone Ranger paced the courtroom and worked his magic for the folks. This was where Andy would find out whether this Lone Ranger lawyer was a trick of some kind or if he really represented that lucky break Andy had eagerly anticipated.

He had to employ all his deceptive skill to keep the amazement off of his face while he watched his attorney argue on his behalf. The man spoke with such passion that it looked like his blubbery face could burst into tears at any second.

Even though it was Andy's life at stake, that didn't do much to help him pay attention to the boring proceedings. Still, he appreci-ated how well the mouthpiece kept everybody's attention while he wrapped up his presentation. Funny, how different it was from the anonymous sentencing hearing, witnessed by nothing more than two local reporters and a couple of cops. Now every seat was taken and he'd overheard a guard remarking that they were reporters from all around the country.

He didn't like having to sit there and listen, but had to admit the guy was a real one-man show. Anybody would think he and Andy had been old army buddies, or maybe longtime neighbors, instead of two men who met for the first time just a few hours earlier inside a solitary confinement cell.

Somehow or other, the attorney had already made the court officially forget about Andy's prison history and crime record, dropping them from consideration in his case. Then he put the Sheriff on the stand and pretty soon the court acknowledged that Andy was mistreated in his cell after his arrest.

"You see, don't you," the little bald guy concluded to the packed room, "that what has clearly occurred in this case is that a scapegoat was made of an itinerant worker." He pointed straight at Andy for emphasis, "simply because he is a stranger in a strange land! Andrew James Carmichael is among us without the natural support of friends and family such as one who resides in the area might expect to have. And it has operated to his *great* detriment! It is opportunism of the worst kind and we must drive it from our midst!"

He swung his arm toward Andy in a wide gesture that took in the whole courtroom. "How is it possible that we permit this young fellow to come here looking for gainful employment and we send him out on the end of a rope?"

"Relevance, Mr. O'Connell?"

Andy couldn't believe it. The bald mouthpiece ignored the judge's question and put his hand over his heart and turned to the American flag displayed next to the judge's bench. It struck Andy that the man had little interest in the judge, the courtroom, or the official proceedings at hand. He was playing to the audience of reporters and the far wider audience they represented. The ones, Andy happily told himself, who were going to make him famous.

"I pledge allegiance!" O'Connell announced in his strongest street-corner voice, "to a Nation built on the concept that every single individual is presumed innocent until *proven guilty!*"

The Judge cleared his throat, "Mr. O'Connell, the theatrics are unnecessary. I am inclined to agree there was an official rush to clear this case and I find that certain illegal liberties appear to have been taken with the defendant while in custody."

"Yes! And of course we all understand why; the Thorntons were liked and respected in this town. Everyone here today wants to see justice done." His smile held for several seconds while his eyes took in every person in the room.

"But Your Honor, I come to you with my heart in my mouth and ask this honorable Court if there still exists inside this profit-ravaged *imitation* of the great country we once were, some last shred of social conscience? With all due respect to those temporary damages to local businesses that resulted from the fear generated by these murders, it is an act of false consolation for the State to sooth public emotions by hanging a straw man!

"Why, it's not merely a question of what this young man deserves, it is a far larger question of what The People of Montana deserve! And I say they deserve to know that the court system they pay for will, by God, be a place where *facts* are the only things that matter!"

"Mr. O'Connell, I suggest you conclude your remarks since I have already told you the Court is favorably inclined toward your client in this matter."

"But the record, your Honor! The record of these proceedings which will stand in the public memory for many years to come. And the record of this case must reflect that my client was beaten and terrorized into a so-called "confession" that no right-thinking person can accept. It's the product of coercion against a frightened and confused young man, beaten and held in isolation, forced to--"

"Mr. O'Connell."

"And *then*, sir, in his most abject despair, he threw himself down in front of the court and refused to defend against the charge. It was not an abandonment of his defense, sir. It was an expression of exhaustion from a beaten man!"

"Mr. O'Connell I've only granted this much leeway because of the—"

"Beg pardon, your Honor, but I tell you, it will not stand up to cold scrutiny in the light of day, sir! Not here in Montana nor in any other place, neither!"

The judge banged his gavel twice, so hard it made Andy jump. "Enough! You will come to order, Mr. O'Connell! As I just said, the Court has only indulged your diatribe out of sympathy for the fact that even though the degree of abuse may be impossible to ascertain, it is clear that there needs to be much be more diligence from the State than has been shown up to this point in guaranteeing the accuracy of any capital punishment. The sentence is overturned, a change of plea from "Guilty" to "Not Guilty" shall be allowed, and the case is set to go to trial in thirty days."

They droned on and on, working out the fine points, but Andy heard the good parts. All the State prosecutor could do was shift tactics and try to argue against allowing Andy's sanity to be tested. The Lone Ranger had already explained how important an insanity defense would be in getting Andy out of there and on his way to his next construction job.

The euphoria that filled him made it impossible for him to sit still, to keep quiet, to play the good client. It felt like itching powder had been poured into his state-provided courthouse suit. This rash of easy victories caused a wave of confidence to fill him. Elation fed him an impulse and then assured him it was a good idea. It was time to put the cherry on the banana split and bring in the Harmless Goofball.

22

The Smoke Code

"Your Honor!" Andy shouted it loud enough to be certain everyone in the jammed courtroom heard it and looked his way.

"Sit down, young man."

"I want to address the court."

"Sir, you have just hired an attorney to address the court for you. This is what attorneys do."

"Yes, but I have something important to say!"

"Counselor, restrain your client or he'll be found in contempt."

"No, I am firing my attorney, your Honor! As of this minute! He's fired! I represent myself."

"It's not that simple, sir."

"Your Honor," Andy's new attorney O'Donnell or whoever leaped to his feet and cried out like a panicked mother. "My client is under terrible stress! I must request that you—"

"I'm not his client anymore, so I can make it public knowledge about the Freemasons and their secret communication code!"

"Bailiff, remove this man to the holding cell in the basement."

"Your Honor, if only I could have a word with my client—"

"Have all the words you want with your client, down in the holding cell!" The judge banged his gavel for emphasis.

The bailiff took Andy under the arm and began to pull him toward the exit. Andy knew if he didn't get it out and onto the record right away he might never get another chance, so he just kept on hollering at the top of his voice. Another bailiff joined the first one to help pull him toward the door. It took all his strength to delay them long enough to get the message out.

"The Freemasons are the ones really running things! You ever wonder why the unions and big business can't get along? It's because the Masons don't want them to!"

The judge began to bang his gavel over and over. It was clear to Andy that the old guy was trying to drown him out. That was an obvious indication that the judge was in on the Freemason conspiracy as well. Of course! Andy thought. Why not? Apparently half the people in power had some connection to the Masonic Order. Naturally that would include this corrupt judge.

But his strength was fading and the two bailiffs were determined men. There were only a few seconds of opportunity left to him. "All you reporters! Freemasons all around the world communicate using columns of smoke! The length, the color, it all has meanings. A thousand times more than old native smoke signals!"

The court was in an uproar now and Andy could see a few of the reporters jotting in their notebooks. One of the bailiffs began to try to slap his hand over Andy's mouth, so he bit down on the edge of his palm hard enough to make his holler and pull it away, giving Andy time for a few choice last words.

They're controlling you! Controlling business! The news! And they're talking to each other in secret about it, right out in front of everybody! Next time you see smoke from a fire, look around for Masons with binoculars!"

They had him now, right at the exit's doorframe, clutching the sides with both hands. Only a second or two more and it would be over.

"They're doing it all *right in front of us*!"

And that was it. They had him in the exterior hallway and out of sight of the court observers.

Since Andy was an experienced hand at dealing with the morality displayed by men of violence when no one was around to consider justice, he felt no surprise at all when the bailiffs struck him to the floor and took turns kicking him until his ribs begin to snap, one by one. Then at last, the best part of his day arrived when the lucky relief of unconsciousness delivered him from evil.

■ ■ ■

Wade Preston switched off his intercom call from the on-duty desk sergeant and immediately wished he had told him something else other than to tell the Shermans they could come on back to his office. But there was a dicey line between the right of a couple of individuals to make themselves extremely unpleasant as opposed to that of citizens exercising freedom of the press. Whenever he had crime news they found to be of interest to their cause, he witnessed the Shermans behaving as if they knew exactly where that line was while they pumped him for the information they wanted. Experience taught him it was usually easier to just tell them what they were after and get rid of them. It wasn't like a lot of people read their magazine, or even knew it existed.

And so this time he immediately regretted allowing them to come on back. At the most, he ought to have gone out to meet them in the lobby, give them two minutes and then walk away. He hated the sensation of coming up with the correct response to something the moment it was too late to do anything about it.

Now the approaching commotion out in the hall told him the ruckus was headed his way. Things got louder and then proved him right two seconds later when his door burst open and Byron and Ruth Sherman came bustling in carrying bundles of legal papers.

They both went into that thing they always did where they would both talk at the same time and try to drown each other out, making it hard to ascertain anything they said. He'd warned them about it a dozen times, but it was a frustrating waste of time.

He decided to use the old combat judo approach and go limp on them, put up no resistance at all, just to see how long it took the pair to burn themselves out on this occasion. Usually once they got onto their high horses it took them a good five minutes of sheer ranting time.

On this occasion it was fifteen minutes before he had to get strong with them and give them the choice: leave right then, or test their theories of press freedom by sitting in jail for disorderly conduct and trying to write their way out of that one. They left huffing about fascists and freedom and country. The only button they seemed unwilling to press was the God connection. Instead they adopted their stance of being offended on general principals and proceeded on the presumption that they were the smart ones, the decent ones, the ones with conscience, the ones who cared in a dimly lit world of greedy fools.

Most of the time, Wade Preston loved his job. He loved it in spite of the fact that it often made him view the general public as a nasty crowd of demanding children, the kind who turn evil on you if they don't get what they want. Fire starters.

He looked down at the bundles of newspapers and legal documents the Prestons left littering his desk. It felt as if the piles each stared up at him, waiting to see what he planned to do about it. The thought made his socket itch so he popped out the phony and put it in his vest pocket for awhile.

He focused the good one on the newsprint, examples of the kinds of press coverage going on out there about Andrew Carmichael. From the state capital, The Helena Independent Record, first page, under the fold: *Murder Suspect In Roundup Dodges Grim Reaper;* The Billings Gazette, first page over the fold: *Montana Drivers Avoiding Hitchhikers;* The Rocky Mountain News, in an article clipped from inside the paper: *Killer Dodges Gallows, Gets New Trial;* and last but certainly not least in Wade Preston's concerns was the latest copy of the Shermans' own baby, The Worker's Monthly. There, in a block print and bolded headline that strained the margins of the page: *Ex-Congressman Saves Montana Man From Execution!*

There was a hero shot of "Jerry the Red" O'Connell under the headline. The picture was so old it was taken back when the guy still had most of his hair and was a good thirty pounds lighter. Still, there he was, glorified in print for all the followers of Karl Marx and looking good enough to scare up a new girlfriend to hide from his wife.

The piece was written under Ruth Sherman's byline, though Preston recognized some of Byron's commonly used phrases. It clearly implicated Sheriff Preston and his department in a saga of rushed judgment and police brutality, compounded by collusion from a judge who could be either senile or corrupt, depending on how you took the meaning of the words.

Preston felt his stomach acid leap into the back of his throat and begin burning its way through him. The editorial staff of The Monthly Worker, i.e. Byron and Ruth Sherman, focused a large part of their coverage on that idiotic diatribe Carmichael screamed in court about Freemasons and signal fires or smoke signals or some damn thing.

It was a show, of course. No doubt all of it was carefully rigged in advance by attorney O'Connell as a set-up for an insanity plea and the basis of a sexy promotional article exactly like this one. Preston had never been in the middle of anything so morally insane. The realization sat in his brain like a nail fired into his head.

Impossibly, according to the article, the Shermans had taken all of Andy Carmichael's babble about a Freemason Smoke Code at face value. Preston ran his eyes down the page as fast as he could take in the words. Andy Carmichael was not an evil man who murdered two lovely people over nothing; this wasn't an evil man who desecrated the bodies of his victims for his own gratification, no indeed. Anyone who thought so was expressing their own mental inferiority. The Shermans cried out to one and all that a "conspiracy of Freemasons" *obviously* represented the major business and political forces of the region. The conspirators *obviously* had Sheriff Preston and his department in their hip pockets, along with most of the mainstream press.

The Worker's Monthly publishers blared their concerns over the exploited workers of the world as their motive for adopting *"the lone voice of sanity in the press"* regarding the shadowy forces that were busily manipulating the murder trial of one Andrew J. Carmichael. The Shermans declared themselves devoted to making this story their magazine's central crusade for as long as it might take. Their stated goal was nothing less than to secure justice for a man who was either an innocent scapegoat or, at worst, a mentally ill individual deserving of compassion and requiring psychiatric treatment in a safe and secure environment.

"This is a new age," the editorial opined, *"with a higher standard of morality than we all had to tolerate during wartime. And if you fail to understand that, you are probably old. You are done. It is time for you to go away and leave the harsh task of educating a civilization of ignorant bigots in the ways of the new society. Leave it to others who are stronger, more vital and more informed than you happen to be. For there is something fundamentally wrong with you if your heart fails to bleed for a lone migrant worker who falls into a trap set by a cabal of evil business and political forces. If you fail to rise in anger against this outdated and wrong-headed Order of Freemasons, who have done so much to amass secret power over the governments and the corporate interests of the world using secret communications, via a secret "Smoke Code" to plan their work right under our noses, then you are <u>one</u> <u>of</u> <u>them</u>. And this holds true whether they count you as a member or not!"*

"Son of a bitch," he said out loud, shaking his head. Maybe it was time to rethink his restraint against shooting them. The piece went on about *"the secret Smoke Code,"* using a simple paraphrase of the stuff Carmichael spouted while he was dragged away. So much for anybody being able to burn their trash in peace.

And there was the whole theory, laid out for the avid readers of <u>The Worker's Monthly</u>: the secret Order of Freemasons were in charge of everything, and to keep the laborers happily working they pitted the state's entire justice system against a single man. Why do that? Because they were the ones who were evil, not the murderer. Since they were evil, they needed no other motive than the satisfaction of doing evil things. And if any reader was having a hard time making ends meet, why, he or she could thank the profit-grabbing capitalists who got rich by keeping the little guy down.

Preston wondered if any of the magazine's subscribers would notice that no explanation was offered to support Carmichael's innocence or to put forth any opposing theories about two heinous double murders. But after ten years as Sheriff, he felt no hope that the public would show interest in handling the hard questions behind this case.

23

Soaking The Heads

The fear was getting toothy by the time Andy's trial got under way. He knew enough to keep hidden under the Harmless Goofball, but the sheer size of the case far exceeded anything he expected. Every pre-trial hearing was a reporter's holiday. National newspaper and radio reporters crowded the courtroom. Fights broke out twice in the courthouse hallway. They were not between reporters clamoring for good seats but by people so impassioned in their opinion of the case that they could not tolerate any other viewpoint.

He picked up good amounts of the local gossip between guards and jail staffers by pretending not to be listening, so he realized the town of Roundup had pretty much divided along two sharp lines, with most of the people in favor of tearing off his head but a small and vocal group who threw themselves heavily onto his side.

Starting with the magical appearance of Andy's attorney, complete strangers continued to appear in his life with a need to defend him the way they would defend their own brother or son. So much of the world on the outside of prison walls made no sense at all to Andy, and so he accepted the aid from idiots who seemed prepared to take a bullet for him. There wasn't anything in his internal store of wisdom to explain the behavior, so he chose to soak in it like a hot bath and let everybody else figure it out.

But on the eve of the hard-won trail, distractions had no power over the looming sense of dread radiating from his stomach and down his legs. Suddenly it didn't feel cute or clever to just ignore everything and run on his own time. He couldn't be certain what triggered the change in him, but it felt like it came from the same sort of clues that he learned how to read inside the joint. He had picked up plenty of things by keeping his eyes and ears open, and warning sensations were going through him.

There was nothing direct, just a shift in the way people looked at him. Through their eyes, he saw a walking dead man who had been granted his piece-of-shit trial just as his worthless attorney demanded for him. He could tell without asking; the general opinion floating around was that Andy would wind up on the same gallows he would have already fallen through if the court hadn't set aside his sentence.

His seeping sense of danger quickly grew once he realized it no longer profited him that he had learned how to read people so well back in the joint. The skill was good for nothing but further torment. People were looking at him with what they thought were blank faces, having no idea that he clearly saw their curiosity about how he might look when they pulled the noose off his body. He imagined workers already assembling Montana's famous portable gallows right out on the courthouse lawn, no more than a hundred paces from his isolation cell.

The vise grip squeezed him harder when one of the reporters, a real wise guy, caught Andy's eyes as he passed in the hallway, shackled and helpless. The reporter had scrawled the numbers *3-7-77* across his notebook and help it up for Andy to see. It was coming from one of the squares, but Andy recognized the behavior from the joint. Inside, men were constantly trying to intimidate each other with every mental game they could come up with. But at least there was some honesty to the game on the inside, because you lived or died by your ability to play it. Make a mistake and maybe get found with a shiv in your ribs, face down in the shower or tucked behind a boiler in the basement.

The reporter was a punk because he threw out his little joke knowing there was nothing Andy could do about it, in chains and under guard. If Andy was ever tempted to wonder whether he might eventually feel some remorse for his victims, doughy cowards like that "law-abiding" reporter reminded him that the world was crammed with people who needed killing. In a world with actual justice he wouldn't even be on trial.

■ ■ ■

Ruth Sherman sat across from her husband and tried not to meet his gaze while Jerry sat at their kitchen table and summed up his plea. "It's just the worst time for marital trouble, you know? She realizes I have this big trial—"

"Your first trial," Byron added.

"My first big chance at the law. So she picks that moment to kick me to the curb."

"Did she find out about your girlfriend here in Roundup, Jerry?" Ruth asked in the spirit of pulling off the band-aid. "Because that had to happen, you know."

Byron picked up her cue and added, "Sooner or later."

"Hey, people! Let's not cast stones, all right? You two are blessed with a great relationship. I know. Most of us never get that."

"Jerry," Byron warned, "opening statements are tomorrow and I don't think you should be concerning yourself with looking for a place to stay. You know, right here on the eve of the trial."

"An *important* trial, Jerry" Ruth added.

O'Connell slammed his palm onto the kitchen table. "Hey! Do you think I don't know that? I had to crawl to get accepted for Public Defender funding on this case! At first that bastard was joking about making me blow him before he'd sign off on letting me represent him!"

"Can you do it, Jerry?" Byron asked in urgent tones. "Because the national press has picked up the case and you're being watched, here."

"Oh, we're all being watched, pal," Jerry grinned. "Trust me. But anyway, sure I can do this. One thing at a time. Right now, I'm focused on the opening statement. When it's done I'll worry about the next thing."

"Then Jerry," Ruth spoke up, "you've got to get your personal situation under control so you can concentrate. Our magazine is committed to his defense and we can't afford to allow slip-ups on this."

"Slip ups?" O'Connell asked, looking hurt. "Such as...?"

"Such as getting caught by your wife so that she throws you out, Jerry" Ruth replied, exasperated.

"Can you stay with your girlfriend?" Byron asked in a hopeful voice.

"Byron!"

"No, really, Ruth. If his wife's already said—"

"Folks, please," O'Connell cut in. "Don't make me say it. Don't make me beg. You know why I'm here."

"There's a hotel right down from the courthouse, Jerry," Byron spoke up.

"Hotel? You guys know how fast that would eat through my paltry salary? Hell, if I could still drive I'd just sleep in my car. Believe me, I would. That's how much I believe in this case!"

Byron dropped his head. "...Shit."

"We're Fellow Travelers, my friends. We have to stick together. I can probably rap up this trial in a week."

"A week?" Byron asked.

"For my half of it anyway. Two, tops. Kids, please. Come on. I'm dying over here."

"Shit," Byron repeated.

"Okay, Jerry" Ruth finally declared. "You can use the sofa. But we're not Fellow Travelers, we're independent publishers. We're helping you because we happen to believe in this case."

"And we believe in everything it means for working people in this part of the country." Byron nodded. "But I'm telling you, Jerry. We're only allowing you a place to stay. You can't bring people over here or interview witnesses here or anything like that."

Jerry beamed. "Yes! Agreed! No problems, kids! Just keep me off the streets for a few days and we'll have a verdict we can all be proud of." He got up and walked over to the front door. "I, ah, left my suitcase out on the porch. He put his hand on the doorknob and sheepishly smiled at them. "In case you didn't want to... you know."

"Okay, Jerry," Ruth said, resigned. "Okay."

Jerry opened the door to reach out and grab the suitcase when several intensely bright camera flashes went off in quick succession, followed by half a dozen male voices, all shouting, "Mr. O'Connell!" "Congressman! Congressman O'Connell, over here!" "Mr. O'Connell! Quick question for <u>The Denver Post</u>?"

Ruth spun to Byron, but he had already dropped his head again, slowly shaking it back and forth while the voices outside rose in intensity and each one tried to drown out the others.

"Our credibility," muttered Byron. "It's resting on this guy."

Ruth nodded. "If I believed in God I'd have to think The Big Guy was out to get us."

24

Getting Bugged

The FBI's Salt Lake City Division covered Montana and the surrounding states. So when the Confidential Informants over in Great Falls began to send in messages about a secret communication code used by the international Order of Freemasons having been plucked off a local wire tap, word went straight up to J. Edgar Hoover. The Boss was staunch in his belief that the FBI needed to be aware of every mode of communication employed inside the United States, whether it originated in the USA or not.

Since there was already a full-time tap on Jerry O'Connell's home line, the Bureau already knew about O'Connell's marital troubles. Agents reported that during his separation he was staying at the home of Byron and Ruth Sherman in Roundup, Montana, where the trial was taking place. It was obviously time to expand the range of the wire taps.

J. Edgar didn't maintain control over one of the world's most powerful organizations by allowing other powerful organizations to operate with impunity inside his territory. If the Freemasons thought they were going to set up a secondary government in the United States, he was prepared to have every one of them jailed, blackmailed, or killed resisting arrest.

He ordered a full-time tap on the Shermans' home phone. The order went down to seek information on defense attorney Jerry

O'Connell's legal strategy, plus anything at all regarding the Secret Smoke Code. The Boss had access to some of the greatest code crackers on the planet, and if he could gather just a few samples of Smoke Code translations, he knew the eggheads could figure out how to read it.

The Bureau's knowledge of the Secret Smoke Code could be every bit as important to the future of America as the capture of the German Enigma machine during the Second World War. The strategy regarding the Code would be the same used by the military during the war, meaning the Bureau would keep perfectly quiet about having the Code, and allow the Masons to keep going along thinking their communications were secure. J. Edgar's opinion was that one well-cracked code was worth a hundred crack agents.

Whatever the Masons might be planning, the FBI had no intention of allowing them to gain the upper hand. They might have controlled the design and construction of Washington, D.C. and all the federal buildings, they might have managed to smuggle their symbol onto the face of every American dollar, but The Boss had no intention of letting them get away with whatever it was they were planning.

The Bureau's resources in the region were ordered to focus on "Jerry The Red" O'Connell and find out everything that his client might happen to know about the Secret Smoke Code. Word was that the killer's mouthpiece planned to use it in his client's defense, but nobody had brought back any details about how it applied to the murder case. This left a major hole in the Bureau's knowledge on the topic. The Boss hated holes.

■ ■ ■

Byron and Ruth made it a point to have the glass repaired on their back door, knowing they would both be away from home whenever the trial was in session. Byron replaced every exterior lock on the house with stronger ones, and they agreed to keep the place entirely locked up from then on, whether they were home or not.

Byron had to credit Jerry for noticing the unmarked car with three men in cheap suits parked just down the street from their house. The ex-congressman pulled Byron outside and away from Ruth, then pretended to be interested in the yard-work while he pointed out the car and whispered to Byron that the men looked like feds. Now both of them had to assume that certain power brokers within the Freemasons had managed to secure major federal interest in the case.

"The question is *why!*" Byron seethed. "It's just a murder trial. Damn it, Jerry, every time you come around things like this happen!"

"Don't make this personal, Byron. I'm trying to give you a heads-up here."

"If those are FBI agents, they're not here because of me or Ruth. We've both been on the public record for years. If they want to know about us all they have to do is order a subscription! Let's go back inside before anymore reporters show up."

Jerry followed him, pretending to cough and covering his mouth with his hand while he added, "Wiretap! From now on, you should assume there's a wiretap on your phone line."

Byron ushered him inside and closed the door. "I guess you'll have to call your girlfriend from a pay phone."

Jerry returned to his usual perch on the sofa. "You joke, but this means something. I agree with you that a local murder case in Montana hardly merits federal interest."

"I agree." Ruth emerged from the bedroom. "What's this about federal interest?"

"Jerry here just noticed three guys down the street who look like they staking out our house. They're not local."

Jerry interrupted. "Listen you two, it's time for you to tell me what's going on with this code. Byron, as a Mason, you owe my defense strategy the important information about—"

"Stop right there, pal," Byron raised the flat of his hand. "I joined the Masons years ago and never rose above the lowest level. Hardly pursued it and eventually just quit. Hell's Bells, I joined looking for a way to push circulation, but it was a waste. You know, I didn't fit in with those people."

He paused and cleared his throat. "The only reason that bastard was able to steal my ring and lapel pin is they were sitting right out. I never wear them and didn't do anything to protect them. I sure as hell never learned any secrets."

"But this code?" Jerry pressed. "This secret smoke thing?"

"Yeah it's secret, all right. I've never heard of it, Jerry. And let's think logically here. Smoke? Is that really practical? I mean, there are plenty of trees in Africa but the natives there preferred long distance communication with drums. I never heard that smoke signals were all that successful with anybody. These days they all prefer electronics, right?"

"No! Not high-tech, the opposite! He says that's how they exist in plain sight and nobody suspects a thing. There are neighborhoods all over the country where residents burn their trash out in back of the house. There are industrial chimneys, household fireplaces, barbeque fires, campfires, work sites. It would be easy to mix smoke signals in with all that and who would give it a thought?"

Ruth laughed. "Well that's a good one! I mean, if it's real, you'd have to admit it's pretty funny to be so blatant, right out in the open, and get the hell away with it! Ha! In front of all of us... I want to learn it."

"Oh you're on Jerry's side now?" Byron challenged his wife. "I'm telling you, if such a thing is real, then only the highest level members get to know about it. That whole organization is built on secret signs and secret meanings, and the higher up you go in the ranks, the more they let you in on the whole game. It seemed like a lot of work."

"Great, Byron. So can you at least get me some contacts inside the Masons who'll confirm this story?"

"Certainly not! Jerry, you have no idea of the things they threaten to do to any Mason who betrays their secrets. Both of you, listen. How do you think it all stays secret in the first place? This stuff has been around for centuries, and I don't know any of it. I don't even know anybody who does, or who will admit to it. *That* is how well these guys keep secrets."

"I guess I'll have to subpoena their head honcho, Grand Wizard or what he's called."

"Jerry, Ruth and I want to see you take a path that might actually work, here. When you talk out of left field like that, you scare me that maybe you don't get how important it is to win this case."

"Oh I get it, Byron."

Ruth added, "Because you're getting a lot of publicity and I can see how it will help you get more work even if this case is lost."

Byron chimed in, "We both need to know you care about winning as much as we do."

"Winning on the merits of the case?" Jerry quietly asked.

"Exactly."

For a moment he just stared at her, then, "*Damn* it, Ruth! I object to anybody getting railroaded by our court system. That's what I believe! But if you want me to think this guy is factually innocent of these crimes, I mean, what can I say? What can I tell you? I'm not, I'm not, I'm not going to sit here and *debate,* you know, whether or not, you know—"

"Shit!" Byron spat the word.

"Don't turn this on me, Byron. A lawyer isn't hired to believe, he's hired to fight!"

"Jerry," Ruth interjected, "<u>The Worker's Monthly</u> has taken a strong public stand on this young man's case."

"What, and I haven't? I'm living on your sofa and betting my career on this case! We can't win on the facts, we have to go for a straight insanity defense."

"Insanity. Wait. That's the first we've heard about this."

"Yeah that's how fast we're moving here. Tomorrow I'm going to start laying the groundwork for the jury, right from the opening state-ment." He lapsed into his professional oratorical tone. "Andrew James Carmichael is clearly a victim of some terrible mental disorder, and somehow it prevents him from being able to exercise self-restraint. Ladies and gentlemen of the jury, you wouldn't hang a man for being without his arms, so how can we hang a man for having a disease that deprives him of his conscience?"

Byron and Ruth caught each other's gaze and felt the wisdom of keeping their mouths shut just then. Old Jerry had just delivered a safety escape for their magazine if things went badly for Andy in court.

If Jerry O'Connell could convert Andy's goofy and inappropriate behavior into genuine criminal insanity, then the issue of his innocence or guilt could be switched for the issue of the how poorly the mentally ill are treated. Byron and Ruth only needed to meet each other's glance for an instant to confirm their shared sense that here was a field they could harvest for years.

■ ■ ■

FBI Confidential Informant of Known Reliability, Number 9 sat in the cab of his new Chevy 3100 pickup truck, which he hoped to keep the FBI from seizing if he could successfully complete his assignment. He sat low behind the wheel to avoid drawing attention while he stared down at the battery-powered tape recorder on the floor of the passenger side, wired to the truck's own battery. All he had to do was run the engine for a few minutes every half hour or so and he could record for as long as he had tape to reload.

He chose the parking spot because it was one block behind the Shermans' house and the radio signal from the bug in their living room light fixture was strong and static-free. He overheard them talking about the wiretap and already knew his Bureau handlers weren't going to get anything that way.

One of his proudest moments took place on that very day, when he picked the new lock on the Shermans' front door, entered their house while they were home, installed the bug in less than one minute and then got back out without being detected.

At one point they were calling back and forth to each other from separate rooms while Number 9 tip-toed back to the exit. It was a perfect experience, addictively good.

The only smear on his sense of accomplishment was that he could not discipline himself to repress the thought: if only things had gone that well on his last job, he wouldn't be stuck there sitting in his truck and working off a debt to old J. Edgar.

He already had one solid nugget to give the boys over in the temporary Field Office. They were set up in a back room over at the school house, and Number 9 was looking forward to dropping the bomb on them. *So you want to know what's going on with the case for some reason? Okay, get this: they're going for a verdict of Innocent by Reason of Insanity.*

"That's right, fools," he imagined himself telling them. "You've got all the power in the world and they still might take this guy away from you and put him back on the street. Where the hell is your great federal authority now? Where the hell are the all-seeing Freemasons now? You dickless, tie-wearing zeros just might get beaten by a stone-broke attorney working alone on his first trial." He laughed out loud at that one.

He raised the ante by imagining himself laughing at them. The thought made him laugh again in spite of the cold, but didn't prevent him from noticing how harsh it was. This reminded him that the engine had been off for quite a while. Number 9 started up the Chevy's 235 cubic in. six-cylinder engine to charge up the sophisticated 12-Volt electrical system and keep the tape rolling.

Once the engine fired up it occurred to him that he really ought to bring in the tidbit right away. Maybe since he was giving them the heads-up about a coming insanity defense, they could flip one back to him and let him take the daytime shift, which would be considerably warmer.

Number 9 muttered a phrase that could get him arrested in a number of jurisdictions and put the four-speed transmission into gear. It had to be worth coming in early to tell them that the defense wasn't playing around with trying to get him a reduced sentence or a lowered charge. They actually had a plan to let him walk.

Number 9 felt so excited to deliver his discovery that for a moment he thought he would be willing to sacrifice the sweetheart of a truck if only he could be the one to deliver the news to old J. Edgar himself, just to watch the expression on his face when he told him, "These guys are going to try to just run this thing straight out, as if the Bureau doesn't even exit." Practically worth trashing the career for the chance to see that old bastard sweat.

But then he hit fourth gear as he sped on down First Avenue and he felt the fat white sidewall tires grip the road like tiger paws. The engine torque pushed him back into the seat and delivered its heightened sense of freedom. The primal sensations made the moment beautiful.

Its effect was to transform his desire for confrontation into an appreciation for the joys of personal freedom. He realized when it came to things that were worth it or not, he had to admit he didn't need to see J. Edgar's face all that bad, what with discretion being the better part of valor, and all.

"Just outlive the guy," he muttered to himself, too crazed to care if he looked crazy. "That's the way to do it. Take your vitamins and just be there when they plant him."

25

One-Eyed Depth Perception

Late on Friday evening, Wade Preston felt his temper beginning to fray after nearly two hours of sitting stuck in the office of Jim Swee-ney, lead prosecutor on the Carmichael murder case. Sweeney was known as "Killer Sweeney" among local law enforcement, respected for his full-speed prosecutions of every criminal facing charges from his office. But with opening statements now completed and the pros-ecution set to begin laying out its case on Monday morning, D.A. Sweeney had the desperate look of a man on the verge of a two-week bender.

"So that's it, then? I'm supposed to nail this guy, who's obviously guilty, we know, using what you've given me?"

"I haven't 'given' you anything, Jim, I just reported what we found."

"Yeah, two bodies here, two more in Canada, no weapon. We can't lift prints from the victims' skin. Wade, you have to get me some-thing! How can I prep you for your testimony if those are the only answers you can give me?"

"They're the facts of the case, Jim, and there aren't many of them."

"I need more, or this thing could land in the crapper!" He laughed. "And that's no shit! Ahem. Sorry. It's not funny. I really need some sleep.""Jim, you need more, I understand. But what, you expect me to have him repeat his crimes only make more mis-takes this time?"

"God-damn it, Sheriff, you sat in court today! You can see what we're up against. I can't use the fact that he confessed, I can't use the fact that he was already sentenced to death, and I've got a defense attorney using a tactic so stupid no good lawyer would attempt it. I tell you, somebody's got to be kidding! They say he's not guilty, but even if he is, he's nuts, so we have to send him to a nice hospital so he can make a miraculous recovery and then walk out a free man while his victims are in the ground."

"Maybe stupid isn't the word for the tactic, then."

"Oh is that sarcasm, Sheriff?"

"Look Jim, I hate this as much as you do. But the problem seems to be that we've underestimated Carmichael's mouthpiece because he's got no trial experience. Maybe we have to bite the bullet and admit that the guy might be onto something with this strategy."

Sweeney poured another slug of whiskey. This time he didn't bother to dilute it with coffee.

"Maybe you should go light on the booze. Your eyes are looking glassy."

"You should see them from my side."

"Okay so maybe that means it's time for us to call it quits tonight. I think we've done all the preparation we can before I get on the stand."

Sweeney stared at the wall and spoke like a man thinking out loud, almost as if he had forgotten anyone was there. "I watched that jury today and I can tell O'Connell is actually getting traction with his Freemason Smoke Code story. If he can get that sort of implication to stick, he'll have a jury willing to buy the idea that this kid has been framed by some secret society."

His eyes refocused as if he had just remembered his point. "Now listen to me, Wade. I've backed you up for ten years. I've never challenged your evidence or tried to implicate you in any wrongdoing."

"Could that be because I've brought you solid cases and I never do anything to give you reason to complain?"

Sweeney slammed his no-coffee coffee cup onto his desk so hard that the whiskey slopped over the side. "Sheriff, this case is a house full of termites! You see what we got here? Freemason smoke codes! Major businesses like Bushmaster Mining and Standard Oil trying to influence the case!"

"Those are rumors. I don't deal in speculation."

"What, you don't 'deal' in a backroom conspiracy to frame an innocent man for no reason whatsoever? Because that's what they're setting us up for. You haven't been paying attention!"

"Oh yes I have."

"Then *give* me something!"

Preston felt his socket starting to itch and burn, the way it tended to do when his stress level got to be more than he could handle. The effects were always worse when he was fighting his own conscience. At that moment he didn't even know why his conscience should be having trouble, but the missing eye had seen something that wasn't visible to the real one yet.

Finally he swallowed and quietly asked, "You mean something I haven't already brought in?"

"That's exactly what I mean."

"Some sort of fabricated evidence?"

"Hey! Hey-hey-hey! You did *not* hear that! Fabricated evidence? What? No, I would not and I did not." He cleared his throat. "But on that note, did you know that modern science is so good, our guys can lift a print from an ordinary object like this coffee cup here..." and with that he rubbed a bit of ash from the end of his cigarette between his fingers, wrapped them around the coffee cup, then removed them and took a piece of cellophane tape from his desktop dispenser. He carefully placed it over the spot where is first finger had just been pressing against the side of the cup, then slowly peeled the tape off and pressed it onto the varnished desktop.

He gently pulled off the tape, leaving a ridged print on the desk's surface. "Then they can transfer it to some other object."

"Some other object."

"Any smooth solid object, actually. A bullet, a gun barrel. Doesn't actually require that much expertise. Most people just aren't aware of it yet. Once you know how, anybody can do it."

Preston felt himself go cold inside. "And this applies to my testimony in what way, Jim?"

"Hey. I *cannot* suggest anything illegal, and I would personally testify in any court in this country that you are a solid law enforcement professional who would also never do anything to rig a case. Certainly not against an innocent man, which we both know he is not."

He leaned close to Preston and spoke in a voice so soft it was almost a whisper. "Imagine if somebody had stopped him before he got here. Think of those people still alive the way they should be. Nobody did that for us, but we can do it for the next victims down the road."

"For example?"

"For example: I would raise a hue and cry if anyone ever suggested you give Carmichael his breakfast before letting him shower, then lifted his greasy prints from his eating utensils and transfer them onto a drop gun the same caliber as the murder weapon."

"A forty-five."

"Right, forty-five. No concern about matching the spent bullets since we can't find 'em without knowing where these people were killed, and Carmichael isn't talking."

"Oh, he talks, all right. Just not about the shootings. Even when he pled guilty he wouldn't say anything about the murder locations."

"Any chance he was already scamming us?"

Preston rubbed the good one and sighed. I don't know anymore, Jim. Guy's such a slippery bastard, I can't figure out if he's stupid or smart."

"Well Sheriff, I think if he gets away the answer will be pretty obvious to everybody. Now the county has plenty of confiscated weapons in the evidence locker under the courthouse. It's only a few steps down from your office. Correct?"

"Yeah you know it is, Jim."

"So how bad do *you* need to see this guy pay? Because I'm telling you, I've been sleeping like shit ever since they found the Thorntons!" He lowered his voice again and spoke in a fair imitation of a best friend sharing a hot secret.

"I tell you, I liked that Mrs. Thornton, Wade. Hell, everybody did. I mean her husband was a great guy, but the missus really had a special quality, don't you think? I mean, you were in there all the time. What did *you* think of her, Wade?" He grinned in a manner that made Preston want to pistol whip him across the face.

Preston stood up and stretched his aching back muscles. "Okay, you've given me something to think about. Time to quit for the night."

Sweeney took him by the upper arm in a grip so tight that if it came from anyone else Preston would have dropped him to the floor. "It doesn't take two eyes to see it, Sheriff. If you can't help the People of the State of Montana with this case, we stand a good chance of watching this guy walk to the highway and hitchhike back out of town. I wonder how he'll treat the next driver to stop for him, Wade? And as far as the public's expectations of us, well, I'm up for reelection next year."

"Yeah. We both are."

"Give me something, Wade. I'll nail this fool to the wall if you just hand me the hammer. The boogie man gets put away and we both get re-elected next year. That's a winner all the way around."

Preston sat silent and unmoving for a long moment. Sweeney had nothing more to offer and just looked back at him with the eerie patience of a cat guarding a mouse hole.

Preston huffed out a deep breath, shaking his head. "Yeah. Yeah. We can't let this guy walk. We can't leave it up to Canada to come and get him and do our job for us. Because that's what will happen if we let him go. They've got a perfectly good reason to extradite him and do the hard work if we don't do it first. But the evidence we have is the evidence we have, and that's all she wrote."

"So bring me the proper tools to do my job, then! I need this done by tomorrow night so I have some time to get ready for Monday."

Preston's good eye was beginning to get the picture. He didn't want to admit it yet, but the image was becoming clear. "Goddamn it!" He shook his head. "God*damn* it, Jim. There ought to be a better way to get justice here. I just can't see what it is."

"*That's* the Sheriff I know! *That's* a man takes his job seriously, and wants the public to let him keep it!" He poured them both the last of his whiskey.

The district attorney favored the county sheriff with the wide smile of a fellow conspirator. Sweeney raised his glass in a snide gesture that made Preston feel like he had just wiped his nose on Preston's shirt.

Preston demurred. "I'm still on duty. Let's keep it legal as much as we can, all right?"

"Relax, officer. The law's on your side. You strike me as a man whose next term of office is guaranteed, soon as we get a conviction on this monster. Hell, you saw the bodies."

He leaned close to Preston and did his best imitation of a confidante. "Now you go recover the murder weapon from the dump site outside town. Why, he must have used a second gun for the Canada shootings, don't you know? For right now, have your damn drink. We're celebrating!"

26

The Truth Or Something Like It

It took the prosecution nearly a week to lay out its case, involving plenty of expert medical and psychiatric testimony as to the particular personality traits revealed in the details of such crimes and the physical power required to do such deep harm. The court recessed on Thursday evening after Defense attorney Jerry O'Connell complained of chest pains. The judge's stated intention was to give O'Connell a long weekend to get himself checked out at a hospital, then reconvene on the following Monday morning. Time for the defense to begin.

National interest ignited in the popular culture on the strength of a threatening idea that strongly resonated with the reading and listening public. The few who owned television sets watched other people sit at a desk and read the same things to them that they heard on their radios, and the story tended to play out in one of two ways, divided along ideological lines.

Conservative publications reported the gruesome crime details, the killer's cold demeanor, the desecration of the bodies, and raised a hue and cry for justice. Progressive publications followed the lead of The Worker's Monthly, since the paper was based in the town where the murders took place, and reprinted full-length copies of the impassioned editorials written by Ruth Sherman, with research assistance from her husband, Byron Sherman. Never had their carefully crafted opinions met such a massive audience.

The New York Times, The Washington Post, and The San Francisco Chronicle led the charge of the major papers in digging deep and getting the background story on Attorney O'Connell's many press conferences promoting the idea of a Secret Smoke Code and the possibility that the Thorntons died because they somehow discovered this secret.

Perhaps they overheard it inside their café? Perhaps that was why they had to die? If so, Andrew J. Carmichael was a convenient patsy to use in covering up someone else's crime. The hasty investigation prior to his forced "confession" and the false guilty plea had seduced the authorities into failing to do their duty, to consider the possibility that someone else could be responsible.

O'Connell warned selected journalists that the brutality of the killings was in itself a message from this most secret of societies. That message warned anyone else who might know about the Freemasons' secret code to understand what could happen if they loosened their lips.

Jerry O'Connell fed the reporters like a kid throwing bread crumbs to geese. He drank up the wide-eyed appreciation that greeted him. The way people hung onto his every word was a slice of Heaven. Under the warm glow of public approval, his deep fears of being unable to handle this mission began to melt. His ex-girlfriend even gave him a call, after the first couple of stories went over the wires. But by that point in the game O'Connell's self-esteem had expanded with every public outing.

The ability to make public proclamations and actually see them the next day in the mainstream press combined with the experience of hearing his name mentioned time and time again on radio newscasts. It all served to remind him of the gritty truth that he could do better than his former girlfriend, some indiscriminant skirt with legs akimbo who dumped him as soon as she thought he couldn't give her what she wanted, and who then came crawling back as soon as his ship came in. Her invitation had no bite this time. It was great to be free of her appeal.

Jerry O'Connell had heard the call. It was the call he feared might never arrive, in this life: the call to arms in a struggle that would ultimately vindicate him. He could only hope that the heart which was already failing him and the high blood pressure that had dogged him for the last few years would allow him to make it all the way to the finish line on this one. The case was a perfect panacea for his life of spoiled opportunities, and he suddenly found himself in the same position as a broken cuckoo clock, accurate for one second twice a day.

Jerry O'Connell intended to stretch that moment. His long background as a decrier of all things capitalist and a supporter of all things collective made him the perfect person to grasp the opportunity of timing in this case.

He played the press like a maestro, and while he initially had to go through the mouthpiece of The Worker's Monthly to get public attention, he soon rose to the point that he could get in touch with any editor or reporter he chose to call. All he had to do was throw them a couple of exclusive facts and give them bragging rights.

Most splendid of all, his lifelong passion for disenfranchised workers, dating to his boyhood, had come across the perfect backdrop for grabbing public attention. Furthermore, it came at a time when he had nearly accepted failure at redeeming and healing the youthful trauma of watching his father get blackballed at work and then broken into poverty, all for simply trying to organize the miserable workforce.

Now with this case's captivating elements of sick murder, implications of rape, and detailed descriptions of defiled bodies, O'Connell fervently believed that the sideshow-loving element of the American population would jump on this story and stick to it like a kid with an all-day sucker.

Through Jerry O'Connell, ex-congressman and current major defense attorney, the country's longstanding struggle between major companies and organized labor was about to find a sizeable place in the mind of John Q. Public.

O'Connell would rise to their attention by broadcasting the contagious concept of wealthy elitists who use ancient Masonic secrets and methods. He did not doubt that even a nation of insensitive bridge trolls was capable of grasping the terrible effects that such conspiracies could have upon them and their families.

Jerry saw a tiny flame that had long been protected and sustained by no one but a few fringe dwellers but was now about to roar up to bonfire strength. He didn't doubt it would be visible to anyone who didn't live underground. He would feed the blaze with stirring accusations that the entire Freemason conspiracy was done to subvert the workers of America and keep them weak. All the while, the fiends in the smoke-filled rooms grew fatter and fatter. Their ridiculous children grew up flimsy and vile, imbued with the conviction that their fecal leavings threw off no unpleasant aroma.

Jerry O'Connell had known for many years that somebody needed to pay for all his troubles. Now, finally, somebody would.

■ ■ ■

Wade Preston stood in the open doorway of the county evidence locker, alone in the building at this late hour except for a few die-hards burning the midnight oil on the upper floors. He stared into the darkened room with the only light a rectangle of hallway spill thrust onto the floor.

This is it, he told himself. *This is when you sell your soul to the devil just to make sure somebody else gets to hell sooner rather than later.*

He leaned forward and dropped his artificial eye into the palm of his hand and dropped it into his left front shirt pocket. His socket was itching and burning so badly, he might just as well have poured itching power into it. But he knew his problem didn't come from any outside material. His socket was burning because it had so many sensitive nerve endings that it was where he felt things first, when they were troublesome things. Now while he stood in the entryway of a room where he knew he could steal a convincing version of the forty-five Carmichael used in the killings.

He avoided the urge to reach into the socket and scratch, but the itching tormented him. He tried to reason with the itch. He emphasized that here was an opportunity to commit the perfect crime because they had no bullets in evidence to compare to it and no way to get them.

But now the itching took on a burning sensation and felt like it was eating his head from the inside. Just in case, he walked over the a janitor's sink and turned on the hot water full force, then took out the eye and rinsed it shiny clean. Likely a waste of time, but the itchy socket didn't take to his explanation.

He re-inserted the cleaned eye, thinking it might do a little itch-scratching in the socket, but when he walked into the evidence locker and turned on the paltry light fixture, he felt as if sand was pouring into his face. *What do I do if Carmichael gets off because I wouldn't help the D.A.?* The itching got worse.

What do I do if he gets away and kills somebody else? The itching and burning nearly bent him over.

What the hell do I do if I break the law, get caught, and he gets convicted anyhow? Maybe we can share a cell?

The itching and burning became so severe he had to pop the eye out again. It felt sunburned in there. With the ceramic eye back in his shirt pocket, he moved along the packed shelves until he got to an open bin where he knew a number of unclaimed weapons were stored. He had seen several good candidates for the murder weapon in the bin many times before.

But the socket was starting to feel so burned inside by this point that he thought he felt blisters forming. He pictured a hot poker closing in on his eye socket and he felt the first tinge of burning flesh.

"Gahhh!" he clutched his socket and pitched forward in pain. "All right! Shit! Shit! All right!" He backed away from the weapons section and staggered toward the doorway, backed through it, then reached in and switched off the light, swung the door shut, pulled out his key chain, and locked the place up tight.

With that he turned his back to the locked door and leaned into it, slumping with relief. He was grateful that the burning sensation was already passing, converting itself to a sharp ache instead.

"Can't do it." He barely whispered the words. "Can't do it," he said again, louder this time.

There was nobody around to hear, so he repeated, "Can't do it, can't do it, can't do it." He moved on down the hallway stepping in rhythm to the chant. "Can't do it, can't do it, can't do it, can't do it."

By the time he reached his office his sense of self worth was able to enjoy a few minutes of relief before the misery pendulum began to swing back the other way. It began when he picked up the phone and called D.A. Sweeney at home. Neither man bothered with the niceties.

"All right, Jim, it's Wade and you know I don't think there's a gun that will work."

"You just come from there?"

"I did, and there just nothing—"

"What do you *mean* 'nothing' Wade?"

"I mean we don't have the right caliber, or rather the right, uh..."

"The right what? Because I've been back in the evidence locker *too*, Wade. I've got eyes *too*. My own son-of-a-bitching *eyes* have seen the weapons there. And we've got about every kind of small arm there is!"

Preston sighed. "All right, then. I'm trying to tell you—"

"Stop right there! Because I'm trying to tell *you*, Wade, I don't like what I'm hearing.!"

"Jim... I can't do it."

"You what."

"I can't."

"Oh you can't."

"No. I'm sorry."

"Oh! You're sorry! He's sorry! Well, *that* makes it all hunky-dory, Wade. It puts a band-aid over the whole damned thing! You 'can't' give me the one thing I need to lock down this conviction, but you're sorry. Hey Wade, can't means won't. You could but you won't."

Preston had no better answer. He stood waiting for Sweeney to go on, but there was a pause that lasted so long Preston was about to hang up. Then Sweeney spoke again. His voice was nearly a whisper, with a metallic edge Preston had never heard him use.

"You had a big thing for Claudette Thornton at one time, didn't you? Don't deny it, either."

"What the hell, Jim? Where'd you hear that?"

"The birdies talk, Wade. They tell me that café was the only place in town you ever went outside of your office and your house. They tell me you sat and watched her whether you two were talking or not."

"Yeah I think the conversation is about over, Jim. This call was just to inform—"

"I know why you called. You had to supervise getting the bodies out of that dump site after seeing the condition she got left there in. You saw the things he did to her."

"God damn you Jim."

"Me? *You* can see your way straight to letting this punk walk out of here! Or just get slapped on the wrist with some third-level charge! Hey, maybe we can get him for loitering, Wade! Get me enough evidence to make that one stick!"

"I'm not paid to rig cases!"

"And neither one of us is paid to put demons back on the street, but that's exactly what we're looking at here! What part of you fails to understand that?"

Before Preston could answer, the D.A. slammed the phone down so hard it hurt his ear. He sat perfectly still for a few moments and waited for the rage to burn away.

Within moments, in spite of the D.A.'s jabs about Claudette, his spirits began to rise. The old socket actually felt like it might be ready to take the eye again, and this time once he got the thing in, it felt good enough to leave it. There wasn't any need to plug it in with nobody around, but experience had taught him the that was the best place for keeping track of the expensive item. If he left it lying around there was always some joker who thought it was funny to steal it.

27

Herd Picks Up the Howl

On the eve of the murder trial, the midnight stroke between Sunday and Monday came especially late for the four men attending an emergency session at the home of Judge Maxwell Summers. The judge was unmoved by the fact that each one had risen before dawn to work on his end of the proceedings. The thorny issue raised by the defense was keeping his Honor up late, so he saw no reason not to share the misery.

D.A. Sweeney, Defense Counsel O'Connell, Sheriff Preston, and Dave Carlton from the local Masonic lodge had each been contacted earlier that evening and told to ignore the late hour and to show up in the judge's living room dressed for court. Summers had no compunction about conducting the process in his bath robe and slippers, but thought it wise to prevent the others from getting too comfortable. The idea being that when people get too comfortable, they start thinking they run things. Years on the bench had convinced him that when people ran things they inevitably wound up storming the streets and setting things on fire.

There was nothing Summers despised more than chaos. He had become a judge for that reason, more than any other, and his years on the bench convinced him that the more control you laid onto people, the better most of them behaved.

Now with this terrible set of murders, the problem was how to keep a lid on things. The Canadians were just waiting for him to make a mistake so they could do the clean up work and extradite Carmichael for a trip through their own system.

He had never tried anyone who was essentially a demon in human form. The dark energy behind the case had effortlessly converted him from a staid jurist with a predictable calendar of public malfeasance into a frightened Dutch boy with all ten fingers jammed into a crumbling dike.

The judicial voice needed to be loud, and Judge Summers had no idea what it was going to say. Any flaw in his procedure that resulted in a distorted verdict had the potential to enflame citizens into breaking the defendant out and lynching him.

"All right, have a seat gentlemen. Mr. Sweeney, are you all right?"

"Me? Yes, your Honor."

"I see you glaring at Sheriff Preston there. You two need a minute outside?"

"No, your Honor," Preston quickly responded. The judge noticed that the Sheriff did a good job of keeping his face neutral, which was something Summers appreciated at trial proceedings. D.A. Sweeney clearly had a bug up his butt about something, but since he didn't answer the question and let the Sheriff do the denying, that was one mess Summers could step around.

"We're not on the record but let's keep it moving tonight. Mr. O'Connell has a radical theory which he plans to advance to the jury if he is permitted to bring it in, and it regards "secret smoke codes," or so called. The idea is that certain high-ranking members of the world's Masonic lodges use it for secret communication."

"That's correct, Your Honor," O'Connell jumped in. "And I—"

"This your first trial, Mr. O'Connell?"

"I don't see what that—"

"*Is* it?"

"Well, yes it is."

"All right, that was your one free slip. Next time you interrupt me you will not like the consequence of it."

"... Yes. Your Honor. May I say I hope my blunder won't prejudice the Court against my client?"

"You starting off my conference here by accusing me of bias?"

"... Well no. Certainly not. Your Honor."

"In spite of Mr. O'Connell's attempts to convince me we are wasting our time, this is a case that will be scrutinized around the country, and I need to sweat the details. So Mr. Sweeney, you're here for the People; Mr. O'Connell for the defense, and the Sheriff is here because he needs to know what's going on if this thing spills over into civil disobedience.

"You gentlemen know Dave Carlton here because he runs the big feed operation outside town, but you might not know he is the grand poo-bah of the local Order of Freemasons.

"The title is actually--" Carlton began, but since he was already looking into the judge's face he quickly stopped himself.

The judge continued, "We'll get the title right if this goes into the record, Dave. Now, Mr. O'Connell over here is going to sit nice and quiet while you tell us that you know about any such thing. You might as well pretend you're under oath because you will be if this goes in."

There was a pause. "Mr. Carlton?"

"Oh! Yes. Well, thank you, Your Honor. First of all let me assure you gentlemen—"

"Smoke codes, Mr. Carlton. Yes or no?"

"Not at all, sir. Ridiculous. Some sort of child's fantasy, if you ask me, and certainly nothing the world's Freemasons have ever employed to my knowledge."

"You're saying it doesn't exist?"

"Of course not, officially."

"Officially? What? Damn it, Dave! I asked you here because you always struck me as a straight-talker. All of a sudden I'm listening to a politician."

"Your Honor, gentlemen, all I mean is that there have been members over centuries of time. Many of them were among the brightest of their people, great thinkers and inventors and engineers. Who knows what they might have created for use among themselves? But what I'm here to tell you... to assure you, really... is that *if* such a thing exists, or ever existed, then the ones who thought it up and put it to use weren't acting in any official Masonic capacity."

"You're saying if they had such a code, it wasn't because they were Masons?" the Judge asked.

"No." Carlton said it with conviction. Then he paused, squinted for a second, and added, "Except in the sense that Freemasonry was what they had in common. The thing that gave them the opportunity to associate. Whatever they did after that, well, people do what they do, right?"

O'Connell raised his hand like a schoolboy. "Your Honor, may I ask a question?"

"Of me?"

"Ah, no. Mr. Carlton."

"Oh Mr. Carlton, not me. There. See how easy it is to be misunderstood if you fail to speak clearly? That's just one of the many things you'll be learning at this, your first trial, wherein a man's life is on the line."

"A guilty man," Preston threw in. "Sorry." He threw up his hands, palms forward.

Sweeney sneered. "First thing you've said all day makes any sense."

"Sweeney, did you *not* hear me, regarding interruptions?"

The D.A. looked like something had just broken open inside of him. "Your Honor! Smoke codes? I've got to try a man for the worst thing most people around here are ever going to know about, and yet the defense gets to, to, to dance us in here on the Sunday night before trial opens, waste our energy?"

The four men kept quiet and waited for Summers to break his gavel on Sweeney's head. But instead, after a tense moment, the judge exhaled and actually smiled. "Yep. You just hit that one on the head. And you keep quiet for now, Mr. O'Connell. Mr. Sweeney believes this is an outrageous theory, a throw-it-against-the-wall-and-see-if-it-sticks theory. I can tell you I personally never heard a word about any secret "smoke code" used by anybody who wasn't a plains

Indian, and frankly I always wondered how they made that work on windy days. You know how much the wind blows out on the plains? What's more, Mr. Carlton appears to agree that the Masons don't use such a thing at all."

"I certainly do. Officially."

"Right you clarified that. So Mr. O'Connell, I think if you're going to make this one work for your client, now is the time for you to knock our socks off. I warn you, if your idea turns out to be nothing more than a loud man in a tall hat, it's going to stop right here in this room."

Judge Summers noticed that the Sheriff, the D.A., and the grand poo-bah looked like they were ready to go home. But Jerry O'Connell dove in like a man after a full night's sleep and two cups of coffee.

"Here's the thing," he began, "I've got a complete code. Not with me at this moment, of course, but I'm telling you, we are going to bring in the secret Masonic Smoke Code *with* specific examples drawn right out on the page! As everybody will see it's too complex for a simple young working man like Andrew Carmichael to have made up on his own. With all due respect to my client, he is not the brightest bulb on the sign. This thing, this code, he got this somewhere. And he says he got it from two young agents of the Freemason Order who were sent to silence him after he broke into the home of Byron and Ruth Sherman and stole Mr. Sherman's Masonic items."

"He's a Mason?" Preston asked, surprised.

"No." Carlton quickly responded. "Apparently he started out with us some years ago but soon quit."

"So," Judge Summers asked, "even if there was a secret "smoke code," he wouldn't know about it?"

"He wasn't around long enough to learn much of anything. Maybe a secret handshake or greeting, something like that."

"So you Masons have secrets?"

"Of course we have secrets, your Honor. But there's nothing to fear from us. Our purpose is to do good work in the world."

"Your Honor, who gets to decide what good work is? I think Nazi Germany felt it was doing good work."

"All right, Mr. O'Connell, that was your *one* free Nazi reference. Use another one, I jail you for contempt. This court will not be manipulated. If you try, you better be so good I don't catch you. You however have been caught."

"Your Honor. I must ask whether or not Mr. Carlton can be believed. I must ask him if it is true that Freemasons not only have secrets, but that they are sworn to protect those secrets. Here's the thing, *even if* they know that by lying they are protecting a guilty person, they are sworn to lie anyway to protect the secrets of their order!"

"Is that true, Mr. Carlton?"

"Oh, please! Those are rituals from centuries ago and nobody takes that pledge seriously in our modern times!"

"Then why use it?" the judge inquired. A trace of sarcasm bled into his voice.

"Well, we just... we have traditions..."

"Traditions of pretending that you're willing to lie, when you're not, to protect old secrets nobody uses anymore?"

"No! Well, yes in a sense, but not the way you..."

The judge sniffed and turned to Sweeney. "Do the People want to weigh in now?"

"We do. And I wonder if Mr. O'Connell is going to have comic book heroes turn up in court after we're finished learning about his secret Freemason smoke code. The People's challenge is how the defense intends to prove such a thing exists when you're got an organization sworn not to tell you? Should we pour hot lead down their throats? You know that's the way defendants were treated back when the Freemasons got started. Short of that, why should they talk for this trial?"

"I'll answer if I may, your Honor. The Defense is going to prove it by bringing in local Masons who care enough about what happened to the Thorntons that they are willing to spill a few outdated secrets to save an innocent man. After all, until he is released, the hunt for the real killer will be suspended."

"I brought back the real killer!" the Sheriff exploded.

It was O'Connell's turn to throw up his hands. "And I'm hired to cast doubt on that, aren't I? We say the Thorntons inadvertently overheard this information and got themselves killed for the trouble. We can't tell you if it was directly done by Masons or just by people who thought they were on the Masons' side. Makes no difference. It is the golden nugget of reasonable doubt and I am confident the public would be outraged to know it was excluded, if it were to be. Now may I try this case? May I present a defense for this boy?"

"The 'boy' is nearly twenty-three, with a violent prison record," D.A. Sweeney grumbled. The judge let that one go.

"Mr. O'Connell, it comes down to this. Without the secret "smoke code," you have no conspiracy. Without that, there is no reason to think those Canadian boys were sent after your client or that the Thorntons overheard anything that got them killed."

"Not that my Order would kill anybody to keep a secret anyway!" Mr. Carlton interjected.

Judge Summers turned to him. "Don't you guys swear to do exactly that?"

"Yes but... but... damn it, we don't *mean* it!"

"Ah. You say it but don't mean it. Tough one to prove though, eh? I'd love to assign that as a debate topic for my law class over in Billings. Now personally, I think Mr. O'Connell is working us over like a horny dog with this one. But like I said, I expect this case to get shoved under every legal microscope in this state and plenty of others. And the fact is, if there really is a secret code of some kind and the Thorntons overheard information about it, and you Masons swear to kill to protect it but you don't really mean it, then the idea that an anonymous third party or parties are responsible for this and presently at large is not unreasonable. If something substantial can be brought in." He pretended to reach over and pick up a gavel, then pantomimed banging it on the table in front of him.

"Bang. The man gets his theory brought in, if he can back it up."

"Your Honor!" Sweeney jumped to a standing position.

"Bang, Mr. Sweeney! Did you not hear me go 'bang' with my pretend gavel?"

"Sir I appreciate your caution, but—"

"*Abundance* of caution, I would say," the judge corrected him. "I will repeat this *abundance* of caution for the record tomorrow, gentlemen. An abundance of caution and respect for the fact that a man's life is at stake. Good night to you. Drive carefully. What are you doing in my house? Go home."

Judge Summers banged the pretend gavel again then stood up and proceeded toward the back of the house, calling over his shoulder, "See yourselves out, gentlemen." He softened the effect by saying it with a smile, but didn't to turn around to display it.

28

The Hard Days

The opening statements took only one day apiece, the prosecution on Thursday and the defense on Friday.

When Jerry O'Connell stood to give his opening statement, he felt the room go quiet. He could smell the sweat in the packed courtroom, whiffed with passing traces of perfume, cologne, and cigarette smoke.

The scene was too surreal for him to feel frightened by the task ahead, his first and only murder case. He swallowed the old voices of self-doubt and memories of desperately trying to re-invent his failed political career with an even later career as a freshman attorney. But today, this new day, he was the state's certified Public Defender of Andrew J. Carmichael in a murder case eagerly watched by the entire nation whether the entire nation realized it or not.

He was past his mid-forties but on this day he didn't feel his age anymore. He was still bald but he felt no self-consciousness about it. He was still a good forty pounds overweight with a lousy ticker, but throughout his presentation of the opening defense he felt like he could step into the ring with a champion and beat him to a pulp. He still refused to return his local girl's phone calls, and it did his heart good to know she was in the audience that day, pining no doubt while she watched him work the room. He played every line with her in mind, but would not give her so much as a glance to let her know he was aware of her.

Instead he addressed the jury while mostly ignoring the rest of the courtroom. He paced the floor while he orated, just the way he imagined William Jennings Bryant would have done in one of his patented bombasts. Jerry O'Connell stared up at the jury in their box and felt in his very bones that they belonged to him. This was his hour and he was the man for it.

"Ladies and gentlemen of the jury, I'm afraid you have a tiger by the tale in this case. You will do far more than judge one man in your duties here. I am going to demonstrate for you that poor Andrew Carmichael is a random victim of the sort of secret crime that usually has no consequence, if it is committed by one of the ruling elite in this country. He is here because he innocently stumbled upon a conspiracy of major businesses and industries who operate a clandestine system of their own that has access to so much power, so much unimaginable wealth, that if you are not part of that rare inner circle, then you cannot be allowed to live if you somehow wander into one of their operations and learn secrets you cannot be permitted to know.

"Poor Mr. and Mrs. Thornton were murdered, all right, but not by my client and for a very simple reason. They happened to overhear something about this secret organization at their café, the Roundup Café, precisely. And they had to be silenced in such a manner that if anyone else out there is also privy to that information, they realize they will only stay alive by staying quiet."

He dropped his voice to a dramatic *sotto voce,* "It has always been that way, until now. Until today, right where we are. Ladies and Gentlemen, Andy Carmichael has learned one of the key secrets kept from us by the hidden government that actually runs our lives, and we will lay that secret out for you right here in this courtroom, one, two, three! The eyes of the world are upon us all here because the ramifications for this discovery are powerful, and wide in their effect!

"A Simple Working Man like Andrew could never conjure this on his own. You will see, because Ladies and Gentlemen of this esteemed Jury, we will explain the secret method of communication that has been used for centuries by certain branches of the Masonic Lodge, or the Freemasons as they're also known, and which is still in use by their highest ranking officers to this very day!

"These are the big ones, no small fry allowed. And do they use the latest in secret spy devices to communicate? Maybe, sometimes. But they can get a message across this country in a matter of hours using a complicated system of smoke signals, and I mean nothing like you may have heard about smoke signals used by certain native groups.

"No indeed! They can speak full sentences! They can express complete ideas and concepts in a form of shorthand written in smoke, using subtle coloring of the smoke column. And that they achieve with chemical concoctions they make themselves.

"Why, they could do it from the house next door and you would think your neighbor had somebody out there burning his trash! How many sources of ordinary smoke can you think of, things that don't make anybody think twice? Smokestacks? Household chimneys? Picnics and campfires? Rural trash burning? Industrial smoke trails? Field burn-offs? We all see it, all the time. Mostly it's just people burning things. But some of it, some of it, ladies and gentlemen, comprises dangerous messages in the Freemasons' Secret Smoke Code!

"And it is the knowledge of *this* that could not be permitted to spread and for which the Thorntons were killed. Although spread it we will, my friends, in this court.

"And so *that* is the tiger whose tail you now hold, you see? You thought this was going to be an ordinary murder trial, but you were warned that the defendant was able and willing to lay out this secret code, and by doing so demonstrate the existence of this hidden consortium of power-grabbing aristocrats. As we will show you here, the Freemasons will commit murder in ways too evil for the decent mind to grasp!

"You cannot understand my client's innocence until you see him in the context of this terrible struggle for power and control over the vast resources of the United States. It's a goal to make your head spin!

"We will *not only* exonerate this young man, we are about to expose the underbelly of the Masonic Conspiracy for Worldwide Domination, all of which is taking place every day, under our noses!

"Ladies and Gentlemen, they know they don't have to win a war if they never have to fight it in the first place! And the best way to guarantee that is to keep the entire population sound asleep in their rocking chairs out on the front porch. They'll be too dumb to notice what's happening, as long as you starve them slowly enough! They treat the population like frogs, knowing you would scream and try to jump out of the boiling water they have in store for you, but that if they start you off in cold water and slowly raise the temperature, you will sit right there calmly while you boil to death.

"We are only six years out from the conclusion of the Second World War. If World War Three is coming, you can bet it will get touched off by these people! They are the ones who would have Andrew Carmichael pay for *their* crimes. Thank you..."

O'Connell scanned the faces of the panel, focusing on their eyes. Within three seconds he was certain there wasn't a dry seat in the jury box.

■ ■ ■

There was the usual weekend break, and then with the passing of another full week, the world was a far different place for District Attorney Jim Sweeney.

Late the following Friday night in the D.A.'s office at the County Courthouse, three floors above the basement-level Sheriff's Department and County Jail, Sweeney shared his third scotch to Wade Preston's first, still untouched.

"You did a good job, Jim." Preston assured him again. "Try to relax."

"I'd *love* to know how I'm supposed to do *that*! We're straddling the damned chasm between what you know and what you can prove. This guy is *painfully* guilty and I had to stretch to get five days out of my case! All we've got is one stinking circumstance after another!"

"Do I hear a reference to the missing murder weapon?"

Sweeney whirled on Preston. "Oh no, you don't hear a fucking 'reference' my friend! You hear a man telling you we could both be out of a job in a few months behind this case and a demon could be back on the street, that's all. We could end up seeing more victims and know that our names are on them. That's what I'm telling you! I could have nailed his nasty ass to the barn *wall* if I had a gun! One *single* forty-five caliber pistol! Any forty-five! The bullets all shot those poor people clean through, likely full metal jackets, and he tossed the shells god knows where, and oh yeah: we don't know the location where they were shot, either!"

He leaned close to Sheriff Preston and blew sour booze breath in his face. "No bullets and no shells means any gun that's the right caliber is the right gun, if you give it to me and I present it to the jury." He drained his glass and slammed it to his desk so hard that Preston was surprised it didn't break. "Damn it, Wade! You *know* he did it!"

"Yeah. I know. I know, Jim."

"Your town needed you. In a dark hour."

"Well, I have to differ on that."

"You what? You *what*? You pulling my leg there, son?"

"No, Jim. I just don't believe the town needed me to manufacture evidence and become a criminal myself to put away another criminal, because then it has to be asked, where does the line get drawn? See that? That's what got me! I was down in that godforsaken evidence locker and that one thing stuck in my... Where's the line, if I do this? Where's the line for us?"

The third juice glass of scotch was thoroughly alive in Sweeney's brain by then. He glared at Preston for a few boozy seconds, then exploded and leaped to his feet.

"Sunday school *shit*? You bringing me that? Is that a joke? We might as well get Satan himself locked up in that isolation cell down there and put his shiny red ass on trial! *This case* is one we don't lose, Wade! We don't lose it!" He stepped to the wall and put his forehead against it. "We just fucking can't. You've been around long enough now. By now you've got a lawman's bead on the range of evil you're likely to find in any normal life, as opposed to the absolute rivers of shit that a man like this has running through his!"

Sweeney began to hyperventilate and had to sit down, panting. He dropped his head between his knees.

Preston glanced at the untouched drink in his hand and set it aside. "Jim I think you better get some sleep, get ready to rebut the defense on Monday."

But Sweeney stayed down low with his hands flat against the sides of his head. He let go with a low moan before he spoke.

"God help me, Wade. I don't think you get it. This piece of garbage could walk on us. I swear to God I'm about to shit myself. I was out there shooting *marshmallows* at the jury! I'm scared the defense is gonna send me flowers!"

He finally raised his head just enough to meet Preston's gaze. "You abandoned me out there, bastard. If I was bigger than you I'd kick your ass to the county line and then set you on fire."

Preston stood up. "I think I heard my dinner bell ring."

"Sure! Might as well go on home, *now*! Nothing we can do about any of it *now*. Rebut the defense? Swat flies, you mean!"

"Okay. Gotta get going. Grab some decent shut-eye, why don't you. 'Night."

Sweeney ignored Preston's exit. He simply stared down at a random spot on the floor stood slightly weaving in place. After a few moments his lips moved in a whisper that was barely audible. "I felt like I was gonna throw up in front of that damn jury, all day long."

With that, his stomach gurgled. His hands went to his mouth and he lunged for the waste basket.

■ ■ ■

Ever since the week before the trial got underway, the Associated Press and United Press International had both been maintaining anonymous stringers in Roundup, Montana. The anonymity was deemed important for allowing the reporters to tap uninhibited remarks from unsuspecting locals or invent deep source comments without having to prove them.

One of the first pieces to emerge from the undercover reporters featured "man on the street" quotes of an avowed Roundup citizen who gave a long spiel about the need for a good lynching to show criminals and communists how they got treated around those parts. The delighted reporter made off with the ranting of FBI Confidential Informant of Known Reliability, Number 6, who was also under cover, spoke for nobody but himself, using the same sense of judgment that got him into trouble with the FBI in the first place, and was only in town to help tend the taps on the Sherman home since he lived over in the State capital of Helena.

But the story was a doozy and had legs on it, as the boys liked to say in the press room, because people didn't have much to focus their attention what with the fighting in Korea putting on such a poor show. In that manner, Number 6 became the unacknowledged voice of Roundup, Montana, a guy spoiling for a fight because the damned case had made him travel to that crap town to run his little snooping errands for J. Edgar Hoover.

The news service wires sang with stories of vigilante lawlessness and capitalist corruption of the law, all floating on the balloons of the Andy Carmichael murder case. The stories were updated every day as new facts and opinions rolled in and were reprinted in newspapers across the country. Every major radio station also had a constant wire service feed, so the airwaves echoed with news announcers reading from A.P. and U.P.I. tear sheets.

Their dedicated social responsibility was promoted as being that of bringing the nation's attention to the fact that the nation was paying attention, and repeat that as often as necessary until the nation paid attention.

Larger issues sprang up from small stories quietly distributed to the press by an amalgam of major business owners in Montana's mining, ranching, and oil industries. These major business owners admonished statewide news outlets to ignore the ridiculous theories of a desperate defense attorney and made passing references to their advertising accounts.

But the days of the Communist Witch Hunt and the backlash it created were already hot across the land. The public was primed to receive theories of vast labor organizations sometimes having their members set up and picked off to intimidate the others into compliance.

This was contrasted to the activities of the clandestine wing of the FBI and their anonymously sourced news tips regarding the crime wave tormenting the nation and the need for steadfast law enforcement, so that children could go grow up in a safer world.

The American Communist Party leaders roused their members to spread the word at work or play based on case news taken from The Worker's Monthly. The local Montana publication had been so friendly to them in years past that the Party leaders did not check their sources, or they would have learned that everything they passed on to their membership resulted from a single source, via the editorial philosophies of Byron and Ruth Sherman.

As a result, a flash flood of new subscription fees poured in. Byron and Ruth found more money into their mailbox in a single week than they had seen in years. Bills were paid, money banked, champagne consumed. After so many years of near-anonymous struggle deep in the journalistic trenches, they found themselves rising each morning knowing their daily work would touch the lives of millions.

Ruth vowed to attend every trial hearing and write new op-ed pieces every day to fill in the pieces she already published prior to its beginning. Those early columns on the corrupting power of capital were the potent seeds of the overall story and they sprouted like magic beanstalks.

There was also, as if by more magic, Ruth's new Sunday guest column in the editorial pages of The New York Times. All she had to do to secure the splendid opportunity of having her thoughts validated by The Gray Lady was guarantee her piece would take the position that something funny was going on in this murder case. She agreed with the editors at the <u>Times</u> that it was imperative to determine whether major capital forces were trying to unfairly affect the outcome of the trial. If so, it would became essential for her to help the <u>Times</u> turn the tide of public opinion and unfairly affect the outcome themselves.

When Jerry O'Connell's Freemason defense theory somehow magically dribbled out, issues surfaced in the national news regarding Freemason influence within the United States and even the state and federal governments. Vital questions about dark Freemason conspiracies sprang up in the popular dialogue. Complexities multiplied while the questions quickly grew branches, the branches sprouted leaves, the leaves fell and scattered to the wind.

29

Vertiginous Until She Met Him

Mazie O'Connell walked out of the courtroom along with the rest of the spectators at noon recess, feeling glad she had traveled from Great Falls in secret to watch her husband on the first day of the defense case. It was her second trip. On the first one she watched him deliver the opening arguments, and it was such a point of pride and pleasure for her that she decided to return for his end of the case. It was worth using up her butter and egg money for the bus tickets to finally see her Jerry excel at something.

The secrecy of her visit gave her some small sense of power amid a life situation that was out of control. A large bonus for her was that traveling to watch her husband at work kept her from feeling guilty about her other activities in stalking him to see if his telephone girl-friend was around while he was staying there in town.

Mazie's first visit not only gave her the pleasure of seeing his magnificent opening oration, but eased her fears a bit when the only people he spoke with outside court appeared to be the Shermans, who he was staying with, and any reporter who wanted to ask him a question or get a statement. Mazie knew Jerry could crack off a formal statement drunk or sober.

Mazie stood five feet two but the people crowding into the hallway were much taller men, so she was concealed among them while she moved through the crowd. They blocked her view so completely that she nearly walked past the tight group of reporters waiting at the end of the hallway for the principal trial figures to come out.

A wave of camera flashes popped amid the reporters, drawing Mazie's eyes to a tall, large-breasted woman in a tight dress who looked like she was going for a role in a Hollywood movie. Mazie pushed her way toward the crowd and got to an open space large enough to see the action. The one with the udders was the cause of the flashes, standing and posing for the men, lifting the hem of her skirt to reveal her legs, above the knees. Her hair was bleached a bright whorehouse yellow and her butt was as big as all outdoors. Mazie had to wonder, how did this B-movie reject fit in with this murder trial?

She backed up against the wall to avoid the foot traffic and pretended to inspect her coat sleeve. From the corners of her eyes she watched the canine pack of reporters slobber over their impromptu pinup girl. In that first moment, Mazie wasn't aware of anything more than her sense of curiosity about the odd scene. That changed right away, now that she was close enough to hear their voices.

"You guys should know," the fake blond announced, "if you want the behind-the-scenes story on Jerry O'Connell, I'm the one to talk to!"

It hit Mazie like a spark: *The telephone girlfriend.* She almost lost control of her bowels. She was glad to be leaning against the wall because she could not move her legs. She shifted her eyes to the reporters to see what their reaction was going to be, but they appeared only mildly interested in the girlfriend's words. The woman seemed to sense their disinterest and raised the stakes like somebody determined to get into the news.

"I'm telling you, we got a relationship going!"

"What kinda relationship?" one of the men called out in a tone that indicated he didn't much care.

She gave them a coy smile and said, "Oh, let's just say I was a vertiginous woman when we met and Jerry took care of that!"

"I don't think you mean vertiginous, lady," the reporter grinned.

"Mister, you don't know me. Are you saying I wasn't?"

"Forget it."

The reporters laughed in derision and began to turn away from her. She called out to them. "You're gonna want to know about this secret code business, and I've got the skinny on that, too!"

With that, there was a noticeable wave of interest from the reporters. They all turned to look at her while she continued.

"I tell ya, this trial has been great for us because his wife stays up there in Great Falls and we spend time together here."

The reporters didn't show much interest at that, so she piped up, "You boys interested in that secret code? I heard him talk about that. You better believe it's real. Who wants a picture?"

She held up her hemline and from Mazie's vantage point it was clear that she exposed her right leg up to the thigh. Mazie couldn't believe her eyes. *Christ, she be doffing her panties in a minute!*

Another wave of camera flashes came from the knot of reporters. The girlfriend acted like she was at a movie opening in Hollywood and soaked it all up. But Mazie found the flashes so blinding that she felt as if they could throw her into a seizure.

She pushed herself away from the wall and made her legs carry her down the hallway, while the male reporters made the predictable response to the girlfriend's beguiling combination of bleached hair, giant knockers, and whorish behavior. Mazie was all the way down to the Ladies Room at the far end of the hallway when she heard her husband's voice call out.

"All right, gentlemen, I have time for just a few questions today!" The reporters flocked to him and circled him with their cameras. He look proud, Mazie noticed, like a man in control of things, like the man she thought she met and married, before he crumbled into a confrontational and unemployable goon with few friends and a list of enemies. At first it had felt like an honor to stand by him in his difficulties, what with all his causes to save humanity. Then he rewarded her with his late night phone calls to women like that one down there near the courtroom door.

It was obvious now that the blonde had been waiting for Jerry to emerge. She ran to him with little bitty high-heeled running steps and took him by the arm. "Honey!" she called out to him while facing the reporters. "I'm so proud of you!"

Strangely, Jerry looked unhappy at her appearance and pulled away from her. She immediately twisted her face into a pout.

"Jerr-eee! Aren't you happy to see me? It's a surprise!" She took his arm again, firmly this time, hugging her giant breasts against his upper arm and, if Mazie was right, deliberately rubbing some of her pancake makeup onto his sleeve.

Mazie watched Jerry recover himself in the manner she knew so well, faking a confidence he didn't feel. All he wanted was to speak to the reporters and get his point of view out to the public through the news, so Mazie knew he was going to downplay his unhappiness about the "surprise" visit. The Bimbo seemed to know that, too, taking advantage of the fact that he was loathe to rebuff here there in front of witnesses.

The thought struck her that Jerry still didn't know his faithful wife Mazie was there. *Gee Jerry, this is a real "surprise" day for you, isn't it?*

Without noticing her own movements, she began to slowly walk back down the hallway toward the courtroom door, toward the gaggle of reporters, and most of all toward her philandering husband, who appeared to think nothing at all of publicly humiliating her by allowing this trashy woman to make a spectacle of them all. Her husband, who had no idea she was there.

She watched Jerry allow the woman to cling to his arm, even as he tried to ignore her and talk to the reporters. He might just as well have shoved a hot blade into Mazie then; the two of them down there actually looked like a couple, standing outside the courtroom together while Jerry made his camera smile and strained to hear to questions hurled by the reporters. *What about this "secret code," Mr. O'Connell? Are the Masons controlling this trial?*

Mazie barely felt herself move toward them. She had no sense of her feet moving. It was as if she floated to the edge of the reporters' circle and stood behind the men in front, watching her husband Jerry and his Nameless Bimbo by peering between the arms of the men in front of her.

The girlfriend interrupted the reporters by calling out, "Better learn all about the Secret Code while you can, fellas. Once I get him out of here, he's mine!"

The men laughed appreciatively, less over appreciation of line and more over appreciation of her breasts. She turned to Jerry and pretended to whisper to him, but did it loud enough for all to hear, "See that, honey? I help my man take care of business!"

With that, the blathering slut hung onto Jerry's sleeve for balance and hiked her hemline to the top of her thigh. It struck Mazie that she'd never seen that much leg anywhere in public outside of a beach or a lingerie ad.

The reporters were good-natured about taking a dozen shots of her all in a row, lighting up the hallway like a lighting storm. Jerry's all-purpose smile never changed while photographs of them together snapped away into the public record. *That's how bad he wants his quote,* Mazie thought, *he'll stand there and let himself get photographed with that strange woman rather than drive her away and lose a moment of publicity.*

Every bit of fear and resentment over her husband's personal failures, business failures, political failures, financial failures, and marital infidelities exploded like a gasoline fire. Jerry had just lost his last chance to prevent disaster by failing to push the woman away. Once Mazie saw him just stand there and try to grin his way past it for no better reason that for the sake of another quote for the news wires, their course was set.

The camera flashes were still popping away when Mazie burst from behind the two men in front of her, both hands clutching the long strap of her sizeable handbag. She ran forward at the same instant that she reared back the purse and then swung it in a tall arc over her head. The heavy purse collided directly onto the head of one flabbergasted barroom floozy.

"Ow! Hey!" the floozy bellowed. "Ow! Ow! Hey, what's she doin'?"

Flashbulbs went off in all directions while Maize circled around and around with her arms, whirling the handbag in powerful arcs and bringing it down in alternate blows on her husband and his bitch. As for the other men, it was permissible public decorum in that time and place to laugh, take photos, even place bets, all while doing nothing to intervene or call for help.

"Ow! Get her away from me! Ow! Is she crazy?"

Jerry looked as if his heart stopped cold in his chest. He gasped at the sight of his wife, uncomprehending, and was too stunned by the very bizarre situation to do more than step back and raise his arms to protect his head. He didn't bother to say a word to her, caught red-handed as he was. Instead he left the girl to whatever Fate she had in store for herself and retreated back into the courtroom, which was off-limits to the public during lunch hour. He pulled the double doors closed, still without making any attempt to speak to her.

The bleached-blonde realized nobody was coming to her aid, so she took advantage of the pause and ran away down the hall in tiny high-heeled steps. Running as fast as she dared in a tight skirt, she moved alongside people walking at the usual pace.

Meanwhile Mazie stood staring at the closed double doors, panting hard. Her arms felt like she had pulled muscles under the shoulders with her impassioned swings of the heavy purse. She realized at that moment that she still held the purse with both hands on the long strap, and the bag looked barely any worse for wear. It validated her policy of owning fewer things but always shopping for the highest quality.

She hoped the reporters wouldn't press her for an explanation and breathed easier when she saw that they appeared to have already decided the fun was over and were on to other things. The District Attorney stepped onto the floor and the crowd surged toward him, so Mazie took the opportunity to leave without having to pose for anymore photos than they already had of her. *Let 'em write their own captions,* she thought. She was confident her husband would remain inside the building, stay in Roundup until the trial was over, and then come back to her in Great Falls and try to fix it all up. Well, he was going to have to replace every penny she spent on the bus tickets. That much was for certain.

She made it nearly all the way out of the building before one young cub reporter chased her down, calling out, "Lady! Hey wait up a minute, will you?" He approached with a big smile, but he was trying too hard. She had lived with Jerry for too long to miss that trick.

"Say lady, anything you can tell me about what just happened there?" He held up his notebook as if that explained his nosy question, like that made it all right, because he had himself a notebook.

It hurt to think. Mazie was so overcome with emotion it was hard to get her brain going. She felt as stupid as if she had just awakened from a deep sleep.

She looked him in the eyes and tried to tell him without words that she was too overcome to say anything just then. This time, unlike her usual experience of everyday life, he actually seemed to see her, to understand the little bit of telepathy she sent to him. She saw it on his face. He took a step back, cleared his throat, and then just raised his notebook to his forehead in a little salute. He turned around and headed back toward the courtroom.

It was the most consideration anyone had shown Mazie in a long time. *If I were ten years younger,* she thought. *But no.*

30

Swan Dive

Andy Carmichael had used the Harmless Goofball since boyhood and most of the time it saved him, though there was the occasional mis-fire. Like all forms of magic, the Harmless Goofball was never one hundred percent reliable.

So far, though, he felt pretty good. He found all the ruckus, as he liked to call it, seductive with its many sporadic glares of public atten-tion. It really helped to get him out of his cell, and he had long consid-ered "out time" to be job one of the incarcerated inmate.

He couldn't imagine how anybody could fail to love the swarming press. In spite of the fact that the attentions lavished upon him were all done with variations on contempt, the strength of the attention itself was so far removed from his months-long state of invisibility that he could not help but wonder how much higher his cache would be inside the joint after all this.

Andy figured he had every reason to expect to trade up, live a hell of a lot better than he had before, in there. Pick his own daddy, somebody who would hire muscle to the horn-dogs off of him. Live like a person.

But this late evening air was dry and hot inside his cell. The radia-tor on the other side of his cell wall made the whole wall hot. He sat on his bunk dripping sweat even though he was stark naked. It was almost as if the coating of character he wore as the Harmless Goof-ball was trapping his body heat.

The bald attorney McDonald or whatever his name was continued to stand over Andy with his male court reporter on his portable stool with his portable transcriber. They both seemed able to ignore his nude condition so Andy made note of the possibility that he overplayed that one, not that he could get dressed now, but it was a good point to keep in mind for future decisions.

The lawyer continued to pump him for information that a smart mouthpiece really ought to realize a Harmless Goofball could never give him. Andy put his invisible feelers out the way the guys in the joint taught him to do when he was trapped in close quarters with a loco bastard. He sat very still and kept a neutral stare plastered on his face, just as if he could see right through the wall. Then he focused on every tiny change in the other guy. Change of voice tone, change of body position, change of attitude, change of personal smell, anything. They were all pieces that could be assembled into a picture of what the other guy is thinking, sometimes things he doesn't even realize about himself. When it got that far, victory was within reach.

"How long do we have to do this, Andy?"

"Sir, we can do whatever you want for as long as you want."

"Oh really? Hey. I'll take that. That's some progress, anyway. Yeah, what I want to do. Let me tell you what I want. It's for you to spell out enough of that code for me to take into court. I've stalled every way humanly possible, but we are way, way out on the limb."

"Well, sir, I'm glad to help."

"The code, Andy. That's the question. Now it's your turn. Go."

Andy chuckled a pleasant little laugh and shook his head. "Mr. O'Donnell—"

"O'Connell, Andy. Jerry O'Connell."

"Mr. O'Connell, you know I can't go anywhere. We're in a cell, here!"

Andy saw the first glint of real panic flash in the lawyer's eyes. It was the second thing you learned to do inside the joint, right after looking for time outside the cell. What you did was learn to gulp back that first flash of panic so it never showed, no matter what. The masters of fear inside the joint had mentored him in reading signs of fear and finding victims that way. Dogs might be able to smell fear the way some people said, but Andy knew human males were the ones who got hard over it.

"Mr. Perzie is here to make it legal, Andy. His transcript is like a ticket out for us. For you."

"Oh, I'd sure like to get out all right, Mr. O'Connell."

"Then recite the code or at least part of the code for Mr. Perzie to transcribe, right here. I will have it entered into the trial record tomorrow morning, Andy."

"Wow, that fast?"

"That fast? Do you understand that I am trying to save your life? This is a hanging state, Andy! It's full of people who want to see you dead."

"Don't be scared, sir. We'll be all right."

"For God's sake, I have to ask, is this thing real Andy? You have to tell me now. I've bought you all the time I can but if I don't give them the code, the entire defense theory goes out with it. Your defense!"

"People seem to like me most of the time."

The court reporter just sat there like a stature while the mouthpiece dropped his head forward and put his palm over his eyes. He stood that way for a long time before he spoke again. When he did his voice was different. More like a whipped dog. Andy couldn't hold back a giggle.

"Andy, do you understand that if we leave here without the Freemasons' secret smoke code, I may not be able to keep you off the gallows?"

"Sir, I may not be so smart but I know if I spill the beans I'm good as dead anyhow. I ain't smart enough to figure my way past it. Maybe you are, I don't know." He shook his head with a sad little Goofball grin. "Crazy," he said. He stood up to stretch, then stepped over to the toilet and urinated in a squatting position while he kept up the grin and repeated, "Crazy, crazy, crazy."

Meanwhile Andy saw it in that first second; a flash of idea on McConnell's bulbous face. The mouthpiece had received Andy's transmitted idea. He was feeling the inspiration. Next he would decide to change from a guilty plea to an insanity plea, citing new evidence of mental defect.

Andy knew it. His invisible feelers were extended so far out they could tell him whether or not the other two guys were hungry.

The Harmless Goofball sat on his cot and softly sang a few little songs while the court reporter packed up his things and the mouth-piece shouted at him. Insults, threats, guarantees of a bad death, all the usual stuff. The lawyer was the one speaking all the evil but he sounded like he was about to cry. *Inside the joint, he'd be dead in ten minutes,* he thought. The picture made him giggle.

■ ■ ■

FBI Confidential Informant of Known Reliability, Number 9 sat in his Chevy 3100 pickup with the recorder turning, desperate to get something the feds actually liked this time. He thought he had them before, but they pressed him for more and sent him back with his tail tucked.

Of course they gave him no idea what he was supposed to look for, just the responsibility of finding it. He'd been in position there for so long that he had nearly idled away his thankful of gas to keep the recorder turning. Just as he was about to take a quick break and sneak off to fill his tank, Lady Luck smiled on him for the first time in months. That was when he heard it. "Sold gold!" he said out loud and pressed the earphones closer to his head.

That planted microphone inside the Shermans' home managed to perfectly capture subject O'Connell's voice—Number 9 figured the hapless defense attorney must have been standing directly under the bugged light fixture. The rolling tape recorded every word.

"Look, there's no point arguing about this! I took a shot with the smoke code, but he froze up. But I know that I can stop this trial right now while we have his head examined."

"What if they don't find him to be crazy?"

"Are you kidding? Assuming the doctors tell the truth, there's nothing else they can say about him. He's on some other planet."

"Are you saying there's nothing to this secret code?"

"No, I'm saying it doesn't matter. If he's afraid to lay it out, we can't use it."

"Or he's faking."

"I tell you Byron, if he can fake it that well, he can fake insanity for the doc."

"Can we quote you?"

"Christ, don't even joke about that."

"All right, all right. We're at the point where the outcome of the trial doesn't matter, as far as this national dialogue we've started. The way Ruth has been writing, I think we can keep it going for as long as we want. Years!"

The voices inside the house went on and on, laying out the trickery of the new defense plan. By that point Number 9 was gleefully anticipating how relieved his handlers were going to be when they heard that the secret smoke code was going to stay a secret. Or at least nothing more than a rumor of a secret, and the Bureau knew all about how to live with that.

■ ■ ■

FBI Confidential Informant of Known Reliability, Number 11 sat inside of his concealed stake-out in the tool shed behind Judge Summers' house. He knew there were other stake-outs going on; hell his number was "11," but he had no doubt that he'd been stuck with the worst one. A stinking tool shed, for crying out loud? No heat, not even any insulation. He could do jumping jacks if he kept the arm swings low, but his body heat escaped right out into the night. There he was, pissing into a can like a captured soldier.

The phone tap wire alone was enough to give him away, leading as it did straight from the house to the shed. He had to think that nobody in the branch office had the slightest idea what they were doing. All the Judge had to do was look outside his window and pay attention for a second, and the stake-out was blown just like that. He could only pray that his walkie-talkie would come to life with the go-ahead to make the call and that he could get the hell out of there.

Operatives had cut the power to the neighborhood for the evening, sacrificing the neighbors' comfort for national interests while they softened up the judge. Phone service was also cut, keeping everybody isolated.

■ ■ ■

Inside Judge Summers' house, the temperature was almost as far down as it was outside. Once again he contemplated going out to the garage and setting up the generator, but these outages usually never lasted more than a few hours. It was unusual to lose the phone line as well as the electricity, but the freezing devil wind was said to be ripping through the region at speeds of up to forty miles an hour, coating everything with ice.

He walked into his darkened living room, moving by flashlight in the deep shadows. When he stepped into the room he gave the light switch a few flicks, just in case. He didn't recall whether or not he had any lights on when the power first went out that afternoon. It didn't matter, the switch was still dead.

He walked over to the telephone on the reading table by the big chair, glad that his bachelor life kept him from having to deal with a woman harping on him to hurry up and make things better. He knew sometimes the thing to do was just hunker down, put your head into the wind and wait for things to get better all by themselves.

He picked up the phone receiver, not really expecting anything, and as he suspected, the line was still dead. He decided he might as well go to bed early and wait there for the power to come back on, so he turned and headed back toward the bedroom.

Just before he passed out of the living room, the phone rang. The loud bell startled him so badly he nearly jumped into the air.

He cursed louder than he would have if anyone else was in the house and turned back to the phone. Within the time it took for one more ring he reached the phone again and snatched up the receiver.

"Hello? Ha-ha, this is odd, I just checked and the phone was out! Who's calling?"

"Judge Summers, this is the FBI. You are being contacted at the direct request of J. Edgar Hoover himself."

Summers' first thought was that he had somehow been named in the Communist witch hunts. His next was to notice that it made no sense for them to call him on the phone instead of picking him up in person, if he was in trouble.

"J. Edgar Hoover? What on earth would he want with me?"

"Nothing, Judge. That's the point. I am to tell you that we're out."

"Out?"

"Of your murder trial. They're abandoning the smoke code theory."

"Oh really. And how do you people know that?"

"We're out, and you are free to try your case any way you want."

"I what? Now see here, if this is a prank call—"

"No prank, Judge. We're out."

"Nobody told me you were in!"

"Good evening to you."

The caller hung up, and Summers replaced the receiver in the phone's cradle while he shook his head and muttered, "Permission to run my trial without the FBI. That's great. Just great." He paced back and forth in the darkness trying to control his sense of indignation. That phone call was the sort of thing they might do to a criminal under surveillance, but sure as hell wasn't acceptable procedure for a sitting judge.

The more he thought about it, the more deeply offended he felt himself to be. He decided it was time to wake up Sheriff Preston and see if he knew anything about this. He walked back to the phone and picked up the receiver.

The line was still dead.

31

Devil In A House Of Mirrors

Early the next morning before the courtroom opened, Jerry O'Connell sat across from Sheriff Preston's desk while Preston stared back at him. D.A. Sweeney stood puffing a cigar as thick as his wrist. They both regarded O'Connell as if he smelled of the barnyard.

"So here I am, gentlemen, as summoned by your royal selves."

"Don't start in on the political crap, O'Connell," Sweeney growled. "We're here to save your ass."

"Save my ass? Gosh, thanks. I've never had my ass saved by right-wing reactionary racists before."

"Racists?" shouted the Sheriff. He looked like he might come flying over the desk.

O'Connell fought the urge to sneer into his one-eyed face. "We all know if this man was a negro, you'd have beaten him to death while 'trying to escape.'"

"You idiot!" fumed Sweeney. "I see how you got yourself thrown out of congress! Hell, your own party fired you for being too pink! So *how* pink does a guy have to be, in order to be too far left for the democrats, Jerry?"

"And Jerry," the Sheriff continued, "you fat little screwball. As a personal aside let me assure you that if you ever call me that name again without a specific complaint to attach to it, then my white fists will beat your white face to a pulp. This means my actions will be racially neutral."

Jerry stood up to leave. "I can see there's no purpose to this meeting." He headed for the door.

"Unless you want to save your client's life," Sweeney threw out. That one stopped O'Connell at the exit. He turned back. "Too late, gentlemen. I'm going in this morning with a motion to change his plea to 'Not Guilty by Reason of Insanity.' So whatever you have to offer, it better be good."

Sweeney sneered. "No, whatever *you* have to offer better be good, pal. Because we will put up every objection in the world. We will demand multiple confirmations of his mental state by qualified doctors who, I can tell you right now, are going to find that he might be evil but he's not *legally insane*. After that, you can take your losing case to the nearest garbage bin, because that's where you *and* your client will wind up!"

"So what, then? You called me here to try to scare me?"

"No," Preston replied, "but we didn't call you here to sit still while you hurl invective, either. So let's all take the high road and follow the Golden Rule. You know, 'do unto others' and all that, shall we?"

O'Connell glared at them for a moment before he responded, "Okay. Fine. Fine. I'm listening."

Sweeney sat in a spare desk chair and blew a puff of contempt in O'Connell's direction. "Here's the thing. We all know your client is bat-shit crazy, but that doesn't make him incapable of knowing right from wrong. I'm confident you can't get him to meet that standard. So threaten all you want, but I don't believe you'll bring home the bacon on that one."

O'Connell nodded. "We'll see."

Preston leaned toward him and quietly said, "We have a better way for you to go."

"*You* guys have a better way for *me* to go?"

"That's right," Sweeney nodded. "Unless you're a big fan of losing causes, because I've been up against the insanity defense half a dozen times and I've never lost to it. Not one time."

O'Connell shook his head. "Is this the part where we all pull out our dicks and go for a tape measure?"

"Too late," Sweeney grinned. "You lose. Because your dick can't match mine, today. I have an offer for second degree murder, along with a guarantee of eligibility for parole in fourteen, sixteen years tops. You can take it or I can send these photos to your wife."

He tossed two eight-by-ten inch black and white shots of Jerry O'Connell in the nude, sprawled atop his Roundup girlfriend. He sat back and grinned. "Now let's see yours."

O'Connell gasped and visibly recoiled, as if this was the one thing he had not prepared himself for. "How did you...? Uh, fourteen to sixteen? That's, that's..."

"More than you could have prayed for?" Preston helpfully added.

"Hell, no! Not... Not unless..."

"Unless we throw in free lunch for you?"

"Hey! Sarcasm is inappropriate in this meeting, gentlemen!"

With that Sheriff Preston stood and leaned right into O'Connell's face. "Sort of like baseless charges of racism?"

"... okay, point taken. You two may not be racists."

"Jesus Christ." Preston shook his head and returned to his seat.

Sweeney picked up the ball. "The simple version is this. You won't get past a jury on insanity, period. You won't. But we can make a plea for Second Degree Murder fly with the court. All parties stipulate. No trial, which means you don't have to risk jury nullification, just a comfy cell for your sociopath and free meals. If you make the wrong choice, then it's good news day for me and I get to watch him hang. If I had it my way, we'd bribe the hangman to make the rope too short so his neck doesn't snap. Then we all get to watch him dance on air for awhile before he shits himself and chokes out. In that case you'll get to be the fool who took on a case he couldn't handle and got his client executed. Build a career on that, you name-calling piece of dog shit."

"Oh and that's not invective?"

"In your case, it's a title. And you've earned it. Unless of course you actually do want to take your 'Smoke Code' defense to the jury and hope your conspiracy brick will fly."

O'Connell glared at him with such rage that his face turned purple. He looked as if his blood pressure could power a fire hose. "You bast— bastards, you— you—"

"Is that a yes, counselor?"

For a moment, he alternately stared at both men, then finally let out a long exhale. "Second Degree, guaranteed? No tricks?"

"We're not going to say it again, O'Connell," Sweeney told him. "You will now either accept this offer or it will be rescinded. Then you can go blow your magic smoke up the jury's ass and hope for a miracle."

"That *is* your defense strategy, isn't it?" Preston added.

With that, O'Connell again stood up. This time he wore an expression that indicated he was about to scoop up bird droppings and have them for breakfast. But he reluctantly stuck out his hand.

"Deal."

■ ■ ■

Four days later, the media frenzy disappeared from the courthouse and moved solely onto the nation's airways and newspaper columns. The fate of Andrew Carmichael and question of justice for his victims became less interesting that the flurry of editorials and commentaries now sweeping national news outlets about whether there was an active hidden conspiracy going on in America, run by the International Order of Freemasons. Masonic lodges all over the country issued denials in the strongest of terms, to which their opponents replied by pointing out that *of course* the Masons would cry foul over the story. *After all, they have a Secret Smoke Code to protect...*

The battle raged on, leaving the left, the right, and the long-suffering middle to swing punches at each other in a contest that had moved past what the right called a botched murder trial in Montana and the left called a victory in snatching a benighted worker from the jaws of an unfair death, and which the middle regarded as simply another useless point of debate between two sides congenitally incapable of dealing with one another on behalf of the country as a whole.

Sheriff Preston returned to his normal office hours to answer countless phone calls admonishing him for failing to make the case against Andrew Carmichael. People were mad as hell and wanted to see heads roll. His explanation that a Sheriff had no power to select specific murder charges did nothing to turn off the vitriol. "You should have brought in more evidence," the litany went. *You should have... You would have... You could have... but you didn't.*

For the first time in Wade Preston's life, he found himself wishing he had fewer scruples. District Attorney Sweeney felt no compunction about reminding Preston over and over that the State of Montana could have sewed up the case nice and tight if Preston's ridiculous attack of conscience hadn't denied the state that one piece of evidence which could have sealed Carmichael's doom.

Now Preston stood in the doorway to the City Hall parking lot and watched his deputies place Carmichael in the state prison's transport van, knowing that as a sheriff and as a man he was beginning a new phase in his life. It would be with him for as long as he lived, and it was the nagging question of whether it had been worth it to show loyalty to his morals, at the expense of a legitimate death penalty against a monster who was never going to do anything but harm if he got back out into the world.

The general tone of his phone calls indicated that he would soon be in no position to make the distinction, once next year's elections were over and the public took away his badge.

32

Montana State Prison, 1956

Andy had turned out to be right about his newfound status in prison, with his credibility firmly established by his multiple killings. The new daddy he found within days of his arrival was an oversized lifer who took pride in having a pretty boy with a reputation for murderous flares of temper but who tossed salads like a chef. As far as the realm of long-term incarceration goes, it was an ideal situation. And since Andy's only satisfaction in assaulting women came through using the same port available with male victims, he found that he wanted for little as a long-term guest of the state.

It took him the first two years of his sentence, but he eventually managed to flirt and blow his way to a nice spot on an outdoor chain gang, doing hard physical work that kept him in good shape and gave the plenty of opportunity to get sunshine and fresh air.

Everything about all of that changed in a heartbeat on the afternoon Andy picked up a discarded newspaper left lying around by one of the guards and read it during his roadside meal break. It was a small article, third page, below the fold, but the words flew up off the paper and stabbed him in the eyes.

Montana State Troopers Get New Insignia. The little headline seemed innocuous enough. Another badge for the authorities.

So what? But before he was able to turn the page, his eyes caught enough of the content to stop him cold.

A new slogan had been adopted by the Montana State Troopers and was going to be inserted on every Trooper insignia *plus* the insignia of the Montana Masons. There it was: *3-7-77.*

It was a confession, a clear and present confession on the part of the State of Montana that they were in cahoots with the Freemasons who once ran the state with their corrupt Vigilante Committee. They were the same bastards who now secretly ran the country, hell maybe the whole world.

Unbelievable! He had to bite his tongue to keep from shouting the news. *They did it! They messed up and showed their true colors!*

At last, the information was verified that he had so painfully extracted from the young Canadian Masonic agents. Here was an open admission of the connection between the Masons and the established authority in the State of Montana. Some fool who obviously wasn't paying attention had okayed this change, and in so doing, the Masonic connection was made plain for all to see.

Andy dropped the paper to the ground. He appeared to stand silent and stare straight ahead, but within himself he was changing at the molecular level. The resigned inmate who had been merely marching through his fate turned into a predatory land shark. He became single in his purpose, without conscience or remorse.

The most important thing in his life became escaping from this unfair prison sentence for his understandable acts of self-defense. The Montana court put him there knowing full well that his story about Masonic corruption of state authority was true, all along, since the Masons had infiltrated the courts along with everything else. In their arrogance they thought themselves to be above retribution. Of course, they were vigilantes at heart and in their origin, so they likely figured vengeance belonged exclusively to them. Knowing that, Andy was instantly starved for vengeance of his own.

If the Masons like vigilantism so damned much, then maybe they need a surprise visit from me...

He sidestepped over to the head guard and gave him his best flirtatious smile. "Hey Sergeant, I'm all tied up in knots over all this work. I need to get into the bushes and knock off some of the tension, know what I mean?"

He saw the guard's hungry look before the guard thought to quash it, so he knew it was safe to continue. "Would that be okay? Because if you felt like letting a minute or two go by so nobody gets suspicious and then stepping off down there, I could, you know, take care of whatever tension you're feeling, too." He looked up at the guard's eyes like a little girl asking for help. He knew if a man had ever had another man before and liked the experience, he would not be able to resist Andy's faux vulnerability and clearly available body parts.

The guard smiled, looked both directions, and said, "Yeah, you go on ahead, sweetheart, but I better stay here."

"Okay!" Andy responded with his best cheerleader's smile. "I'll be back in just a few minutes."

"Yeah you'll be back or I'll come get you."

"I'd like that."

"Not the way I mean it, you won't."

"Okay. Couple minutes to myself, then right back to the shovel."

"Yeah, and I want a carton of cigarettes on my desk by tomorrow morning or I write you up for a walk-off and you get switched to indoor work."

"No need! No need!" Andy grinned, moving away in a hurry. "I'll be right back. And your cigarettes are as good as there already!"

The guard sniffed to show that he wasn't impressed by Andy's display of pleasant temperament and still didn't trust him one bit. It was more for show, in case any of the other workers were taking note of things. The guard's theatrics didn't matter at all to Andy, who knew there wasn't going to be any need to give away any cigarettes because he wasn't going to be around for the guard to torment him over it.

As soon as he was out of sight in the bushes, he took off running through the thick overgrowth that lined the highway. He kept his profile low while he ran like a man possessed. His honor position on the road crew was hard won, and something he would never see again, even if they caught him. But first they would have to do that, and Andy Carmichael had no intention of ever returning to that place. He visualized his new mission of revenge while he ran along, and it kept him strong and determined. Having a quest was better than having a good prison daddy because what it lacked in creature comforts it gave back in spades with a heady sense of purpose.

A single string of numbers had stood his life on its head. *3-7-77.* Andy understood it cryptic message as well as any of them. *We're here and we don't even have to hide it anymore! We own you. And if you ever forget it, then these are the dimensions of your grave.*

Suddenly, dying in the sort of act of righteous vengeance he imagined was infinitely preferable to one more day of his well-padded prison life. Who knows, he thought, maybe the bastards even sent those two young incompetent agents in Canada because they knew he would overpower them and wipe them out. Hell, they probably used Andy as the executioner against those two kids because they had done something wrong in the eyes of the other Masons. What a bunch of Einsteins.

So they had been after him all along because he got too close to the truth with a single unfortunate break-in job. In the years since, they had grown so cocky and arrogant that they couldn't resist their little in-joke of putting the truth right out there, *3-7-77,* just as plain as the Secret Smoke Code they hid in plain view. Obviously, the Masons were into a mode of amusing themselves by taunting an ignorant public and doing it as an open secret.

The sense of being on a mission powered his legs long after fatigue would have slowed him. He ran hard. He ran for the sake of revenge. He ran to correct a terrible wrong that had been done to him. And now that his memory had successfully reshaped his murders into acts of self-defense, he ran for the sheer joy of having a clear cut enemy, for the sense of purpose it gave him. Andy figured the old Vigilante Freemasons would understand that part of his thinking perfectly well, if they only knew.

Part Three

Dastards In The Night

* Seattle – Late August, 2001 *

33

Don't Go Up In The Attic

Shelby Preston sat on an unmarked cardboard box amid the attic's organized chaos, then steeled himself and popped the lock on the large steamer trunk. He lifted the creaking lid and stopped at the same place where he had stopped on three prior attempts. He never got farther than peering down at the packed compartments filled with old clothing, stacks of photographs and a thick pile of yellowing newspaper clippings. The old trunk came to him while cleaning out his late parents' home, and he took it with him out of an odd feeling of obligation to his uncle Wade Preston, a family member he never knew. In the past, each time he tried to go through the box, this was the point where the thought of his uncle's suicide cast a pall over him.

Today curiosity overrode his feeling of superstitious dread and combined with his need to prove he could handle this challenge. That evening, a rare argument with his wife Carla had sprouted after dinner when she chided him for leaving the chore undone. In spite of feeling defensive about the whole topic, Shelby had to admit it had been up in the attic unopened for a long time.

The thought of learning more about a desperate person's point of view felt dangerous, as if he might somehow catch a suicidal spore drifting up off of the old papers and fall into a bout of despair himself. Although he was still a toddler back when his Uncle Wade died, his own lifelong struggle with dark emotions had kept him at a distance from the story behind it.

He reminded himself that this was a piece of superstition and nothing more. His success as a private investigator was partly due to his lack of such metaphysical concerns. He had always ferreted out the truth by searching for evidence and sticking to facts. But his compulsive nature also caused facts to stick to him, and until this evening he had avoided accumulating any sticky points of information about his uncle's suicide. He had never learned what triggered it, just something about a case from Uncle Wade's days as a sheriff in Montana.

Shelby had promised Carla several times that he would get the job done. She was convinced that some of his torment about having no family would be eased if he took apart that last bit of his family history and dealt with it. He didn't necessarily agree but he was out of ideas for stalling, so this time instead of bailing out on the project he reached in and pulled out the newspaper articles. His hunch was that they had been saved because they were about his uncle's big case. He gently pulled the stiffened papers apart and glanced at the first few. Within seconds his suspicions were confirmed; they all featured stories about the murder trial of a young escaped convict named Andrew James Carmichael.

It quickly became obvious to Shelby that the case was a much bigger deal in its day than he ever heard from his parents. As Uncle Wade's only brother, Shelby's father had taken his brother's death especially hard and never wanted to talk about it.

Some of the articles were just from local Montana newspapers and magazines, but their were also copies of <u>The New York Times</u>, <u>The Chicago Tribune</u>, <u>The Washington Post</u>, and <u>The San Francisco Chronicle</u>, plus a spate of old political magazines that were important back in the day.

Until that moment, all Shelby had known of the case was that some drifter committed terrible murders fifty years ago back in a cattle town called Roundup, Montana, where Uncle Wade was the sheriff.

Within a few minutes of picking up the first yellowed newspaper, that picture began to clear.

Most of the articles were written around the time of the murder trial, and it had manifested as a major battle for the minds of the reading public between political forces on both sides of the aisle. Once Carmichael's attorney pleaded him down to lower charges and got him off with a minimum of fourteen years, the Canadians gave up in disgust, knowing their own case against him would have the same problems. The cost and the clamor wasn't worth the vengeance in their eyes.

The disposition of the case did nothing to quell the verbal war in the press. For many weeks afterward, the raging commentators continued to assail one another with scorn and derision. It struck Shelby that whoever saved those articles included them with the trial stories to put it all in perspective. A short stack of smaller articles were from 1956, five years after the end of the trial, concerning the new changes in insignia for the Montana State Troopers. That was when they added the numerical phrase, 3-7-77 to official state trooper badges and emblems. No explanation was given and nobody seemed to know what the phrase meant. By then it was taken as a nostalgic throwback to the long-gone pioneer days, to the Vigilante Committee that once ruled the land. Nothing more than that.

The last four articles were only from the defunct weekly newspaper, The Weekly Roundup, and had small articles noting that the murderer who was convicted in Roundup five years earlier had escaped from his work crew. Back then, certain people were concerned that he might come back to the area for some sort of revenge. But in later articles there was no word of him ever showing up around there.

Only one article offered Shelby real insight into what happened to Wade Preston – the last one in the stack reported that in the wake of Andrew Carmichael's escape and the failure of the authorities to track him down, the same town sheriff who weathered voter dissatisfaction after the Carmichael trial and had been permitted to keep his job suddenly didn't want it anymore. Sheriff Wade Preston quit five years short of a halfway decent pension and instead moved out of the area. The article noted that the outgoing sheriff was asked whether he was going after Carmichael as a vigilante. He refused to answer.

And that was it. End of story. If Uncle Wade went after Carmichael, somehow there was no record of it. Shelby knew a few more facts than the papers reported, but it wasn't much. Broken bits of information had slipped out through his mother or father over the years. He knew Uncle Wade spent the next few years haunting police stations in the southwestern states, convinced Carmichael was down there living in hiding somewhere off the grid.

Uncle Wade had also publicly complained that he had information the authorities refused to act on, regarding four more murders he was certain were done by Carmichael, after his escape. But other men had been arrested and "confessed" and now rotted behind bars. Nobody would reopen the cases. Uncle Wade quickly became a notorious crank, a figure of gossip and ridicule.

Shelby had never understood why Uncle Wade took his own life, but now a picture of his depth of despair began to emerge. It turned out that Uncle Wade's demise was only a short time after he learned that nothing he could do would bring Andrew Carmichael to justice. He sat down alone inside a small tent pitched in an isolated arroyo outside Manitou Springs, Colorado. There he picked up his Police Special and fired a .380 Magnum round through his right temple. His body was found days later by hikers.

With that news, Shelby felt as if his heart dropped to the floor. This was the sort of emotion he had sensed might explode out of this wooden chest and which he had been trying to avoid in the first place. It left him cursed with knowledge that raised questions even stickier than he had feared.

Because he had to wonder what triggered Wade Preston's final despair. Did it have something to do with the Carmichael case? And what ever happened to Carmichael himself? How did he manage to just walk off the planet? From the looks of it, nobody ever tracked him down.

Most likely dead by now, he thought. *And so there ought to be records somewhere.*

He stood up and stretched his back before making his way downstairs to tell Carla about the new case he had just assigned himself. She'd been running his office throughout the years of their partnership together and she knew all about his way of working. He trusted her to recognize this as a mystery he couldn't walk away from. He grinned at that and thought, *serves her right for sending me up there.*

Shelby's compulsive nature made him a natural private investigator, and as of that moment, the late Andrew Carmichael had just gained his very own stalker. Of course all that only mattered if there was any way Carmichael was still alive out there somewhere.

34

Scorpion John

In slot number nineteen at the High Noon Trailer Park in South Phoenix, out in a tiny isolated patch off of West Carver Road, seventy-
two year-old Scorpion John sorted through the junk inventory filling
the yard out behind his doublewide. He knew every piece in stock
by heart, but the solitary work helped him remain calm when the old
anxieties hit.

It was growing so much harder, with the long passage of time, to
wait out the kids when they were out on the road working the suckers.
He had only had them around these past two years, but they were
already indispensible. Of course the boy was in his thirties now and
the girl right behind him, maybe late twenties if he recalled right, so it
wasn't as if they needed babysitting. Still, they were his children and
they had made it a point to look him up after everything and all. And
so naturally anytime he had them out on a work detail he couldn't help
but feel antsy until they got back with the stuff.

Anxiety churned away behind his expectation of a the kids and
the bonanza they would bring. The small part of him that knew and
acknowledged the wrongness of what he was doing to them sounded
like the insistent jingle of a silver bell hung above the entryway, a
cheerful warning but a warning nonetheless. Unseen fears swarmed
like a band of shoplifters and made off with his sense of ease. They
reminded him at the gut level that the gambler in him already knew he

had asked too much of chance and leaned on his little piece of good luck for too long.

He had set up shop in a sweet spot and made the mistake of doing it as if sweet spots weren't prone to move around, when he knew better. When the sweet spot inevitably moved along, he was left behind. He had been on the long end of a twisting downward spiral when the surprise goodness arrived in the form of a late-life gift: two kids showing up friendly and eager, apparently willing to forget all about being abandoned as children and left to a life of poverty and abuse with their alcoholic mother. He knew this was a whole lot more than anything he had earned from them.

The old con knew without having to give it a thought; even if they could avoid resenting him for leaving them with nothing (although he reminded himself that it was a long time ago, after all), there was always the question of how much he could reveal to them about the rest of his life since then. The only way to know where to draw the line was to slowly push forward. So he took them in and they acted like they had always been family and he began to reveal himself to them slow and steady, like an inmate digging out with a spoon.

The bubble had not broken yet. That fact alone had come to impart a sense of providence on his side. Two years down the road and the miracle long shot of having two devoted young adult kids somehow continued.

Still. Old Scorpion John could never shake the uneasy feeling that the kids might keep his truck and make off with the goods. In the back of his mind he didn't believe it possible that they weren't full of resentment over his abandonment. He had heard plenty of men talk about karma in the joint, but he generally took it as pleasant bullshit for imitation smart guys to run their mouths about stinking karma like it meant they knew something special. Like you meet guys inside there who are all that damn smart, anyway. Geniuses in striped jumpsuits.

But the kids had been so small when he left, it had to have affected them. Especially Debra, painfully named after her slut mother by her slut mother, and Derrick, named by Andy after an oil derrick for the obvious.

It was true that sometimes he felt the urge to sneer at both of them, knock the girl to the floor and do her like a pig and pipe the boy upside his head until he gave in and tossed him a salad. But he recognized that as his old inside-the-joint thinking and he was usually successful at leaving that sort of thing behind. Such attitudes were mostly behind him.

He didn't want to rock this particular boat. Having minions was good. Perhaps too good to be true, not the sort of thing that tended to work out for him as a rule. He knew this about himself. Inside or outside the joint, having a minion was like holding a snake by the tail. The snake is always close enough to hurt you. Try to get away and it can whip-run in a sideways tornado and be on you in a heartbeat, fangs to femur.

It was not his strong suit to tolerate things he couldn't control. It came from being in the joint, of course. A man gets good at life behind bars to find himself bad at life outside. As if there is some cosmic rule that says you can only have one or the other. The experience of having his kids hunt him down and yet not show him hatred for abandoning them to their crazy mother, why, that was something. It opened him up inside. It was a pleasure he had never expected to enjoy in his old age, to have the opportunity to spread his knowledge about certain things to a couple of born crooks like those two. Within days of their arrival he had both of them fully wired up and under his control. As minions they gave his aging arms a nice long reach out into the world. *Puts pepper in your pecker,* he would have told the boys in the pool hall if he still went down there.

It was best for them to come back alive, but he had no skill at fretting over a distant loved one, whether or not he was willing to shoot them in a card game. Now that his failing kidneys kept him tied to regular dialysis visits at the local free clinic, all he could do was trust that the careful lessons he had impressed upon them would guide them in scoring well and avoiding capture.

Still he could never rest easy until they got back with plenty of pur-loined goodies and cash. The junk business served as a good cover to launder stolen money. The road work was necessary and involved the risky acquisition phase, and also the fun part because of those same risks. But that was a younger man's game.

Andy had done his time. If there was an arrest and conviction in the cards for his well-trained travelers, then so be it. Let them take the next round of years lost to the midnight screaming and the clang-ing steel doors. He hoped to spend the rest of his nights drifting off to sleep in the silence of a trailer park backed up to the desert hills. He needed more than anything else to spend his days as Scorpion John and never go near the name of Andrew James Carmichael. That was his in-the-joint name. The name of a lowly convict. His slave name.

Scorpion John was going to sting the customer every time, but he never stung hard enough to cause anyone to get seriously interested in who he was. He could smell that kind of suspicion a mile away, and if life in the desert had taught him anything at all, it was that all kinds of things could be hidden out there, actions taken, objects buried. The secret was to be careful about every little step. To be deceitful above all things. In these days of unexpected bounty, life in the old doublewide was just as pleasant and tolerable as a man might expect it to be, with his health fail-ing him and his strength draining like water through a sieve.

What the perfumed touch of an expensive weekend hooker had once brought to his senses, he now obtained from and was equally gratified by the nightly silence outside his windows. Sometimes there were even crickets. The thing about the desert was the silence.

The thing about prison was the noise. His first encounter with prison bowled him over him with an avalanche of sound that put the fear of death into him. Upon his initial arrival, a fog of noise rolled out of a cell block packed with anti-social males. The open-tiered cage boasted the acoustical properties of steel and stone, so that the effect of the noise blast gave a powerful message: *your life just took a nose-dive.*

Nothing got better after dark. It was then when most of the foul things occurred, the kind best obscured in darkness. He would have laughed, that first night – if he had been someplace where a laugh couldn't get him killed – at the span between myth and reality.

In the myth, popular prison movies showed prison inmates going to sleep after lights out. Some guy down on the end of the tier has a harmonica. He plays "Shenandoah" slow and sweet while everybody slips off to dreamland. Maybe a little nookie gets stolen in the shadows by two passionate fellows who waited all day for lights out. But other than that, everybody needs their rest. A guard strolls by and dangles the end of his nightstick against the bars, annoying but still quickly over, and that's about it for the night in movie prison.

In reality, trapped in the bowels of the actual place, it soon became apparent every space was inhabited by the same dense fabric of noise, night and day. It hammered at his ears from that first moment, long before he learned how to separate out the thousand sources. Some of it was merely chaos, but in the midst of it there also emerged a language familiar at the instinctive level. The language was unique to large jails and old prisons, and sounded out in screams.

Newbies who wanted to stay alive quickly learned that the most important screams were the ones with the darkest causes. They told savvy listeners about lethal places to be avoided and terrible things to ignore.

It took longer to learn the full language of the screams: The soprano scream of a rape victim suffering a sudden sneak attack; the muffled scream of a man coming out of a nightmare; the scream of indignation from a man who has just caught another man messing with his bitch; the scream of a guard who has backed too close to the cell bars; the screams of a man having a psychotic break; and those very special, useless screams for mercy from a victim being dragged to a "black area" where a hole in surveillance will allow his attackers to maim him at their leisure.

This form of sonic torture was also paired with the reverberating clang of metal doors up and down the rows. The omnipresent noise was a sharp stick constantly jabbing at the ears. Enter crazy, exit crazier. Every scrap of inner peace left to him when he first walked into that place got scrubbed away by the unceasing noise.

More than anything else, it was the memory of it that kept Andy out of there in the days since his departure. It spurred him to stay on top of his game, to remain willing to commit any act his aging frame would allow, if only to remain free of the clanging doors and screams that must be ignored. For this reason it was easier to hold the kids in secret contempt for trusting a man on the make like him, as opposed to feeling the weight of his crimes against them.

It would be a lot less painful if they got nabbed and had to be the ones to do time instead of him. As young newbies, they would both have that natural coating of insulation around their sanity such as most people started out with in the joint

He wondered whether he ought to generate an argument with them so he could lose his temper and see how much whipping they would take. But he immediately recognized that thought as part of his inside-the-joint thinking and reminded himself he was off of such things these days.

Scorpion John experienced a little squirt of joy in spite of himself when he heard his truck engine rev two times with the clutch engaged. Derrick, then. Down shifting and grinding the gears in that special way his dumb ass always did when he made the turn into the driveway.

He glanced out the front window, hanging back in the shadows. There was the boy at the wheel and the girl in the other bucket seat. Both alive and well, obviously no cop troubles on this trip.

And there would be loot. They knew better than to come back without it. They would at least have the basic goals set out in his plan, but more if they wanted to see daddy happy. He hadn't felt this good since he was a kid making his first break from that road crew and taking his hard-earned Golden Walk.

35

"Slow Justice, Made By Hand"

It was three a.m. when the attic light flicked on. Shelby Preston padded up the stairs in his bathrobe and stocking feet, holding onto a glass of milk he had already forgotten. He had enough self awareness to realize he had activated his slightly compulsive side with the thought of merely checking to be certain all the papers were properly stacked in the trunk. He knew how flimsy the excuse sounded and was glad he didn't have to use it on Carla. But he headed off his guilt with the thought of the self-evident value of neatness and efficiency.

He also accepted the fact that he now stood with the trunk lid wide open, feeling its flaky wood in his fingers. He stared down at the yellowing stacks of newspaper articles, carefully replaced just as they were first discovered. It struck him that he ought to have known everything would be in position as long as he was the last one to handle the contents.

He sorted out the few articles that concerned the suicide, small pieces written in the stilted language of society's discomfort with the topic. By this point he knew his reason for returning was a ruse and that he couldn't wait to begin compiling answers to his uncle's story. It had been kept uncomfortably in the background for many years, but as he stood looking down into the open truck Shelby knew priority had shifted to the task of getting some answers.

All his life, people had commented on his tendency to get stuck on some fascination or other and work it on a full time basis. He either chewed the information out of it or got distracted by something even more interesting. Shelby didn't see himself as overly compulsive; he figured if the people who refused to practice neatness had their way, the entire world would look like a landfill.

Life before his switch into private investigations had been a long list of meandering career paths that all felt like they were designed for somebody else. Until his compulsive side met the needs of private investigation techniques he had never felt he was completely himself.

This made his career change to licensed private investigator the best move of his life. The profession called for insights, information, and stories he only had available because of his meandering career path. It struck him that his present line of work offered the possibility of discovering the true reason for Wade Preston's untimely death.

The recollection of his father's shame over the suicide still stung him. Ditto the question of what could have thrown a self-reliant lawman into such a state of personal despair. The notion hit him that if he could find mediating circumstances of some kind, perhaps everyone's own memory of the stigma would be released. The thought went through him unchallenged. He didn't stop to ask who else was left to feel any stigma besides himself.

What if his uncle's actions were understandable, at least on some level? What if sense could be made of his final choice?

Shelby didn't know why the impulse took control of him. He never knew why. It just did, the way strings animate a puppet. Under its power, he snatched up the lower third of the pile where the few articles on Wade Preston's suicide were gathered. After culling them from the rest of the batch, he tucked the others right back into place and the rest was a matter of procedure.

First thing to do was soak every fact from those old publications, then use the names and dates to begin an online search for Andrew Carmichael, or any living relative. The articles didn't take much work, they were short and there were few.

The breakdown was that everybody at the time appeared to assume that Wade Preston simply fell into such despair over his inability to get the case opened up that he gave up on life. From Shelby's vantage point half a century later, not only did the explanation fail to hold water, it looked like a clear case of manufactured opinion. The articles revealed little more than that the reporters and editors of the pieces unanimously bought into the idea of the suicide as an obvious result of his failed struggle to reopen the old case.

The articles made is plain that the worst explosion of outrage for his uncle was the second time Andrew Carmichael walked off of a work detail. Wade Preston's interview comments decried the fact that he was even on a work detail at all, the second time. This was a man nearly hung for multiple first-degree murders, bargained down to lesser charges, then apparently forgotten inside the prison system and allowed to insinuate himself into a position of potential escape.

There was mention of an internal investigation by the state into rumors of there being established avenues of escape from the state prison, something called "Golden Walks." If anything more came of the investigation into the matter, it was somehow kept out of the press.

He was struck by the long distance between those times and the present. Back then it was still possible to effectively silence public knowledge of important things by closing off the small throat of the day's media. Shelby's experience assured him those journalists had only been people doing their jobs and this was only one small story in their working lives. But the bits and pieces left him with a strong sense that something vital was missing. The picture of Uncle Wade shooting himself because he was frustrated by legal bureaucracy might play well to strangers but to him it was badly out of balance.

He still had clear memories of his father and his uncle as strong and self-reliant men. He could imagine Uncle Wade being obsessed with the project, but the notion that suicidal despair just because he couldn't put an escapee back in prison was too much of a stretch. Even though he remembered Uncle Wade through the lens of a boy's perception, the aura of strength around him was strong.

Downstairs, following his excited summary of the information in the attic trunk, Carla sighed. "Tell me I didn't just nudge you into another one of your causes when I sent you up to the attic. I was trying to get things done, not start up a campaign."

"Come on, Carla, don't say that. This isn't a 'cause,' it's a discovery! Uncle Wade's memory was all but flushed out of the family. My dad's sense of shame about it colored the rest of his life."

"Exactly. And I realize with your parents gone and no direct family left, there's a—" she shook her head and switched directions. "Are you attaching more importance to this than there is?"

Shelby smiled. If she was asking questions and not making demands, that was a signal she might be persuaded. "I don't have any way of knowing if it's important or not until I get into it, but it's an adventure. Not for a client this time, this one would be for me."

"Mm. How much time we looking at?"

"A week. In a week, I can nose around enough to know if there's anything there."

"So you're telling me I need to book out your whole schedule for that week? You have four outstanding cases."

"Right, but they're all at a point where they need time for their principals to make a move. They can wait, Carla."

"Because I'm the one answering the phones and listening to people's paranoia if they think you could be moving faster on their case."

"People always think you could move faster on their case. We live in a culture of self-entitled whiners... Not that they don't have genuine concerns... Which of course they do, whiney or not... You talk now."

Carla sighed. Fourteen years of marriage gave her enough insight into her husband's processes to know he was already glued to this one. There was a certain look that came over his face when it happened. She caught it as easily as she once noticed changes in her sleeping daughter's breathing.

Early in their partnership, before they ventured into marriage, she would have resisted him on something like this. Time and experience had taught her that as frustrating as his bulldog stubbornness was, it was part of the reason they had a success in their business together. The harder his interest was glued to a mystery, the faster he tended to chew it down to the facts.

To Carla it really was like making sure one's dog had plenty of chew time on a good sized bone. Not that she thought of personal time as a bone, but rather that men just hunt better when you treat them like that. One of Carla's daily coping tools was the viewpoint that the quickest way to get her man off of a fixation was to let him play it out.

"Okay, if I book you out for a week with your clients and hold off on intakes, are you promising that's it? Don't put me in that position where I have to stall them a second time. That's when they go paranoid and show up here. Spew all over the office."

"I don't want to do that."

"You don't see it, though. I'm the one at the office."

"Okay, you're right. You are. I don't want you taking crap from jerk clients."

"More than usual."

"Well yeah."

"So a week?"

"One week."

It was a dance they had more or less perfected over time, but for the occasional misreading of some subtle clue. The dance gave them each room to step forward, with graceful built-in twirls that transferred the lead from one to another. Then the came the moment to step back. They moved together in directions neither quite intended but somehow suited them both.

■ ■ ■

The hours melted in Shelby's little home office. It was where he did most of his real work, since the storefront office with the shingle over the door was a prop, as far as he was concerned. It paid to keep up a bricks and mortar presence, but he would have gotten nothing done there with distractions swarming him.

In the quiet of his actual working place he slipped into a bubble of concentration. Time was measured only in terms of research goals, one small task after another.

With all the nationally linked crime databases available for searching, finding out whatever became of Andrew James Carmichael wouldn't take any fancy methods or illegal software. Somewhere on the public record, he had to have left a trace while he was alive.

Shelby had long since purchased mass-research software and adapted its programming to his own people-search routines. On his first full session of working the question, he ran searches and collated the results from people-search engines, social media searches, job applicant web site comments, prison/police record search, federal investigation search, and then...

An amateurish little site for wives of prison inmates, all genders welcomed, offered branches of comment lines that were wide open for public reading. It continually amazed Shelby to see the things people would post in an open forum, shielded by nothing more than a screen name.

"My father killed people in the US and Canada and served fourteen years, then ran off. They never caught him. How is that our fault? Does that mean we can't have his insurance if he left it to us? D."

Bingo. Hits on five qualifiers by a sweet little routine that recognized the connections between those first four hits and the correlation to that last whiny sentence. Shelby's modification to the search program included a scanner for statements of victimhood, on the theory that crooks were all either victims of terrible abuse or at least perceived themselves to be. Except for the professionals who build and maintain the criminal justice system, who else but a crook had the time to learn all its ins and outs and then figure out how to game it? The people who love them, that's who.

Even the smartest crooks will leave tiny footprints in spite of all their cleverness and persistence if you bring the right viewing glass to the game. The resulting pattern explained itself.

Shelby's focus deepened. The internal territory became familiar. With his custom program's five distinct hits on that one website comment, he already felt certain whoever posted this was a relative of Andrew Carmichael. The odds of coincidence were too small to figure.

If a child of Carmichael's was trolling for funds resulting from the father's insurance, then somewhere out there on the public record that person was likely to have used his or her real name, and not just an internet handle, tied to the facts of this case.

Half an hour later, there it was; a minor arrest report nearly three years earlier on an uncharged incident in Tucson, Arizona. One Derrick Carmichael, then twenty-six, and his younger sister Debra, then nineteen, were detained and later released when police accepted Derrick's explanation for striking his neighbor to the ground as a natural rage reaction because the neighbor was taunting Derrick, claiming he and Debra were living together as lovers.

While both subjects admitted to being roommates, they insisted it was a legitimate situation, and a natural one after having been abandoned together by their father Andrew J. Carmichael when they were small children. Shelby winced; this Carmichael fellow seemed to have the devil's luck. Because the officer noted that Derrick claimed his father was an absconded convict who had been on the run when he sired both children, and yet nothing was said in the police report about any sort of follow up regarding his location. Shelby could only shake his head. Unbelievable.

Both claimed that they were still children when their mother was imprisoned on a scam gone bad. Derrick took control of his sister Debra, six years his junior, and if Shelby read between the lines a bit, it seemed that the pair slipped through the county system and nobody did much to find them.

Bingo! thought Shelby. Two kids, then: Derrick and Debra. Derrick Carmichael, now late twenties, and sister Debra, early twenties. Most likely still together. A few more search runs indicated they had not turned up dead anywhere, but somehow they appeared to live off the public record.

No matter, now. Their address was changed just a few months after that police report to a mail-drop place offering customers an address that sounds like an actual place. There was no record of any business registered through there, nothing on any searchable database connected to it.

Fair enough, brother and sister citizens. Nothing wrong with underground communication by old school postal means. All depending on the messages themselves of course, but hey, we are who we are. As for that address, the was no apparent physical need for the user or users to have it. Nothing in the searchable records tied to that address, no official communications of any sort. It fit the profile of a drop box for things secret and/or illegal.

The odd part was that the box wasn't in Tucson, it was in Phoenix. Why Phoenix? He wondered. Was one tactless neighbor's taunting enough to drive them away? That didn't sound right. Both were defiant in the incident. Neither one went to Phoenix to take an on-the-books job, or there would be employment records, tax records, insurance records, perhaps licensing records. Oddly enough, neither had a driver's license. At least, not in the Carmichael name. Was somebody helping them operate on the down low?

Shelby realized he had reached a point where computer skills weren't going to take him any farther. The next steps had to be done in person. And if by some chance he was on a wrong lead, then he needed to find out as soon as possible to minimize wasted time. After all, he only had the one week, and this was Day One.

That put the starting question in stark relief: once he located the two younger Carmichaels, how could he approach them? He certainly couldn't risk blundering into their lives with a random phone call. Likewise, he couldn't sub out the job to another investigator, somebody local down there. If he did, there would be no way to control the methods used.

No, this job called for personal observation under disguise. He felt glad when his thoughts arrived at that point. Suddenly he felt hungry for action. It would feel good to leave the electronic world and hit the street.

36

"Sunny Sin City"

Some people are born with a perfect ear for music. Shelby wasn't, but he had a skill that was sometimes just as good. Shelby Preston could sleep on a plane the way a man sleeps on a plane when he gets paid to sleep on planes. Even in turbulence, he snoozed, through the crying of babies, he slumbered, through the shuffle and shove of passenger altercations, he stopped short of snoring but otherwise slept like the dead. If a flight attendant gently touched him, seeking to determine whether he was out cold, Shelby opened his eyes, spoke with that person in pleasant terms, then politely dismissed him or her and closed his eyes again, only to fall right back to sleep. Seasoned travelers gritted their teeth in envy.

On this trip it turned out to be an especially vital skill, after a night of sleep lost to preparing for the last-minute trip and in making it to the airport for the pre-dawn flight. Carla wanted to drive him, but he felt guilty enough about running off on this personal snipe-hunt to insist she stay home and sleep while he made his way to the airport by cab.

His promise to her that he would only take a week away from work was made to a woman without whom he could never have made a go of his investigative business. It was her organizational skill and her head for business that allowed him to indulge his talents for research and examination. She would use her skills to move things around and carve out that time for him without allowing things to fall apart, all to buy him his one week window, and only because he told her it was personally important to him to go. He had to stay inside that one week period.

He awakened when the plane bumped to a landing, feeling rested and only slightly troubled over not having time for a quick shower. It wouldn't matter to anyone but him; the disguise in his briefcase was toned down several notches below his level of attire. It boasted an expensive but convincing wig of matted hair and a carefully pre-aged set of grungy clothing, ratty shoes, and fingerless gloves that appeared to be so filthy, anyone would think twice before wanting to touch him.

The disguise had worked several times in the past. It would render him close to invisible. All he had to do was avoid attracting trouble over loitering while simultaneously looking as if he would panhandle anybody who made eye contact with him.

Part of the reason he loved his work kicked in; he noticed his heartbeat rising. He loved the anxious thrill of making an invisible cruise through a subject's home territory, the incognito drive-by.

He grinned more or less to himself and did not say out loud but only muttered, "Adrenalin. Breakfast of champions." He couldn't avoid a single snort of a laugh at that one. Then he breezed on out of the terminal towing his travel bag with one hand and gripping the briefcase with the other.

Routine screw-ups of his auto rental reservation did not tie him up in frustration because he felt no grogginess following his excellent nap on the flight and he had no inclination to be contrary with anybody.

The car's GPS took him out of the airport without confusion after it reset itself twice just before crucial turns, announcing it was "recalculating" as if that was a big accomplishment and going into "lost signal" mode when he passed behind a large parking structure. Eventually he followed its guidance to the southbound I-10 and headed for what it told him was South Phoenix, just before it dropped its signal again.

He reset the destination and trusted the device to get it right now that they were away from the parking garage's satellite interference. Beamed up again, he made his way toward the little storefront mail drop with its image already clear in his mind from their website photo.

He wasn't eager to burn his limited supply of personal time in a cold-butt stakeout, but the mail drop was a logical place to start. The day was still young; it wasn't even noon yet. He needed to check the place out, at least. Watch the foot traffic for subjects Derrick and/ or Debra Carmichael-slash-whatever last name they preferred. Sniff around.

■ ■ ■

Scorpion John hit the mini-mall's private mail drop at around lunch time, and as usual he had all his feelers out, standard deployment style. It was a matter of long standing practice for him these days, something he rarely gave a conscious thought. Decades as an absconded convict had imprinted certain vital driving habits. *Check all rear mirrors from the moment you leave to get the mail, don't stop there until you're sure no one has followed, then get in, collect the mail, and get out. Don't make conversation. If someone speaks, answer politely, act like you're in a hurry, and rush off.*

He hadn't stayed out of prison for so many years by being careless. All his mail went there. No home address on anything but the physical utilities, and those bills were in the name of the fake identity on his driver's license, one Jonathan William Havers.

Twenty years earlier, during a down time when he was destitute and every penny counted, he had put together ten thousand dollars in carefully resold stolen items to raise the cash for a new identity. He believed it to be the salient reason he was still a free man, courtesy of an ersatz namesake who died as an infant and offered him his second life as Scorpion John W. Havers, the *King Of Roadside Doublewide Resale Shops*.

It was a hot early afternoon, with the dry air working its way up to the hundred degree mark, but he loved the heat. It baked the stiffness from his bones and tended to keep people indoors, with their blinds closed against the glare.

Fewer people on the street equaled fewer potential witnesses to see something amiss, get curious, maybe make a few calls. He avoided moving around too much because it increased his exposure to random people, any one of whom just might know a thing or two that could come back to bite him if he let it.

But against the backdrop of his doublewide and the miscellaneous junk items piled around the property, he was firmly established as Scorpion John. People didn't even look at him there, really. They only saw the clown he played for them. He could tell that people saw him as a piece of the whole picture about that place, with the junk car parts and the broken appliances and used electronics, Mr. Junk Man, grizzled old desert rat who spent his days selling crap from his air-conditioned trailer and who passed the cool evenings wandering the landscape to troll for more inventory.

Never mind that a one-man junkyard was hard to beat as a place to launder cash and get rid of stolen bounty. It did far more than merely support him, it gave him an identity to play off on the rest of the world, even to cops. He had half a dozen city cops, county deputies, and highway patrol officers as regular customers, and it warmed his heart beyond measure to know that they laundered the cash from their graft activities by spending it in places like his because he only dealt in cash and he kept very poor records.

With his invaluable help, buyers could spend untraceable cash for untraceable items and never run a penny of it through a bank account. Scorpion John also made it a point to offer a wide range of smaller items that he stored inside the doublewide and sold on the sly to no one but the most familiar customers – the ones who knew to come around to his back door and use the shave-and-a-haircut knock.

Now that he had the kids as gofers, things were much more like they were in the old days, while he was still strong and in peak condition, right after his second and final escape. It hadn't taken him long at all to befriend the doublewide's owner, get him to forge a new will, kill the older man while he slept, and take over the place in the role of his cousin and only family. The desert swallows up bodies like a snake digesting a mouse.

Those were the glory days, hiding in the open, prowling for theft opportunities and selling the goods, sex anytime it advanced his concerns of the moment. Most everyone he came across during those years was physically weaker and slower than he was, certainly less skilled at the savagery of street fighting. To move around the city was to stroll through a cascade of instances where he could amuse himself by silently speculating who among them it would be the most fun to kill.

Discipline forged behind steel bars and a bone-deep terror of returning to prison stayed his hand from the serial violence that might have compelled him if life only granted him the chance to fully express himself. Back then, each and every day was marked by a healthy physical feeling and a sense of possibility, in terms of how he might choose to fill the day.

The initial discovery of the old doublewide's owner had been a fine payoff for his careful reconnaissance work, weeks spent intentionally starting random conversations with frail-looking people until he got one to admit he was alone in the world. With that bit of information received, then from that moment on the old guy's doublewide was already his property.

That was a long time ago. Nowadays he got occasional tweaks of pain over the thought that he had since grown older than the man he murdered for the property. It might not haunt him at all if old age was a tormented time for him, but he still felt good enough in spite of the kidney difficulties and the dialysis that he wasn't ready to give up the ghost. That caused him to wonder if maybe the old guy hadn't been ready to go, either.

However, during his second life as Scorpion John he had watched enough oldsters wander into his yard to know many of them lived in physical pain. It helped him to remember the old owner as a guy who was on his last legs, practically begging for it to end. On that basis, he was a Good Samaritan and the property was little more than a fair payoff for services rendered.

Inside the mail drop, he went through the quick routine of opening his box and retrieving the few pieces of mail. He got back out the door by keeping his face down as if he was reading while he walked along. A guy in a hurry. Everybody understood a guy in a hurry. It wasn't bullet-proof but it usually deflected dumb questions and random conversation.

The mail drop was a necessary exposure, since the best way to receive all bills was in paper form, even when the providers clearly wanted to do business online. He got past that one with each company by employing the ageism of the youth society against them; he claimed to be unable to understand the internet. People loved to condescend to him and to find his ignorance cute. They bought the story because it gave them a little rush of feeling how much younger and smarter they were. In the expert thievery of his heart, Scorpion John figured no matter how much people might look down on an old ex-con like him, plenty of them would steal or even kill to be younger and smarter, themselves. Thus he maneuvered them to aid in constructing the paper wall surrounding him by offering them nothing more than a whiff of their own extended youth in return, hiding from them behind the role of a dumb old guy who just can't fathom modern technology.

Outside, on the streets, he was like an actor who wanted to avoid being recognized while he was out in public. It took too much effort to constantly be presentable, agreeable enough to pass as a local small businessman. He was best viewed against the backdrop of his colorful junk yard full of reclaimed items. Then if his eyes got a little crazy, it was only a bit of added color. Might even boost sales in some cases, with the ones who noticed it perhaps fearing they somehow caused it and therefore buying a few more things, just to make nice.

He walked quickly without looking so rushed as to attract attention. As a standard deflection procedure, he sorted the utility bills over and over while he moved along, using the action to keep his eyes down while he made his way back to his truck. He didn't notice another man getting close to him until he felt the presence just behind his right shoulder.

Just as he began to turn toward him, the man spoke, "Scorpion John, right? Great to see you, I'm just on my way to your place. For the, ah, pottery and stuff."

As Scorpion John, he automatically smiled his over-the-counter expression while he kept on walking and replied, "Right-right. Howdy. Yep, back in a flash. Doing the mail, here. I'll be out there all afternoon. See you there."

He forced himself to lock eyes with the guy for an instant, brightened his smile just a tad and threw in a quick wave. It was his best combination. Shut them down but leave them happy. He kept on walking and was glad when the other guy took the hint and dropped it.

As a matter of long habit, he filed away the obvious wig on the man and the fact that his clothing was too consistently soiled to be believable. Some guy in hiding over something. Maybe another runner? *Via con Dios,* pal. It isn't the Scorpion's problem.

Give it another ten minutes, he thought, then once they were back at his place, sure, let's all sit and talk, stand and walk, shoot the breeze, maybe even do some business. Hey, all welcome. Bring the kids.

Nevertheless, as a routine caution he stopped at a rare working public phone and called his own place. When Derrick answered he told him to put his sister behind the counter and move himself into the background. It made the place seem friendlier and helped keep people from getting on guard.

He assured Derrick that he would be back there in five minutes to explain. In the meantime, he felt certain both of the kids could be counted on to do this much, anyway. He didn't know why, but instinct told him it was true.

That thought made him smile throughout the short drive back home. He arrived ready to open the shop back up and maybe do some business, feeling at ease over having made another excursion without trouble. The deep breathing of his relaxed state lightened his head and caused his cheeks to feel flushed, as if he had just completed a healthy jog somewhere nice.

37

A Harmless Old Man

Shelby Preston's scalp itched something fierce under the wig, but it was worth the discomfort to get the effect of transforming his short, sandy hair to the greasy black strands of a born jailbird. The look fit this location like the right key for the lock.

He regretted not removing his clothing before slipping the grimy costume over them. Heat somehow intensified in that little junk yard, as if the tall piles of goods stifled the breeze. He kept up the pretense of shopping around among surprisingly good pieces of random stuff while he waited for the old guy to notice he was there. The sign at the gate proclaimed "Junk Items! Scavenged Items! Recycled Items!" but a lot of it looked pretty new to him. He wondered how much the owner had to pay the local constable to avoid questions.

There was a young woman out in the yard, moving stock items around and eyeing him on the sly. She wasn't too bad at her surreptitious observation but Shelby would have trained her better. The large slightly older fellow who watched him from behind a couple of scavenged junk cars seemed to think he was hidden from sight. Either that or he was less eager than the female to disguise his actions, maybe secretly spoiling for a fight. He looked tough enough to handle himself. If these two were Derrick and Debra, the fact that he found them could prove to be a mixed blessing.

He could have hurried things along by knocking on the door of the mobile home-cum-junk shop, but after the lucky break of spotting the old guy at the mail drop, he didn't want to appear too eager. This "Scorpion John Havers" as the property papers listed him, was the right age to be Andy Carmichael himself. He didn't want to do anything to tip him off.

The sun continued to beat down and the wig and costume became items of torment. He debated approaching either the female or the large male, but he had already spoken to his suspect and saw no reason to complicate things by bringing in the kids, especially the tough-looking guy. He was about to give in and approach the front door to get things moving along when he heard a voice call out behind him.

"Hey there! You was out at the mail drop, right?"

He turned and saw the same old guy framed in the doorway, affable enough now that he was on his home turf. The guy smiled like a salesman ready to move some inventory.

"Hey, hi. Mr. Havers. So I came on out after running into you. Reminded me I need a few things for my yard."

"Yeah!" the old guy nodded. "That your mail drop too?" The question sounded innocent enough.

"Ah, no. Not yet. I'm thinking about getting my mail there, but I want to make sure it's the closest one to my place."

"Oh? Whereabouts you live?" The question fit the conversation, but Shelby felt a flash of insecurity as he realized he hadn't prepared his cover story. There was nothing to do but improvise. "Center of town, pretty much."

"Well this is the south side. There're definitely more places closer to you."

"Right, right. But I like to come down south here a lot."

"What for?"

"...Desert hiking."

The old guy grinned at that. "What, on purpose?"

"Sure. Great exercise."

The old guy laughed out loud and stepped down into the yard and sidled on over toward Shelby. "You health nuts! I met a guy once who slammed his fist into an iron plate ten times a day, every day, just to build up his hand for karate! So I asked him if he ever considered just buying a gun, ha-ha-ha! So what can I interest you in, here?"

"Oh, mostly the pottery. I manage a little apartment building and we need some stuff for the front yard. So you're Scorpion John."

"Yeah you already recognized me back there."

"Right, right. Just making conversation."

"Plenty to talk about with the stuff here in front of you," the old guy grinned. It was not a friendly expression.

Shelby felt a nasty rush of adrenalin. Scorpion John Havers was one suspicious bastard; somehow the man already had his antennae out for trouble. Shelby couldn't imagine how he'd given himself away so soon. He dismissed it as the old guy's general level of paranoia, but he once again resisted scratching his head fearing his whole hairline might move with it.

The owner inched close enough to throw a punch. "Maybe you want to use a few of these oversized pots? People like to plant them with cactus." He patted one of the large terra cotta pieces with his right hand, drawing Shelby's eyes to his ring finger.

The ring bore the Masonic emblem. *Son of a bitch!* The thought hit him so hard he struggled to keep his face calm. If it wasn't exactly proof of Carmichael's identity, it was a major clue.

The ring gave an impression oddly out of context with the owner. It was not impossible for "Scorpion John" to be a Freemason, but Shelby had never met one who needed to resort to palming off what appeared to be stolen second-hand items just to scratch out a living. From everything he knew about the Masonic Orders, if members were discovered to be involved in crime at all, it would most likely prove to involve large banks, major architectural projects, and massive amounts of money – not purloined yard ornaments.

Carmichael liked to pose as a mason, back in the day. Had a real fascination with them. Suddenly Shelby's senses began to overwhelm him while it struck him that he had most likely just confirmed Andrew Carmichael to be alive and well, after more than forty years. Not only that, but the man was living right out in the open with grown children, and they appeared to have seen fit to reunite with him in spite of the fact that he abandoned them as children.

Shelby had never seen a stakeout that produced so much payoff with this kind of speed. It felt like holding onto the door of a taxi that was already accelerating down the street. So all right then, jump right in. At least he wouldn't have to wear the costume again after that. Once confirmation was reached, there was nothing left to do but bug on out of there, hit the showers, and call in the *gendarmerie* from a reasonable distance.

"Okay, well I see some good stuff here, so let me look around a few minutes and I'll let you know what I'm interested in." Shelby tried to smile like a tired working man who manages a lousy apartment building in a desert community where nobody gets paid real money.

His act seemed to satisfy Scorpion John, who made it a point to move away and give him distance. Very professional, he noticed. The guy had been doing this for awhile.

Shelby did his best to appear to be inspecting things, bending down for close-up views of smaller items. He stalled for time to recover from the surprise. If he was correct, then he was standing a few yards from a man who scammed the system for an easy sentence after multiple murders, then frustrated his uncle's efforts to find him and bring him to justice for many years, possibly with a other victims since.

If the internet age had existed back then, Wade Preston would have found Andrew Carmichael forty years earlier. Shelby felt a wave of anger and grief wash through him. Andrew Carmichael murdered people for personal amusement, then disappeared on the relatively short and easy sentence placed upon him. During all of the time Wade Preston lost from his future, Carmichael had been living free and easy as a desert rat.

And all that only pertained to those things Shelby knew about a young killer from decades earlier. What sort of life would a man like that be expected to live, out on the loose with a past like his? Even back in those days, Andy Carmichael's behavior was too bizarre for him to sustain relationships. The lifestyle of desert junk dealer would suit such a man well.

After all, that personality trait was unlikely to change. Who was willing to bet on the prospect that he had put himself on the straight and narrow after escaping prison for the *second* time? Who would bet anything they ever wanted to see again that he had simply been peacefully living there in his miniature junkyard, for all those decades?

Shelby tried to imagine what sort of threads held a family like the Carmichaels together. There was nothing familiar to him in their situation. His and Carla's only daughter was such a lovely chip off her mother's block that her strong rapport remained solid with both of them, even after she went away to college. In contrast, if this man was really Andrew J. Carmichael, then he would probably be wise, for as long as the kids remained there with him, to lock his bedroom door at night and do all his own cooking.

38

Watchers Watching Watchers

FBI Confidential Informant of Known Reliability Number 5248 felt more than a little ridiculous while he walked under the scrub wood archway that bore the sign, "Scorpion John's." The video glasses issued by the Phoenix Office were out of date, clunky fake sunglasses that were so oversized they looked like goggles. He briefly wondered if an ironic stance would be best way to go, and if he shouldn't just fasten a little note to a toothpick and glue it to the middle of the frame, saying "camera lens" with a little arrow pointing right at the hole. People might decide it was a goof and let their inhibitions down anyway.

If Number 5248 wasn't so desperate to avoid a third strike on his meth cooking, he would have told them where to stuff it on this whole assignment. All he knew was the Bureau liked Scorpion John for a list of nasty things, none of which could be pinned directly onto him but nevertheless put him in the vicinity of violent crime often enough to raise questions.

Number 5248 found that part to be the most troublesome aspect of this whole assignment, because he supposed the Bureau's description of his Target Subject could just as easily fit onto him. It was bad enough to let them make him a lapdog, but at least it would have been nice to help take down somebody really bad. A real baby killer or something.

Instead, it was some old guy with a little junk business. For the great Federal Bureau of Investigation, it had come down to this, making the world safe from gnarly junk dealers.

Still, the old guy had somehow gotten marked for surveillance, and all Number 5248 knew was that you didn't have to go to prison to live your life by prison rules. Somebody could ask him whose side are you on and he would see the answer staring back from any mirror.

As it was, he could only swallow hard and stroll on into the yard and wander around among the stacks, just do it balls out. Pretend everybody wears thick sunglasses with hearing aids built into the side rails. Remember the goal of getting anything good enough to advance the investigation and get this particular Confidential Informant off the hook with the Bureau.

He saw the proprietor standing close to some grungy guy who looked more like he might be there to get rid of something rather than spend money. Number 5248 knew money by the smell and this threadbare fake Elvis or whatever he was didn't have any. But the pair appeared to be having an intense conversation, so Number 5248 fake-browsed his way over into their vicinity. The best he could do was try not to look at anyone straight on, fearing they would take one look at the old school video sunglasses and break out laughing.

He had to wonder why the FBI wouldn't have the absolute coolest stuff anybody could imagine. Federal budget cuts? Had it come to this? How else to explain using crap from third-tier retail stores? He wouldn't have been surprised to learn that the last model of their "secret spy camera" required an extension cord and a dish antenna on a helmet.

When he got close enough that he could overhear the two men, he turned on the eyeglass recorder with his pocket remote. Scorpion John seemed to have asked the customer why he was wearing a wig and a costume. Number 5248 deliberately looked away from them to avoid raising suspicion, but held still to let the microphone inside the sunglasses pick them up.

"Ah, okay, well you got me," the customer said. "I was trying out this disguise, you know, getting used to wearing it around."

"Planning on robbing a bank?"

"Ha. No. No, to tell you the truth, I've got this problem with my wife, and I'm pretty sure she's got a boyfriend, so I'm gonna hide and, you know—"

"Catch her red-handed 'cuz she'll never spot you in that wig?" Scorpion John showed a wide I'm-just-funnin'-you grin.

"Yeah. Pretty embarrassing, how you just spotted it right off like that."

"Well we see all types here. You learn to see through all kinds of things. Like I say though, don't matter who they are, it's the cash does the talking, ha-ha!"

"No, and I'm sorry if the question was too personal."

"No, I was just playin' here. You asked where I got my ring, I ask where you got your wig, get it?"

"Right, right, I'm sorry, I just noticed your ring and I've been interested in the whole Freemason experience, so I thought you might give me a pointer or two about joining."

"I'm no mason, I wear this ring to remind me."

"What about?"

"A long time ago, one of the high mucky-mucks in their organization messed up and let me find out about a secret way of signaling they've used for centuries and it still works today. But it's complicated. The ring helps me remember to run the code sequence through my memory enough to keep it in mind."

"A secret code? But you're not afraid to talk about it?"

"Why should I be?" He laughed out loud. "I talk about it all the time and nobody believes me anyway. The secret's safe with me!" He laughed again.

"This code, how does it work?"

"I only tell people this much: they use smoke."

"Smoke?"

"I'm telling you!"

"What kind of smoke are we talking about?"

"Name it! Chimneys, smokestacks, incinerator fires, field burn-off fires, camp fires, picnic fires, how many you need?"

"Wait, smoke signals? Like in western movies?"

"No. Far more complex. The height of the smoke column, the color of the smoke, the density of the smoke are highly controlled and carry whole ideas."

"So how do you know which smoke columns are messages and which ones are just smoke?"

"I tell you, when you know the smoke code, it's like somebody who's illiterate asking how you can tell real words from random marks on a page. It's that obvious. Now you mentioned these large pots?"

"The pots! Oh! Right. I'll need all four of those large ones over there. Ah, here's two hundred dollars, I know you prefer cash."

"I do not prefer cash. Cash is all I take."

"Well. There it is, so you can hold them for me, and I'm on my way back home to get the truck. Meanwhile, you're paid in full, so just hold them for me until I can come around tomorrow."

Scorpion John laughed outright at that one. "Hey, you can leave them here 'til next week!" He took the money and reflexively counted it. "*This* is the way I like to do business. Buddy, I need ten customers a day like you."

■ ■ ■

Number 5248 scurried back to his car walking as fast as he dared to go without appearing to be making a getaway. Excitement ran through him while he pulled off the goofy hidden camera sunglasses and jumped into his vehicle. Surely, he thought, this would do it for him. Surely a secret code employed by the International Masonic Order would be worth enough to the FBI to get him sprung from informant duty and let him go back to his essentially law-abiding life. Number 5248 had no doubt that as much as the Bureau loved to spy on people, access to a secret code used all over the world had to be enough to push their buttons.

39

Catch Up To The Past

Back in Seattle on the following day, Shelby played video he shot the day before. It showed the Phoenix Police responding at Scorpion John's place following his visit to their headquarters to let them know an escaped murderer had been living openly in their town for many years. He had wondered out loud to the desk sergeant how the conservative people of Arizona would take to finding out their police department let this guy slide for so long while he lived among their citizens. And that, Shelby was careful to emphasize, was only what was already known about the man. What if, Shelby asked, he turned out to have continued his criminal life at the expense of the people because law enforcement never bothered to hunt him down?

They had three cars at Scorpion John's place within the hour. The rest was documented on digital video from Shelby's smartphone. As soon as he got back home, he hooked up his phone to his desktop computer's full-screen and showed the capture to Carla, who couldn't believe their good luck in finding him and getting him captured so quickly.

"Damn!" she said with a pout. "I knew I should have gone with you. I hate to have missed this."

"You didn't miss it," Shelby grinned, "watch!"

The screen came to life as the third car was just pulling up to the trailer. All six cops moved in on the trailer's door with their shotguns and handguns drawn.

"Is that him?" Carla asked when the elder Carmichael answered the door.

"You bet. Watch this though." The audio didn't come across clearly, but they could see that Andy was told to step outside and immediately placed in cuffs while his Miranda rights were read to him. "Here's the best part!" Shelby said in excitement.

"That's his son, Derrick, with his daughter Debra standing in back of him. Here we go!"

At that moment the son charged at the officer who was walking the senior Carmichael back to the squad car. Derrick managed to get in a single roundhouse punch to the side of the officer's head, knocking him to his knees. A second later all five remaining officers swarmed him and flattened him to the ground. "I count about sixteen body punches and eight solid blows to his head for Carmichael's boy," Shelby smiled.

"Wait, what's she doing?" Carla asked when Debra came running out of the house toward the melee. Just as the officers were climbing back to their feet, she took off after them in a flying leap and took two of them to the ground with her. "Is she crazy? Oh, and look – she's getting it almost as bad as her brother."

"Yeah, but I can tell you I could hear the punches hitting her brother and there wasn't any sound from the blows to her."

"What, you think they went easy on her for being female?"

"Probably. Why not? She's smaller, anyway. I think they went easy, considering she could have broken somebody's neck."

"Wait, she's still fighting them!"

"Watch the female officer on the right side."

"What's she got, a Tazer?"

"Yep. Watch her go down."

"Owee! On the ground... are those convulsions?"

"Hard to tell. Sure took the fight out of her, though."

"Weird, she's fighting for her brother the way an abused wife fights for her wife-beater husband."

"He's been her protector since their mother disappeared."

"Disappeared or died?"

"Died, disappeared, gone."

"Okay you know I have to ask this, I mean, given the range of human behavior we've had come through those doors since we opened up shop... Oops, now the brother's acting up. Boom, he's down too. Anyway, he's her biological brother?"

"Right. Same parents, if you can call them that."

"She was young enough to be helpless. He was all she had."

"And their father was a sociopath which means he's still a sociopath, and their mother is whatever kind of person you have to be in order to abandon your son at fourteen and your daughter at seven."

"God, Shel. Oh, look – they've got both of them hog-tied, now."

"Yeah they say those plastic strips are a lot more comfortable than the steel ones, though."

"There they go, one car for each of them."

"Want to hear the funny part?"

"Hard to see humor here."

"Get this: it's strictly a coincidence that three cars showed up for the arrest. They weren't coming after his two kids."

"I get it. Up until then there wasn't anything to report."

"Nope. You had to figure they were into something dark and nasty, but that doesn't equal an arrest warrant."

"There they go," Carla narrated, "all three squad cars pulling away." The video ran out and she turned to him in amazement.

"Shel, this is the most unbelievable thing! That man was an escaped killer. Your uncle spent years trying to bring him to justice."

"Yeah. Now I'm pretty sheepish about how long it took me to get motivated to open up that trunk."

"It's like your mom knew you would investigate it someday."

"Maybe. More like now I'm so glad you bitched me into doing it."

She kissed him. "Nothing like a man who's big enough to show gratitude. Sexy as hell. It could get you laid."

He laughed and put his arms around her. "Hey if that's the case, we should go on the last leg of this thing together and make a little getaway out of it."

"Sounds good, except we own a business. There are no get-aways."

"Field work! It's how you travel guilt-free! And if in doing such field work god-forbid a little bit of getting away should happen to occur, I think there's not a court in the country that would convict us. I go back to work here instead of taking the rest of the week, and we'll push the trip ahead. Next week or the week after..."

"Any chance this thing plays out in the Caribbean?"

"No, but I heard Roundup, Montana is lovely this time of year."

"The state prison's nowhere near there. What's left to do in that little town?"

"I found this old barber in Roundup, and he knew my uncle. Cut his hair! The guy's still alive."

"Must be pretty old."

"Says he's ninety-two. Been retired for twenty-some years but he still rents out the shop to other barbers. He's willing to meet me at the shop and tell me what he remembers. I tell you, Carla, this guy is still sharp as a tack. He says if it wasn't for his eyes, he could still cut hair! It would be great if you were there too."

"Hey, when you put it that way..."

◼ ▦ ◼

Andy Carmichael paced along the solid walls of his one man cell and tried to figure out how the old Scorpion John identity managed to fail him like this. At first he thought the FBI tracked him down and used that fellow in the bad disguise to verify him, but the cops said the guy was civilian, a freelancer all the way from Seattle. Nothing made sense.

He tried to find out what happened to his kids, but nobody was telling him anything. All he got was a quick hearing to confirm his identity and an order to ship him back to Montana State Prison up in Deer Lodge.

Later that night, one of the young guys in the next cell down the row claimed he was listening to the news when he was picked up, and that old Andy was semi-famous. There was a big controversy blowing up over whether or not a man Andy's age ought to be rearrested after being free for so many years.

At first Andy wasn't sure he heard the kid right. He had to ask him to repeat it. But there it was again: no, grandpa, you're kind of a hero to some people. They think the state ought to leave you alone. That Sheriff's nephew ought to mind his own business."

"Sheriff's nephew?"

"Says his uncle was the Sheriff who arrested you and died trying to find you again. Says he tracked you down for him."

That one put Andy right down on his cot, where he could only sit and stare. The Sheriff's damned nephew? What could he possibly want after so many years?

"What you in here for, boy?"

"Fighting with my girlfriend."

"Yeah? Well, you get a message to the press for me, I'll pay five thousand dollars to your attorney."

"How does that work?"

"You send me your lawyer's name. When I get a reporter coming to interview me, I'll know you kept up your end and I'll get him the money."

"How do I know you'll pay?"

"Because you'll know right where I am, where anybody can get to me."

"... deal."

40

Camouflage Smoke, Multiple Colors

The next day, Andy realized they must have set bail for the kid early that morning and that he really needed the defense money. Messages began coming in early that afternoon from reporters attached to daily papers in the state capital and several TV and radio outlets. The Phoenix police granted him one hour with a group of them that evening before his transfer to Montana, and he used up every minute.

He emphasized that he had been living a quiet life as a law-abiding citizen and ignored questions about many unsolved property crimes in his vicinity. He managed to set fire to the Masonic issue again by teasing reporters with knowledge of the Secret Smoke Code, withholding the code key but making certain they understood the principal. He could see on their eager faces that the story was a real idiot tickler.

Internet chat room use was still in its infancy, but there was already a dedicated corps of net users who made it a point to live the lives online and try to influence public opinion or at least the opinions of the others on the comment line or at least the opinion of the commenter they were arguing with. The opening themes were mainly along political lines, with the more liberal users crying out against returning "such a frail old man to prison after so many years," while law-and-order types reminded readers that the "frail old man" was a multiple murderer who showed his victims no mercy and twice escaped prison. He was living out his old age, they cried, while his victims had died young. The attacks flew back and forth with a depth of bitterness that made it seem as if the fate of humanity hinged on the outcome of every posted comment.

As soon as Andy arrived back at State Prison he began to work at relieving his shell-shocked condition by embracing the familiar routine of incarcerated living. He set up his lines of in-house contacts using funds from the small prison bank account his *pro bono* lawyer was able to set up for him. Old age brought few benefits behind bars, but at least his hearing had deteriorated to the point that the clanging, screaming din of prison living no longer tormented him as much as it once did. He found in his deteriorated condition he could retreat into his thoughts and reduce the entire world of sound to an unpleasant fog that could not be ignored but could at least be tolerated.

Andy had stashed more than enough cash to pay for a top notch attorney, but he knew his case was so open and shut that it made little difference who spoke for him. The old time desert rat turned a schooled junk dealer's savvy eye to his own situation and sized up the odds.

The realist in him knew he wasn't getting out this time. So the best option was to retain the funds that would otherwise go to an expensive lawyer and instead use the money to soften up life behind bars as much as he could. Special favors that a man his age could no longer expect to obtain on his knees or even his hands and knees could nevertheless be obtained via a steady flow of cash. His prison bank account linked up to the prison dispensary, with its laughably inflated prices, where he moved out a steady flow of cartons of cigarettes priced only slightly less than the heroin available elsewhere around the prison.

Andy had quit tobacco a few years earlier when the cough became permanent, which made it easier to handle the goods without tapping the supply. Inside, the cigarettes were better than cash.

Something about the ciggies, though; a man who would swipe your cash roll without batting an eye will walk right past your carton of smokes. Along with the worldwide prison inmate's ban on the rape of children, the stealing of a man's smokes was accepted by all as a sign of a man who was to be reviled. Andy doled out the cartons with careful political awareness and quickly linked up with the Alpha-dogs who knew their way around. First thing he needed was access to accurate information about things in the outside world.

He put out feelers and learned his son and daughter had made bail and would stand trial for assaulting the officers. There wasn't any-thing he could do about that, but they had their freedom until their tri-als, anyway. Even if they got sentenced and had to do time, they'd be better off behind bars than a man his age.

The one pleasant surprise for him back in prison was that nobody seemed to care anything about him one way or the other. He was just tossed in with the general population and promptly ignored. The guards either hadn't read anything about his case or simply didn't care. There was no special security put in place around him, and the prison seemed to think his age was the strongest obstacle to any further escapes.

They were right about his lack of interest in escape; he had other things in mind besides getting out. The best part of the plan he was already forming was that it would unfold while he remained in the joint, leaving him with the world's best alibi and plenty of access to dialysis and other medical care.

He hit the prison library at the first opportunity and looked up every-thing on the available public records for the Seattle private investigator who tracked him down. It seemed unbelievable that the guy had such a grudge over things that happened so long ago. Andy had never expe-rienced a family relationship that gave him any insight into such strong feelings from one person for another. He couldn't shake the vague suspicion that there was a trick of some kind at work in this.

So this Shelby Preston was a nephew of old Sheriff Wade Pres-ton, who apparently spent years trying to track Andy. Obviously the sheriff failed to penetrate Scorpion John's identity, heh-heh-heh.

"A fucking P.I.," he muttered, shaking his head. No formal connection to law enforcement, just some P.I. with a wife running his business while he tracked down the cheating husbands. It had to be a fluke that such a person managed to find Andy. That only happened because Andy got a bit slack about keeping up appearances, if he hadn't gotten soft, he was certain nobody would have ever located him at all.

Once he knew that much about Shelby Preston, Seattle P.I., the rest was a matter of setting up a scheduled visit from the boy. Derrick. He instructed his volunteer attorney to send Derrick a plane ticket for a visit for the next day. There was no doubt in his mind that the boy would come and that he would do as he was told, now that he needed Andy's help with paying for a defense.

At the thought of Derrick's defense, Andy could only shake his head once again. The only reason he needed it was because of his useless gesture of going after that cop during Andy's arrest. Andy considered it to have been equally ineffective and repugnant as the thought of the boy running at them naked and trying to butt-fuck the nearest officer – and honestly expecting that to come out well, somehow.

He hoped the kid was too dense to realize that it was now in Andy's interest for Derrick and Debra to remain free, so he could have gofers on the outside. Early life experience had shown Andy that prison was far easier to tolerate if you still had influence on the outside world. The feeling of being able to make things happen somehow lifted you up outside the walls and eased up the claustrophobia.

And just in case the kids lost their court case for jumping those cops, he needed to get them busy while they were still out on bail. Derrick would cooperate in hopes of getting his defense money and his sister would do whatever she could to help. Meek compliance was all she had ever shown Andy since the pair arrived on his doorstep two years earlier.

■ ■ ■

The visiting room didn't require a glass partition, but there was a small wall running down the middle of the long table where Andy and Derrick sat facing one another. It effectively prevented visitors from passing contraband, but Andy barely noticed it. All he needed to pass was information. As soon as they escorted him into the room, Derrick was already seated waiting for him. Andy sat, pulled his seat close to the table and spoke to Derrick in a low voice without bothering to greet him first.

"What did you think you were doing, jumping those cops?"

"Hello to you too. Thought you might appreciate the support."

"Support?" Andy nearly yelled it, so he quickly glanced around to be certain he hadn't irritated a guard. He dropped his voice again. "How did you 'support' anybody, getting yourself arrested? And your sister, for shit's sake? Does she have to do everything you do?"

"She's loyal, Dad."

"Andy," Andy sighed.

"Andy."

"We'll see if she's loyal or not. Now you two are gonna need thousands to get off on your charges, maybe suspended sentence and a parole, nothing too bad. I can help you get that. I've already got my lawyer making calls for you. He'll get you set up with some eager kid out of law school who wants to make it their mission in life to defend you."

"I'll never forget your loyalty, Andy. Debra too. We just lost our heads, I guess. I think we both thought we were fighting for you."

"Okay enough about that. You call my attorney and get the funds for plane tickets, then you two get up to Seattle. In fact, I'll have his office handle the tickets. You get the flight information from them and just head for the airport."

"What's in Seattle?"

"Shelby Preston, Private Investigator, that's what. Got a wife helps him run his business. Got a pretty daughter in college someplace."

"What about them? Andy, please. Don't ask us to go off on a revenge hit for you. The cops will look straight at us for something like that. I mean, the first thing."

"Yeah I thought you might worry about that, but revenge isn't worth money, whereas the thing you're going after is worth a fortune. An unbelievable fortune. More than enough to set you both up for life, and to make sure I get anything I need in here."

"What are we supposed to steal?"

"Information. That's all. It's invisible. Almost impossible to catch you with it." Andy leaned as close to him as the partition would allow and spoke in a hoarse whisper so soft that nobody else could hear him. "This guy Shelby Preston is a top-level Freemason and he has the key to the Secret Smoke Code used by Masons all over the world. There are black ops groups here and in Europe who will pay big for a simple but effective way to code messages."

"What are we supposed to do about it?"

"Snatch him and his wife and get the information out of them one way or the other. The code key. I have part of it but you need it all. Once we have it, I can put out the word and you can sell it to the highest bidder. You and your sister can retire safe and sound while I eat decent food and watch my own shows on my own TV."

"Well, what are we supposed to do in Seattle? Grab them and torture it out of them?"

"Maybe not. Maybe you can threaten them, scare them good. Here's the incentive, you tell them one or two pieces of what you already know, so they realize the secret is already out anyway."

"Is it?"

"Don't worry about that. Here's what you need to know. They talk in complex messages based on smoke columns, the thickness of the smoke, the length of the column, the placement of one column in relation to another. Most of all, look out for changes in smoke color. Example, putting up a column of white smoke and then releasing one big puff of yellow next to it is a warning to get out of the area, that you are about to be attacked."

"They can say that? From a chimney or smokestack or something?"

"Listen, they can give you instructions on how to build a bomb or invest your money. The thing is the code key. It tells you exactly what each symbol means according to the length of smoke, the thickness, the color, the number of columns. Also the chemicals to make each color."

"Holy Christ. You're serious."

"I'm serious about you two running up to Washington state, next flight out. Just go back and pick up Debra. Once you get to up to Seattle and find this Preston fellow and his wife, have Debra run her rape victim routine on them. This is just like any other rape scam, except this time you aren't after their money. Once she gets them distracted, you move in and overpower them and make him tell you what he knows."

"Do you care what happens to them after that?"

"I care that you get the code key and then escape without being caught, that's what I care about. The rest is bullshit. The code key will make us the kind of money that fixes everything."

"Seriously though, who'll buy it?"

"Any black ops organization on the planet who doesn't want FBI decoders to read their communications."

"Maybe the FBI itself?"

"Ha! That would be funny. Why not?"

"Do the Masons have bodyguards around him or something?"

"Why would they? They don't even know that anybody outside the Order is aware of the code in the first place. They hide in plain sight and trust in secrecy."

"Wow. Andy, when you make a plan..."

"What's the problem?"

"Nothing, nothing. I just— I mean, even if I get Preston to talk—"

"He'll talk. Threaten his wife. Stick her once or twice to get him moving. I know you like that."

"I just can't believe the Masons are going to let us walk away. Surely they'll come after us."

"You mean if Preston or his wife describes you to the cops?"

"Well, yeah. I mean, there's Masons all over the world. I don't want them chasing me."

"Well then, once you get the code, maybe you best make sure they don't talk." He covered his mouth and whispered, "Remember, that code is worth millions of dollars. If anything happens to me in here, that's all I have to leave you two. But you can make something out of it. Just get the code out of him! Do what you have to do, that's all. Anything you have to do."

Half an hour later, alone again in his cell, Andy felt a deep rush of satisfaction he hadn't expected to experience inside the joint. This form of incarceration was new to him, with his ability to reach beyond the walls. It really gave meaning to the word bittersweet.

Big, dumb Derrick was a bloodhound on the scent, now. He would drag Debra to Seattle as instructed and she would help him trick the Prestons into letting them get close enough to strike. Then with Derrick's adrenalin even higher than when he flipped out and jumped the police officers, he would pour all his fear and frustration into the act of torturing information out of Shelby Preston and his wife, which they would never give up even if tortured all the way to death, since you can't tell what you don't know. So much for Andy Carmichael's reply to Mister Nosy P.I. Preston and his dime-dropping ass.

If Derrick and Debra failed, others would go and do the job for them, because Andy didn't doubt that Derrick would talk. His two moronic kids were as good as on the trail of the Prestons at that moment, bound to spill the beans to other desperados when they inevitably stopped in a bar to fortify themselves.

Thus if they failed, there would be half a dozen other strike teams aimed at the Prestons, all of them trashy bastards who never had enough money and constantly prowled the streets looking for a score. Let the Prestons survive that. Like the old country song bragged, "I got friends in low places."

It would be Andy's final fuck-you to a world that never showed him much. And to him that was reason enough for whatever destruction he could possibly perpetrate, an epitaph done not in words but in action.

It did Andy's heart good to know that as of that moment, even if the prison doctors denied him his dialysis and he crashed, the busy-body

Shelby Preston would still hear from Andy Carmichael one more time, and in a big way. The wife, too. Hell, the daughter if she was around. The way he saw it, somebody needed to pay for all his troubles. Now, finally, somebody would.

41

What We Do Is Understandable

Debra Carmichael was asleep in the same bed where the old man used to sleep, in the back bedroom of the old doublewide. She wore nothing but an oversized T-shirt and was startled awake when brother Derrick strode in and slapped her naked fanny.

"Ow! What're you doing? I'm trying to sleep!"

"Get up, we've got a flight to Seattle in three hours."

"Seattle? What are you talking about?"

"I think the Lord has sent us some payback, some *compensation* for seeing the old man get busted and hauled away before we could put him down and claim the insurance."

"I thought he wouldn't sign the papers."

"He would have, eventually. Now we can forget all that. There's tons more in Seattle."

"You better tell me what you're talking about, because I'm not going—" The impact of his open palm with the side of her face stung like a strike from the flat side of a board. She recognized the signal as showing her the need for patience and therefore waited for him to explain.

"The old man somehow came across this secret communication code that the Shriners use. They do it with smoke. Various kinds of smoke."

"Shriners?"

"Shriners, Masons, Freemasons, whatever. I think they're those idiots who have conventions in town and ride around on little motor scooters with those stupid red hats that look like sippee cups. It's an act, get it? If they act stupid in public, people won't peek into what they really do. Genius, really. They've use this code for secret communication and its never been broken. Think of what people would pay for that! Underground types."

"Terrorists?"

"Well not necessarily. What do we care what they do with the information, anyway?"

"...I guess."

"The P.I. who busted Andy lives up there with his wife. He knows the code key. He's a top level Mason. So he's going to give over the information, that's it."

She perked up at hearing that. The idea of fair play was basic to her, and the investigator had really messed up their careful plan to skin the old man. Her desire was strong for reclaiming some of the fair play life denied her young years. That desire sometimes put stiffness in her spine. It had given her enough strength to stand up to her brother when it came time to make him quit climbing into her bed whenever he felt like it.

"I think it would be good for that guy to fix the money hole he put us in. I mean, if he could have just waited a few more weeks, we'd have been done and out of here. Old Andy's already been out here longer than there's been rocks. What was the rush, anyway?"

"Right. So payback is a bitch for Shelby Preston. He's gonna tell me the code key. Hell, he's gonna write it out for us! The old man's mouthpiece set us up with tickets, so let's go. We'll pick them up at the airport."

The pair was aboard their flight three hours later after being thoroughly searched and then passing through scanners so thorough they checked for everything but motive. Once their ascending plane leveled off, Debra turned away from the window and whispered to Derrick, careful to faintly brush her lips against his ears. "How will we know if this guy is giving us fake information?"

She watched Derrick break into his it-feels-good-to-be-smarter-than-everybody-else smile and felt a small rush of satisfaction over having caused his response. Things went so much smoother when he was happy. This had always been so, but now that it was different between them, she was careful to continually make him feel good using little things instead of the big thing. The soundtrack for this new wrinkle in their relationship was that of a piano tuner constantly stretching the strings to keep the music on key.

"Not that he would necessarily lie..."

"We'll know because I already have a piece of it!" He pushed his forearm against hers, rather dismissively, she thought. As if he was indicating his awareness of her flirtations and was brushing them aside. A gush of nausea twisted in her stomach and she felt herself blush. She looked down to brush away non-existent dust on her shorts.

"But I'm not gonna tell the guy which piece I know. That way I can check him to see if he's lying. So now he's got no way to know how much of it I already have."

She leaned toward him as if she was groping under seat, habitually pressing her upper arms into her sides so that the neck of her T-shirt fell forward and revealed her compressed cleavage, then pretended to change her mind and sat back down, using one hand against his upper arm to steady herself. "What kind of secret code?"

"Smoke. Fucking *smoke*. They have this long and complicated list of meanings for every kind of smoke there is. How tall the smoke column is, how many smoke columns, how wide, what color."

"Didn't the Indians do that?"

"No, no, this is genius. Complicated. The old man says they can even do the alphabet, tell jokes."

"What about when the wind's blowing?" Debra asked without thinking. She felt an icy stab of alarm arrive an instant too late; the words were already out. She hated herself for the fact that she couldn't seem to learn. She knew better than to challenge one of his plans, especially at the beginning. The trick was to wait until things started to fall apart, then offer helpful suggestions after he got scared and he was ready to hear ideas.

Her little burst of shame over such stupidity made her feel so penitent that she kept her face pleasant and her eyes wide while she politely listened and showed genuine interest in his thoughts. Most of what he said ran together for her, the same way that most of what other people said also ran together, but the way of the passive follower sustained her.

She carefully pretended not to notice her bare forearm lightly pressing against his on the armrest. She could make her breathing produce microscopic movements that were just enough to brush against the tiny hairs on his arm.

"Okay, you think I don't know? Think the old guy didn't tell me?"

"I didn't say that," she made her voice sound tired and a little weak the way he liked.

"Here's one. It's an example of one he'd better give me straight or I'll make him squeal." He dropped his voice to a whisper and brushed his lips very faintly against her ear. The touch was so faint that it might not have been his skin touching her; it might have only been the warmth of his breath.

"Okay this one is a warning: It's one long white smoke column with a single yellow puff next to it. The yellow comes from a second source. It's warning you to get the hell out. Run. As in you're being watched."

"Does it say who's watching?"

"No, just you're being followed."

"Followed or watched?"

"Okay the idea is, it's a heads-up. You know, the rest of the message comes next, and you can tell them whatever you want."

"You can find people who will buy this?"

"Can I find people? Hey I don't 'find' anybody! I put the word out, is all I do. A few trusted underground people. You let the power of it filter out there and then take bids. Everything by phone, electronic funds, never meet anybody."

"These guys finger paint in the air with smoke."

"With the whole world right there around them and nobody knows anything."

She was glad to see him beaming at the thought of this secret knowledge. The look of pleasure on his face was especially reassuring because she was getting hungry, and Derrick always took them somewhere nice for dinner when things went his way.

■ ■ ■

FBI Confidential Informant of Known Reliability, Number 9116 had the official utility truck on loan from the City parked three houses down from the Preston home. The fake repair site was set up according to strict instructions, for authenticity. He made it a point to move around the job site like a man used to working on the clock at a job he had done a hundred times. If asked, his story was that he was inspecting lines beneath the street to compile a city report whose purpose it was not in his pay grade to know.

What Number 9116 knew for certain was that this deed for the Bureau had the power to work genuine magic in his life, to transform a third strike and life behind bars into a bad memory and a blue sky. Chicken-shit charge, to be sure. No harm done. No blood spilled, no valuables moved. A crime of philosophy, truth be told. So if boosting this investigation for the feds could serve as a Get Out Of Jail Free card, he only needed to know how high to jump.

It was a busy work site, with a generator running outside the back of the truck and a vent hose reaching down below the street through the open manhole cover. A folding metal frame held yellow plastic tape printed with "Caution – Work Site" and surrounded the manhole, set off by the orange cones. A small gas-powered cook tank had a gallon of hot road tar ready to go, and a gas-fired steam hose stood by with a variety of steam wand attachments. *Don't worry, folks, gonna clean up any mess.*

Since Number 9116 had only worked at a formal job in an actual office for those first few years after high school, back when he was dicking around trying to do things on the straight and narrow, the role-playing aspect of this stakeout was more fun than he would have imagined. *Look at me, folks, a real working stiff.* He had to appear to be a guy with a responsible job without actually doing the job itself. If this was what it was like to be a movie actor, he mused, those boys out in Hollywood had a good thing going.

His watch told him it was time to call in for the afternoon. He leaned into the truck cab and spoke into the dash microphone.

"Check in: 9116."

"9116, go ahead."

"Still nothing at the house since they left this morning. But I tell you, I put up smoke every time one of them drove past or even showed at the window. They never looked twice."

"They're outside the grid for now. We confirmed they drove to the airport and flew to Montana."

"So I should pack up the tent here?"

"Not yet. We expect two subjects to arrive there shortly. Once again, you make no contact at all. Just work the smoke. We're tracking their rental's GPS and we'll notify you when they get close."

"What composition this time?"

"Use sack number five in the tar pot. Double-check for listed ingredients: auramine, potassium chlorate, baking soda, and sulfur. Get the steam generator heated and ready."

Gibberish. Nobody told him what any of it meant, of course. Smug bastards.

42

Instincts Of The Feral

Shelby and Carla Preston flew from Seattle to Billings, Montana, then drove to Roundup in a rented car. The little town was barely bigger than it was in the days of the Carmichael murder trial, back when it spent a few weeks in the national eye as a symbol of the nation's divisive stances on crime and punishment.

The people of Roundup gave the Prestons a warm-hearted welcome everywhere they went. Even after fifty years, the locals seemed to have a soft spot for the story of their late Sheriff Wade Preston and his attempts to recapture the killer, along with a simmering rage for his crimes against their people. The general tone was one of amazement that Andrew Carmichael had managed to hide in plain sight for so long. Somehow the fact of his capture seemed to remind everyone of the levels of frustration Wade Preston endured in trying to rouse interest in recapturing him.

It turned out that Chester the Barber was still an active force in the region in spite of his age. The younger barbers who ran his shop worked with the citizens to put together an informal "Sheriff Wade Preston Day," with flowers decorating the shop and a local reporter to snap photos for the online edition.

Carla held Shelby's arm and confided, "Looks like the people around here have a soft spot for you by way of your uncle. Maybe you've got a bigger family than you think."

Shelby felt his throat tighten at the thought, but before he could reply, a man about his age hesitantly stepped forward and cleared his throat. "Uh, Mr. Preston? My name is Carl Richter. I live in Phoenix, but when I heard about this little celebration going on here, I flew up to meet you in person." He took Shelby's hand and firmly shook it.

"Well thank you, Mr. Richter, but what would make you go that distance?"

"It was your uncle, Mr. Preston. He was the only one who believed in my case against Carmichael."

"Afraid I don't know anything about that."

"Yeah, people don't. I know Andy Carmichael killed my younger sister in Colorado Springs twenty-five years ago. It was called a suicide but it wasn't. The police didn't have enough to go on and they lost interest. But one day I called your brother and told him about it, so he came to Colorado to investigate it himself. Mr. Preston, after he got all the facts in, he agreed with me. This guy Carmichael never went straight while he was out, he just got better at hiding his crimes."

"So my uncle thought Andrew Carmichael was still committing murders even after he escaped?"

"Yes. My sister's and a couple of others as well. Once he got a real picture of the crime scenes, he was convinced Carmichael was alive and well and committing crimes with impunity."

Carla whistled. "Shelby, that's what put him in such despair."

"That and something else," Richter added. "He claimed that he had the chance to put Carmichael away for life or maybe get the noose, back during his trial, but that he blew it."

Shelby felt himself grow defensive. "How could he have blown it? He didn't try the case, he just made the arrest and testified."

"Yeah, but he talked about getting pressured to produce a fake murder weapon. The prosecution knew that they had the right man, but wanted his help because their case wasn't air tight. Your uncle said he was sorely tempted, but then he refused, and the defense was able to plead down to lower charges and get a light sentence. That light sentence was why Carmichael was able to escape."

Preston exhaled. "Wade took the blame for the fact that Car-michael was able to create more victims when he could have been locked away instead."

"He refused to use corruption to put the guy away, even though they knew he was guilty. And because of that, Carmichael winds up escaping and killing again, and meanwhile Uncle Wade couldn't get anybody to listen."

"It was a real political football," Richter added. "What person in authority wants to pick up a case that will make everybody involved look bad? Easier to hope the sheriff was crazy and Carmichael was dead somewhere, just blow it all off. I came here to honor your uncle. He was the only person outside our family who believed my sister never committed suicide. We've owed Wade Preston a debt of thanks for a long time."

Shelby felt like he had just taken a blow to the stomach. He thanked Richter for coming and gave him a hug, then took Carla's arm and walked him over to one of the empty barber chairs. She urged him to sit and stood protectively by him, waiting for him to swallow everything he had just heard.

■ ■ ■

"9116? Come in?" the voice cracked over the cab radio.

"9116. Go ahead."

"Suspects approaching your position, adult male and female, twenties, conspiracy to sell information promoting terrorist activity. They're driving a rented Ford Focus, dark blue. E.T.A. five minutes."

"Got it. Roger. Whatever. I have the right chemicals, the tar pot is bubbling and the steam boiler's hot."

"On our signal, allow a continuous column of steam to rise. Leave the column in place and wait for our second signal, then pour the bag into the tar boiler. Let the smoke flash for one second, then kick the lid closed. We want a single ball of yellow smoke."

"What's it mean? ... Okay, no problem. I've done those."

"The issue here is one of timing. We need to be certain they see your work to determine whether they know the secret code or not. If they react and turn around, that will be proof. Have your truck ready to follow them until one of our tail cars can take over. We'll have the site cleaned up."

"Just get me the signals at the right time, I'll take care of it."

"Stand by..."

■ ■ ■

The FBI leak in the Seattle bureau was an on-site contractor with a good security clearance and a bad gambling problem. Thus his sideline as a purveyor of information to WikiLeaks, TMZ, the National Enquirer, and an increasing share of the Euro-Indo-Chino market for pop culture infotainment. As a stylist, he made an art of his betrayals, giving only the minimum required to generate cash while retaining certain irrelevant details. In this fashion he retained a sense that was not the same as a sense of honor, but none-theless an acceptable form of honor's moral equivalent as filtered through a world view.

So when he leaked the fact that the Freemasons had some kind of secret code done with special smoke signals and that they had long employed it around the world, a small flash mob of fringe-dwelling online journalists showed up in the Prestons neighborhood, magically aware that the FBI was conducting surveillance on the Preston house in the form of a fake City Utility work site.

"Fucking hackers," the faux-City worker was caught muttering while he glared out from his faux work site.

The neighborhood was one of those where an outrageously expensive house can look surprisingly humble, in the drive-by. The Prestons' Craftsman home was clean and cozy but too modest to hate, and the few tweets that went out in that direction didn't catch any blowback from the online collective regarding undeserved wealth.

General online concern swirled around questions about the FBI's interest in the case. Why a stakeout? Why the secrecy? What was being hidden from the people?

The edgiest of the online journalists employed hidden cameras several generations ahead of the government-issued clunky junk. A fake gardener edging the lawn down the street had a perfect long distance cam in his baseball cap. The pizza delivery car was wired with lipstick cameras inside and out, with special hyper-sensitive microphones. The jogger huffing down the sidewalk and stopping to do deep stretches wore sunglasses that almost looked like they had normal frames, but which snapped photos with ten megapixels of resolution, more than enough to be effectively forgotten on the ground while focused on the truck, and retrieved later.

Even though the reporters' posts were being ignored by the mainstream press, dark corners of the online community began to go active: special private chat rooms too new to have been infiltrated by law enforcement combined to boost public awareness while like-minded political bloggers began to light up private emails, secret texts, even an occasional voice call to spread the word: *the reactionary P.I. from Seattle who cruelly caused an escaped killer to go back to prison in spite of his years of successful evasion of the law is being staked out by the FBI at his home. The reason for the surveillance is that he knows details about a secret communication code used by the Freemasons in their unquenchable desire for world domination. This fellow might not be a part of the country's richest one percent, but he's obviously their stooge. We Resolve, As A Community, to refuse to employ Preston Investigations for any of our P.I. needs! Solidarity!*

The task ahead for these concerned individuals was to get samples of the Secret Smoke Code photographed in clear focus and in good light, and then spread around the world at light speed, crushing this latest attempt by the rich and powerful. A tweet in favor of the convict Andrew Carmichael was a tweet for The Rest Of Us! as someone among them chose to label their group.

The Rest Of Us! cyber-evolved into a full-fledged movement and began to collectively knock at the door of general public awareness.

Members of mainstream media outlets protected themselves from accusations of age and irrelevance by paying strict attention to the edgy fringes of their incoming tweets.

"Trending is Ending!" trumpeted the hair triggers among the blogosphere. The real trick for Generation Gadget, as blog-implanted agents of the gadget-makers named their target audience in a multi-media blitz, was to *be aware of trends that are about to trend but have not trended yet.* And the only way to clear the decks for fresh stuff that hasn't trended yet is to *get rid of the trending crap because it only gets in your way.*

The power of this concept was amplified by the public's ongoing enthusiasm for not having crap in their way. Thus the great granite ball of public awareness began to inch forward. The sentiment: "I may have crow's feet but I'm still cool" began to add its desperate energy to the general mix. It fueled the emerging bubbles of public knowledge about a Secret Smoke Code completely unknown to the morons who relied on commercial media. The rumor grew legs and ran toward critical mass until it blew up in a mainstream media star burst while it went viral online. It was clear nobody with an uplink wanted to be one of the morons.

43

Unknown To Morons

"Stop the car!" Debra hissed. At the same moment she grabbed the wheel and forced Derrick to pull to the curb.

"Oh what the *hell*, Debra? What are you—"

"Look!" she pointed straight ahead. There, just a few houses down from the address that their car's GPS told them was the home of Shelby Preston, was a utility truck with a worker busily tending various pieces of machinery.

"That working guy? What's the problem? Are you going off your nut?"

"Look at what he's *doing*, Derrick. Look at the column of steam coming out of that machine of his. And just as we rolled up, he put out a huge puff of yellow smoke."

"So?"

"*So*? You're the one who told me about the code, dummy! A long white smoke column next to a single puff of yellow smoke. Remember?"

"You saw him do that?"

"Yeah, and I don't know why you didn't see it too. we're both facing the same way."

"Shit. I was busy driving."

"Well that right over there is a warning, and we're probably the only two people around here who know that except for the P.I. and

Freemason friends. Thing is, is that warning for the Prestons or is it for us?"

"Us? Who would warn us? We don't know anybody around here."

"I don't know, maybe the Masons themselves. Maybe they want to give us a chance to turn around!"

Derrick stared at the workman and his smoke display, then exhaled hard and smacked the steering wheel. "Damn it! I wish Andy was here. He'd come up with some kind of plan to get the code key anyway, whatever the warning is about."

"Well, he's not. Somebody knows we are, though. I want that money too, but if we walk into this thing blind then maybe we're too stupid to stay out of jail anyway."

"Don't talk like that. I've kept us out of jail so far, haven't I?"

"Right. But look ahead of us. What the hell is that guy *doing*, Derrick? I think somebody knows we have a piece of the code or they wouldn't use it on us."

"Or it isn't meant for us and the warning is for the Prestons."

"That's just as bad! It means the Prestons have been warned now and that somebody else knows we're here. What does that do to the element of surprise for us?" She put her hand on his arm and squeezed hard enough to signal that she meant business. "Maybe we can come back later, but we have to get out of here until we find out what's going on."

Derrick hesitated a moment, then let out a huge sigh. "Son of a bitch, dude." He turned the wheel hard and stepped on the gas, pulling a U-turn and taking off away from the house. "I can't believe we got this far and we're quitting."

"It's not 'quitting' to back off and get in touch with the old man again, make sure we're going into this thing right. If this code is worth so much money, then we better walk up on them with something better than the rape scam."

Derrick drove their rental car out of the neighborhood and toward the highway entrance. "Okay, I'll back off for one day. We'll call the prison and get Andy on the line, see what he has to say. But tomorrow,

I'm going back whether you come along or not. I'll jump that guy at his own front door if I have to."

"So we can go have dinner now and get a hotel, right?" She touched his arm as if to promise something without actually promising anything.

Derrick sighed, suddenly disappointed with the entire day. "Yeah. Shit. We'll get a room. Just for the night, though. Tomorrow, I'm going back one way or the other."

■ ■ ■

When the ersatz City Utility truck squealed away from its work site and followed the young man and woman in the obvious rental car down the street, the undercover online journalists through the neighborhood moved as one, capturing the truck's pursuit of the couple as the end button to the earlier shots of white and yellow smoke. Half a dozen video stories were uploaded to internet outlets in seconds.

A fake biker who had been making a show of changing his bike chain suddenly popped it back in place and rode off in hot pursuit of the truck. He was rewarded for his physical prowess and journalistic determination when an unmarked police car loomed around a corner and zoomed between the truck and the young couple's car, then forced their auto to the side of the road. The truck kept on going down the street, leaving the fake biker as the only one to capture video of the couple being pulled from their car, placed in handcuffs, and hauled away. One plainclothes officer drove them off while a second drove the impounded car after them. The biker missed the chance to follow the truck back to its destination, but all that would have told him is that the utility truck was being used by the FBI, and the savvy bloggers already knew that much.

Word poured forth onto the leading-edge news blogs, not the irrelevant trending ones, but the vital and edgy *pre*-trending outlets that only people who were not morons knew about and sometimes read. WikiLeaks was left in the dust as the creaky old corporate entity it had allowed itself to become, while the blogosphere's cognoscenti spread the hottest new word: *The FBI has obtained the Freemasons' Secret Smoke Code and is using it on Americans!*

The tantalizing stories featured photographs of one of the Secret Smoke Code messages: a long white column of steam with a round puff of bright yellow smoke roiling the air next to it. Although the ubiquity of digital cameras had so far failed to render a clear shot of a single UFO anywhere in the world, nonetheless this picture's photographer captured a clear and perfectly recognizable shot of that one piece of the code.

Shelby Preston was forgotten in the boil over. The non-morons seemed to reach the unspoken agreement that he was no longer an interesting player in a story that was now far larger than any individual. The opportunity to confront Preston and try to make him tell whatever he knew was suddenly far less appealing to The Rest Of Us! than the idea of staking out the FBI headquarters in Seattle. They set up a flash mob to occupy the street in front of the building and set about publicly shaming the Bureau by making a toilet of the sidewalk.

By evening, there was a good-sized congregation of protestors carrying handmade signs demanding that the FBI reveal the secret code to the American People and guarantee the populace that the code would never be employed against citizens. The reasons for such a ban were not laid out by the protestors.

When one mainstream journalist approached them and asked why the FBI shouldn't have secret codes, he was shouted down and photographed with an awkward expression on his face. The picture was posted online and captioned, "A DINOSAUR MORON" and he became the living face of the impotent mainstream press who knew nothing about this edgy pre-trending story.

44

The Tale Too Good To Die

Andy returned to his two-man cell from the latest meeting with his attorney and tossed the sheaf of papers that the lawyer had left with him onto his bunk.

His cellie was nice and young, twenty-four or so, and as eager to please as any kid who wants to keep his ass in one piece. Once Andy had picked him out of the general population, it cost him nearly five hundred dollars to make the necessary arrangements to have the kid savagely beaten, then transferred to Andy's cell and warned there would be more beatings, worse beatings, unless they got word back from Andy that the kid was the world's best cellmate.

Now the kid quickly sat on the bunk beside him and laid his hand on Andy's thigh to show that he realized Andy was upset about something. Andy reached over and fondly tousled the kid's hair. "I'm tense," was all he needed to say.

While the kid blew him, Andy relaxed and sorted through the papers the attorney had brought him, print-outs from online news magazines and blogs. He shuffled through them one by one, but they all seemed to say more or less the same thing. The mainstream news had finally noticed the blogosphere's focus on a supposed "Masonic secret code" and was debunking the notion and ridiculing the sources of the story. The blogs shot back with accusations of massive cover-ups and conspiracy. They decried the major media for supporting this obvious attempt by big business to continue deceiving the beleaguered public.

When comedians began to post jokes on YouTube poking fun at The Rest Of Us!, the blogosphere converted into a virtual stadium filled with screaming supporters on both sides of the issue, hurling invective like inmates throwing feces back and forth across the tier.

There was no longer any mention of Andrew Carmichael or Shelby Preston anywhere in the maelstrom. This, according to Andy's attorney, was good news for him. "The sooner they forget about you, the sooner we can get to work on getting you out of there."

Andy wasn't fooled by such sugar talk; he was there for the duration. The guy just wanted to stay on the payroll. But that was fine with him. He had the money to keep him on retainer now that he was saving a bundle by not helping out the kids, who had to go and get their dumb asses arrested for the interstate trafficking scheme Andy had pulled them into.

They were obviously as guilty as he was, and there was no way they could avoid going down on the charges. Therefore there was also no way he was going to waste money paying for a defense on a case they couldn't win.

It was unfortunate that they couldn't perform his task as instructed regarding the Seattle P.I., but Andy had a hard time believing Derrick when he said nobody else had been told. Andy knew the kid had no discipline and loved to sit at the center of a circle of drinkers and blow it out his ass. Trust bad luck and Murphy's Law to see to it that nobody else was after Shelby Preston for details on the Secret Smoke Code.

As far as the prison futures that were guaranteed for Debra and Derrick, Andy thought it might be for the best. They were young enough to still have insulation around their internal wiring, meaning they could stand a few years on the inside. Things might get a little weird for them sexually, but Andy had picked up a few clues here and there watching the two of them interact and thought maybe weird sex wasn't all that unfamiliar to either one. Inside the joint, perversion was a handy survival skill.

Leaving them to their fate was easier for Andy when he considered their failed attempt to get him to sign life insurance papers. He figured the only logical explanation for their ridiculously friendly treatment of him and their obvious attempts to get in close with him had been intended to put him off guard. Why, as far as Andy could tell, this Shelby Preston fellow might have saved his life by getting him away from those two before they had a chance to hatch whatever plan they had in mind.

Defense money? Those two needed to get real and start earning their way to a Golden Walk. Hell, prison life would toughen them up and teach them a few survival tricks at the same time. The way Andy saw it, they were getting just what they needed. More than likely they would one day thank him for it.

At that point the oral sex began to take over his concentration and it occurred to him that he might be able to achieve an erection this time. He lay back on the bunk and mentally returned to his favorite getaway spot, a poolside cabana tended by a strapping young towel boy who happened to look exactly like the new cellie. And for the next few minutes there in the privacy of the solid-walled two man unit, Andy Carmichael's life was as good as any old con with failing kidneys had the right to expect it to be.

■ ■ ■

Chester's Barbershop down on Main Street, just above 1st, was packed with old-timers who came out to meet Shelby Preston, nephew of the late Sheriff Wade Preston and the man who found Andrew Carmichael so easily after the authorities failed to apprehend him for so long. There way no way for Shelby to determine whether they were there out of affection for the man's memory or guilt over his treatment by the town's citizens.

Shelby accepted a free haircut from one of the newer barbers, and he and Carla relaxed amid a friendly crowd who didn't seem to want anything from the occasion except to put some kind of a cap on the story of Andrew Carmichael and the old Roundup murders.

Before Shelby's haircut was complete, old Chester himself came hobbling in, all ninety-two years of him, still slim and straight. He introduced himself graciously and it was clear that the younger barbers had a soft spot for him. He never had to raise his voice when he spoke. As soon as his lips began to move, everybody else just naturally stopped talking and listened. Shelby tried to remember the last time he had seen any elderly person who was neither rich nor famous granted that sort of respect.

"Your uncle was a good man," Chester told him. "He had a hard row to hoe with getting the people of this county on his side. He took that job so serious. One story said he stopped a fellow on the highway, pulled him out of the car and told him he knew how the guy was beating his wife. Then he struck the man so hard he didn't get up for awhile, so he wrote him a speeding ticket and tucked it in his pocket and left him there."

Everybody laughed and whistled at that. Chester paused like an experienced storyteller until they were almost quiet again, then went on. "Nobody wanted that Sheriff job, but he took it and did his best for years. He had to earn people's respect, what with only having one eye and all."

"One eye? My uncle had only one eye? Wow, that detail somehow slipped out of the family memory."

"I'm not surprised," Old Chester replied. "He had a very good glass eye somebody made up for him. Most of the time you couldn't tell. Some people didn't even know, I guess."

A smile came over Old Chester's face. "I had to learn the hard way not to use the electric scalp massager on him, though. It relaxed his face muscles so much that one time it actually made his eye pop right out."

And with that opening, Old Chester launched into "The Tale Of The Hairy Eyeball," which by this point he had repeated so many times he could tell it in his sleep. The old master of the clippers and comb knew how to deliver it to make it a real crowd pleaser. Everybody laughed just as hard this time.

- The End -

15035843R00170

Made in the USA
San Bernardino, CA
12 September 2014